Joan Livieri enjoys traveling with no schedules. Baseball and golf are her favorite sports. Always a reader, it ignited in her imagination with passion to write. She and her husband settled in a small town in middle Tennessee with its moderate four seasons and friendly people, Joan now lives alone. Though never lonely, with books for company and feeding stray animals that happen by.

Joan Livieri

THE MISSING DUKE

AUSTIN MACAULEY PUBLISHERS™

LONDON ∗ CAMBRIDGE ∗ NEW YORK ∗ SHARJAH

Ordering Information
Quantity sales: Special discounts are available on quantity purchases by corporations, associations, and others. For details, contact the publisher at the address below.

Publisher's Cataloging-in-Publication data
Livieri, Joan
The Missing Duke

ISBN 9781685626693 (Paperback)
ISBN 9781685626709 (Hardback)
ISBN 9781685627409 (ePub e-book)

Library of Congress Control Number: 2023913635

www.austinmacauley.com/us

First Published 2024
Austin Macauley Publishers LLC
40 Wall Street, 33rd Floor, Suite 3302
New York, NY 10005
USA

mail-usa@austinmacauley.com
+1 (646) 5125767

Chapter One

1837, Salisbury (not far from London)

The ballroom at Penumbra Manor was aglow with its crystal chandeliers, lighted candles appearing to turn its prisms into stars. Generously arranged yews in brass urns graced the walls between floor-to-ceiling windows along with massive vases of gardenias emitting their appealing bouquet. Colors from ladies' gowns were reflected from windowpanes as they danced across the parquet floor, mirroring the evening's radiance.

A variety of meats, poultry, sausages, cheeses, and fruits, along with puddings, cakes, tarts, and raspberry puffs won praise from elitist guests.

The orchestra played into the late hour—this celebration for the Duke of Grenfell's twin sons' five and twenty birthdays being a colossal success.

The Duke of Grenfell, highly esteemed by his peers, known for not only his integrity but a constant kind temperament—yet not without a backbone of iron when necessary. The duke knew that Lady Eudora Weston, the Earl of Sherbrooke's daughter, coveted the title of Duchess of Grenfell. She planned on wedding Derrick, his firstborn, to achieve that aspiration. Sadness crept into his being for his wife that had died, leaving him with two twin boys to nurture. If his Elaine were here, they would talk and perhaps arrive at a way to discourage Eudora's thinking—telling that she should set her sights elsewhere and that Derrick was not for her.

Eudora approached the duke. Her peach gown cut low with its neckline allowing the fullness of her breasts to be eye-catching. Her sleeves puffed to her elbows with lace tight to her wrists as the gown full with layers of scalped ecru lace down to the hemline, permitting the peach color to shimmer through. Her peach slippers matched her gown—tapping one foot as she waited to speak with the duke. He kept his expression pleasant.

Eudora recognized his indifference toward her, that he was extending her a gentleman's courtesy.

"You look lovely, Lady Eudora."

Gushing sweetness, knowing others standing near could hear, curtsied, looked up and gave one of her best performances, not the least intimidated with the Duke of Grenfell. "Thank you, Your Grace." She fluttered her eyes. "I know that it is improper for a lady to request a dance from a gentleman, but you seem to have missed signing my dance card." She pouted, "Will you honor me with a dance, Your Grace?"

"I say, Grenfell," one of his guests crowed, "what a lucky chap you are to have the most beautiful lady asking you to attend her."

George Richard Staunton, Duke of Grenfell, bowed to Lady Eudora and offered her his arm. He said not a word but began to lead the dance. She smiled in her practiced inane way and spoke on the sly without breaking her smile. "Your Grace, I must speak with you in private as soon as possible."

Surprised, but not showing it, the duke nodded.

"May I meet with you in your library after this dance?"

Again, he nodded.

Satisfied, Eudora swayed, letting her head fall back enjoying the rest of the dance.

The Duke of Grenfell closed the door. Eudora was waiting. One lighted lamp left dark shadows in the large room. Still, the soft light offered inviting warmth that the duke did not enjoy at the moment.

"I would be remiss to leave my guests for more than a few minutes. What is so urgent that we must meet this eve in private?"

"I will get right to the point, Your Grace." She offered no softness in her voice, "For some reason you do not like me. I can feel it. So let there be no mistake," her lips thinned, "it is of no consequence as I will marry Derrick in the near future and hope for your blessing."

The duke's eyes turned stonier never leaving Eudora's face, said, "I don't appreciate your playing one brother against the other. Delbert is in love with you, yet you want a commitment from Derrick. You are willing to wed Derrick only to become Grenfell's duchess." Without preamble, his voice held not a vestige of sympathy, "If Delbert were my first born you would have set your sights on him."

Haughty and not the least disconcerted, she replied, "You are quite perceptive, Your Grace. In fact, I would prefer Delbert as he would be easier to control while Derrick has a forceful streak." Fingering her pearls, added, "Just so you know I shall be the next Grenfell duchess."

Wanting to put an end to this preposterous conversation, the duke smiled, "Let us return to the dancing."

"Trust me, Your Grace; I will obtain my long-held dream. Derrick will come around."

"I have every confidence in my son. You need have no concern from me if Derrick chooses you to be his bride, he will have my blessing."

A tall man moved into the dim light, his tone carried a touch of sarcasm. "I find that seeking respite from the warmth of the ballroom has allowed me to find myself the main topic in your conversation." Directing his message to the exquisitely coiffed young woman, he lowered his voice, "Listen well, Lady Eudora, I will decide whom my bride will be and when to wed." He gifted a deliberate bow, and then said, "My apologies that it will not be you. I trust this will put an end all further discussions."

Taken aback, but quickly gaining her senses, she reached for Derrick's arm. "You misunderstand, my lord. I just wanted his grace to know how important you are to me." Her voice turned pleading. "Surely, you cannot think for one moment I spoke seriously. After all, it was at his grace's insistence that I meet him here."

"Stop! No more lies… enough. Quit fabricating, I was sitting here thinking how wonderful this evening has been when you entered. I was about to reveal myself to you when Father entered and closed the door. I heard him inquire about your urgent need to speak with him." Derrick didn't smile. "Let me escort you back to the ballroom."

Spewing venom, Lady Eudora Weston vowed, "I do not need your escort. Both of you will regret this for I will not be cheated."

The duke said nothing but Derrick, tilting his head, said, "Is that a threat or…"

Delbert tapped on the door and walked in, smiling. "I saw you come this way, Father, and…" Spying Eudora, then Derrick, he lost his smile. "Is this a private party or may I join?" Delbert, wearing blue satin pants and coat with heavy ruffles covering the front of his shirt with the same frills exposed at his wrists, was the opposite of his twin. Derrick, wearing black pants with a subdued silver-gray vest and with fewer frills, did not come across as a dandy like his brother.

Eudora rushed to Delbert, wrapping her hands on his arm. Big tears formed with one rolling down her cheek. "Oh Delbert, I was just telling the duke and your brother that it is you I want to marry. They refuse to accept my decision. His grace wants me to choose Derrick."

"Don't be a fool, Del; it is not as Eudora says," Derrick's voice softly warned. "She is using you. Don't yield to her nonsense."

Delbert narrowed his eyes. Leaving Eudora, he strutted toward his brother. "You can't accept that Eudora rejected you, can you, my overconfident twin?"

The Duke of Grenfell was not to be denied his power. "It is time for us to return to your celebration. We will discuss this later. As it is, we have been gone far too long." He walked toward the door, turned, and said to his sons, "This is a family matter and is to remain so. We will continue to host our guests. Lady Eudora, I think it best you attend to the ladies retiring room until you are able to get yourself together. Of course, you are welcome to be part of the festivities."

Eudora glanced at the duke and then turning to Delbert with tears for his benefit, said, "I would rather go home. Delbert, will you see to my coach and tell my father that I have a severe headache?"

"Yes, of course, my dear. I will see you home."

The duke's words, cold and exact, intervened, "You will stay with your guests, Delbert. Lord Sherbrooke will see to his daughter."

Needing time to gather her wits and not daring to push the duke further, using her breathless voice, cooing to Delbert, "No, my sweet, his grace is right, you must remain with your guests. This is your party and must not leave because of my distress. I will be fine. Thank you, dearest, for caring."

Derrick walked away, he could not endure Eudora's false and disgusting exhibition. Tomorrow, he would talk with his twin. "Father is right, we best go. Are you coming, Del?" Acting complacent, he left the library with his father.

The duke gave Derrick a slight nod before moving across the large foyer into another direction. He erased concern from his features. The music playing; he heard happy voices and hoped this evening would soon end. It was a blessing that all the weekend guests would be departing after breaking their fast in the morning. Until then, there would be no opportunity to settle this night's misfortune with his second-born son. Thinking that this was one celebration he won't forget.

"I say there, Grenfell, I thought you may have tottered off to bed," one of his guests teased, "not that I would blame you. I'm ready to call it a night."

The duke smiled as he led the man back to the ballroom. As a proper host, he would never hurry his guests but assure them they were welcome to stay as long as they wished.

Chapter Two

Two days after the birthday celebration

George Richard Staunton, aging gray-haired Duke of Grenfell, sat at his massive oak desk in his private study. Unnatural lines of anguish accented his handsome features as he thought of the differences between his twin sons—knowing he could trust only one.

Derrick personified innate integrity with powerful strength in mind and body, yet a gentleness augured deep within him. He would be an excellent steward.

Delbert, born ten minutes later, carried within him a cruel nature. His flagrant behavior of thoughtless acts and pranks toward household servants and also small animals were deplorable. Being bitter as the second son, he often masked his resentment cunningly with no embarrassment or apology, causing the duke no end of grief.

There was a light knock on the door and Derrick walked in. He wore an old pair of black kersey riding breeches, his boots marked with dust and his cambric white shirt hung loose around his tapered waist. Smiling, he said, "I was with Rutley. I think Monticon will give us a foal soon."

Here at Penumbra Manor, their country estate, Derrick often donned old clothes to extend a hand to Grenfell's stablemaster, Rutley. During his growing years, Derrick had spent time working with Grenfell's cattle. There was nothing about a horse he didn't know and it was Rutley's training that Derrick willingly absorbed the old man's teachings.

"Monticon is a healthy mare. We should have another grand colt, especially with Acadia *King* as the sire. You were right, Derrick, encouraging me to purchase her."

Derrick slid onto a chair across from his father, his tone changed from positive to unenthusiastic, "I tried talking with Del, but he has his mind set on Eudora and thinks I have ulterior motives. I tried to get him to slow down in his pursuit, but to no avail." A grin crossed Derrick's mouth. "He said I sound like you. Where is he, by the way?"

"He's over at Sherbrooke. Eudora sent a note and he left immediately; that's why I summoned you. This will be an ideal time to acquaint you with the dukedom that only you must be privy to. I cannot stress enough how important this knowledge necessitates extreme secrecy."

"Father, please. You are well and healthy and have years ahead of you. I have no yearning to carry the title."

The gray-haired man rose, moved to the door and turned the key. He twisted the handle to be sure it was securely locked. He walked to the windows, checking from the second-floor level, scanning the usual tranquil expanse of lawn and gardens. A breeze waved the trees leaves causing their shadows moving back and forth on the grass. Appearing idyllic, it didn't match the duke's present disposition.

His interest piqued, Derrick rested an ankle across his knee, knowing this mysterious nature was quite unlike his father. "Something is bothering you, Father. What is it?"

The duke didn't sit at his desk but took the chair next to his son. "I ask that you do not interrupt me, no matter how inquisitive you will become. When I have finished, we can discuss whatever is unclear."

Perplexed, Derrick nodded.

"As you know, these sixty thousand acres of Penumbra goes to the firstborn son upon my death. Everything I own automatically becomes yours—my titles, Penumbra, the London house, all fall under entailment."

Derrick had grown up hearing this from his governess and tutors. He never gave them importance as it was years and years away. As a boy all he wanted was to be a stablemaster like Rutley and be with horses every day. He held back his smile, giving his father his attention.

"From you it transfers to your son, or if you should die before a son is sired, then these lands and titles would supposedly go to the next in line."

"I understand."

"No," the duke shook his head, "no, you don't. There is a proclamation that declares Penumbra cannot be inherited without precise Staunton proof. A decree was attached and recorded for eternity by the then Sovereign because our ancestor was an invaluable servant and was so rewarded. Over time more land was added, either through marriage or purchase, but the decree applies to ownership without end as long as proof is provided."

Stunned, Derrick stared at his father.

The duke continued. "Should no Staunton heirs fulfill the specifics, it is written that what we own reverts to the Crown." The older man could not withhold a smile. "I have faith in your fulfilling your duty to our family. You are a Staunton and we Stauntons have for two hundred years met the decree's stipulation."

Derrick shifted in the chair, captivated.

"It is time for you to value the Staunton tradition in name as well as handling all its properties and investments. It is my duty to apprise you of the good and the bad in caring for Penumbra—to know of its widespread responsibilities." The duke's voice held sorrow. "Know this, Son, I cannot stress enough—because you will have power beyond your imagination, your life can be in jeopardy from many envious and greedy people."

Derrick jumped up; unable to remain silent. *"What?"*

"Sit down! Listen carefully. When you inherit Penumbra, your life will dramatically change. Though integrity is the Staunton commandment, there will be times we are faced to cross that thin line to protect our interests." The duke's tormented voice raised hairs on Derrick's nape. "Presently, my greatest concern for you is Delbert's resentment of being born second."

Derrick felt an acute sense of disbelief, hurt, and then distress. "I trust your words, Father, yet it's difficult to think Del would turn against his family."

So there could be no misunderstanding, the duke knew he must stress the gravity of his reasoning. "Heed my warning—you are aware Delbert is devious and vindictive. Those shameful characteristics of his will, in the future, bring grief and disgrace upon our good name if you are not on your guard. It will be up to you to be alert for every eventuality. If possible, understand it before it happens and meet it head on with Staunton strength and power."

"I know Del is discontented. We've never been very close, but I presumed it was because my love for horses never interested him. I recall his being deceitful to enhance his own well-being—it didn't seem important. I thought it was Del being Del."

"Surely you know that Delbert felt cheated being the second born son?"

"Truthfully, Father, my interest was in the stable with Rutley. After all, it isn't my choosing that I came before Del. His feeling cheated has to be understood and lived with. He'll always have a home here at Penumbra. I accept the fact that I am your heir, no more than that." He smiled, "I'm pleased that you have a long life ahead of you."

"Thank you, Son. With you in charge, I am sure the Staunton legacy will persevere." Their eyes met with mutual respect.

"Now," said the duke, "I have something to show you. Except for a few necessary people, this is the best kept secret in the aristocracy. I must have your word that what you learn today, in this room, remains only with you. As the next Duke of Grenfell, including Penumbra lands, you will be its guardian."

"You have my word, Your Grace."

"Excellent… as there will be a time *when* you will be called upon to show proof that you are a true Staunton, the true Duke of Grenfell and a trusted emissary of the Crown. This will be your proof." The Duke of Grenfell removed his coat and dropped it on a chair. Next was his cravat—this he tossed on top of his jacket; lastly, he removed his shirt, hastily dropping it where it lay half on the chair. His broad chest was still firm for a man of his fifty-three years, he exuded vigor.

Derrick was at a loss not knowing why his father was undressing and without his valet.

No longer as, when the duke raised his bare right arm, on the underside of it Derrick viewed a red mark. "Son, this tiny mark is *our* insignia, the Staunton identification. No one can steal my identity. It is the proof needed to claim and hold all our lands, properties and titles. Because of this, we are free from any taxes or debts incurred by the Crown. No one can draft any claim against us. This revered dispensation was bestowed on our first ancestor, Derrick George Staunton, because of his devoted service as liege to his Sovereign centuries ago. The decree remains ours and can only be overturned if proof is established that any heir has no Staunton blood in our veins."

"This insignia allows me the esteemed privilege with three other similar persons left that are still able to prove their heredity. When I die, you must have this identification so that no one can take what we have worked and strove to maintain. Be aware the value of what we have haunts many of our king's closest associates *as* well *as* an envious group of scoundrels. A change in the realm cannot expunge the records that are stored in the Abbey and are well protected."

"One thing more," his voice hardened, "when it comes to scoundrels, I regret to also have to include Delbert. Never forget that for one minute. Be on your guard."

"But if Del hasn't this proof, he can't inherit. Wouldn't it be wise to let him know?"

"No, never! This information belongs only to the titled steward of Penumbra and Grenfell lands. This is what gives you the power to do well and keep the Staunton name valued." The duke began dressing. "Some properties are not entailed giving Delbert an income. I have every intention of having added in my will that the castle and its lands in Scotland be his to do with as he chooses. But only on my death." Donning his coat, he motioned for Derrick to follow.

At the end of the room, the top half of the wall was covered end to end with a hunting tapestry. Below the tapestry built flush into the wall were the sets of oak cabinets. Some had glass doors and some were flush with carved images of trees. There were rows of drawers with brass handles that need no rays of light to bring out their brilliance.

The duke opened one of the cabinet doors and removed several volumes of books. Reaching inside, he said, "The back of this panel will slide with an exact amount of pressure applied in each comer at the same time. Your hand span is now large enough to enable you to do that."

Derrick heard the movement of wood slide—it was a muffled sound. Then he heard it slide again as it closed.

"It is important that I know you can do this. Try." Derrick tried, but had no success.

"Try again putting an equal amount of pressure in each comer on the right side only."

"I'll get it this time." Applying pressure as his father instructed, he felt the wood panel slide from his fingers. He turned to his father and smiled.

"Excellent. Now gently slide it back into place sealing our hiding place." Again, it worked.

"Now I want you to open it and remove whatever is in there and bring it to my desk."

Derrick returned to the duke's desk carrying a small soft pouch, a tome, a heavy stiff leather bag and a black leather case.

The Duke of Grenfell picked up the stiff bag and spilled the contents of gold sovereigns upon his desk. "When you are the duke, these are to be left untouched, but always available for an emergency. This very bag belonged to our benefactor, Derrick George Staunton." He smiled at his son, "You were named after him." He pointed to the tome, "The First Staunton was the strongest. He started Penumbra. It is all recorded here, the good and the bad. It's believed that knowing our history keeps us strong. You will add facts under your stewardship. It is *never* to be taken out of Penumbra Manor." Lifting the black rectangular case cover, the duke couldn't have stopped the tremor in his hands if he wanted to as memories of his taking the jeweled necklace from its velvet cushion and placing it on his wife's lovely neck.

The necklace with tiers of rubies, sapphires and diamonds, sprinkled with inlaid emeralds was stupendous and no matter what Staunton wife donned it, everyone fortunate to see it adorned turned that Staunton duchess into a walking goddess.

"I've heard stories about the Grenfell jewels, but nothing could prepare me for their magnificence. How can the necklace, bracelet and earrings with all its dainty silver filigree be so elaborate and yet not the least ostentatious? It's no wonder people have talked about them." Derrick's eyes were bleak, "Poor Del, how often he said he'd find these."

"Know, Son, that none of this on my desk belongs to us. They belong to Penumbra and Grenfell. We are only temporary guardians. The jewels are priceless and you must never give up control or sell them. They are part of our heritage and must forever be protected. These stones have been sought after by many you will discover when you read our history. Castles, villas, armies and ships have been offered in trade for them, but no Staunton would ever relinquish them. Remember, not even your wife is to know where they are kept."

"Did not mother ask you?"

"No, she never asked and I would not have told her if she did." The duke smiled, "I valued that in her as it was love that we shared and not the jewels."

"Be assured you can trust me."

The duke picked up the last small pouch and removed a gold ring that looked as if it had a bubble on it. Holding it before his son, his demeanor grave, said, "This is the Staunton crest and is nearing three hundred years. It was designed; engraved and completed twelve years after the Sovereign decreed these lands to his loyal liege. This ring and its crest can never be duplicated. The tool that cut these special grooves was destroyed when the engraving was completed. Our crest is on record in the Abbey. Only our barrister, James Barslow, is fully cognizant of the documentation, but only that. It is our seal and signature of ownership and must never leave this estate. Its use must always be administered here at Penumbra Manor, thereby keeping it safe and available for the next heir."

Derrick stared at his father. "I had no idea the depth of secrets and the onus that you carry and have constantly presided over."

The duke spoke with pride. "I have relished fulfilling my duties and have tried to continue the legacy our ancestors empowered to us. I have always tried to be fair, but diligent in sustaining our legacy to its highest tradition. It is with honor and gratification whenever I do affix my personal touch upon it. Remember, Derrick, it is our secrets that keep us safe. It has been the Staunton way and why we must always, unconditionally ensure it continues under each of our stewardship. We must pass it on to the future Grenfell heirs in the same healthy, powerful condition as when it was received. Each duke has left his own mark trusting the next will do the same with added success."

"I will follow and obey the unwritten Staunton laws and never let you or our ancestors down." He added with pride, "The crest, Father, it is the one burned under your arm?"

The duke nodded.

"When must I do the same?"

"You tell me when you're ready. It must be soon. I can't stress enough that you never reveal it to anyone, especially to your twin."

"You need have no worry, Father. All is safe with me."

"I had no doubt. Please return everything to its safe place." He moved toward the door and reminded Derrick to relock it so the servants wouldn't enter. Adding in a severe tone, "Remember, not a word to anyone."

"What has been told and shown to me today will forever remain my secret."

The duke departed. He heard the key click in place—satisfied.

Gathering Staunton's heritage, Derrick shook his head. *Could Del be resentful of me being first born? Delbert, please let Father be wrong about you.*

Chapter Three

Two weeks after the birthday celebration

Two grays pulled the curricle at a comfortable pace. Unsatisfied, Viscount Delbert Stephen Staunton flicked the whip, stinging their backsides.

Piqued, Lady Eudora Weston exclaimed, "For heaven's sake, Delbert, slow down! My bonnet is about to blow away. My curls will be a tangle."

"Well, all right," he griped, "but only for you. These beasts need to feel a bit of leather."

Eudora did not agree, but why argue when she had other vital chicanery on her mind. They'd been traveling on Penumbra lands for over two hours and she had to find a place where they could stop and talk without possibly being seen by any of Penumbra's tenants. Taking hold of Delbert's soft upper arm, she gave it a little squeeze, instantly comparing him to Derrick's solid muscle. She cringed and wrinkled her nose as she removed her hand. "Let us stop under that big oak so we can visit undisturbed."

Delbert's impish grin made her cringe again.

"Yes, my dear, as you wish." That's what he liked about Eudora— there was no guessing about her intentions. His smug countenance assured him that she longed for him. His mind tumbled, jubilant that Eudora had chosen him over his sanctimonious twin. Jerking the reins, he steered the horses under the shade of the oak with its abundance of new spring leaves. "Does this meet with your approval, my dearest?"

Eudora turned her head so Delbert couldn't see her roll her eyes and bite her lip.

Despising him was something she was finding more difficult to disguise. They had been seeing each other continually since that horrifying night in the library. A night not to be dismissed—she would have her revenge. To become the next Duchess of Grenfell required having this whiny jackanapes beside her. Confident he would do as she proffered or else she'd accept another's proposal and be a countess, but it was being a duchess... *the Duchess of Grenfell* that mattered. She wanted its prestige.

Delbert halted the horses; the reins fell at his feet and reached to draw Eudora to him. "Please, Delbert," her voice syrupy, "let's walk a bit. There is something I would first discuss with you. Something significant you must hear."

He ogled his lovely lady; his body relaxed and lithe, "Are you going to tell me I may be allowed to ravish you?"

She knew she had to be very careful with her reply; he could turn snappish and cruel.

Tweaking him under his chin with her gloved hand, she favored him with one of her teasing smiles while fluttering her dark lashes. "Now you know that is what I'd like more than anything, but it is simply improper until we are wed."

"Then why won't you set a date?" He waved his arms. "Why shouldn't I speak to your father about us?" He pulled a handkerchief from his sleeve to dab at his face. "Tell me why, Eudora. Why?" Today he donned a dark rose coat with silk ruffles—his feathered hat sat halfcocked on his head. "Stop worrying about the duke. He'll end up giving us his blessing."

Eudora closed her eyes, stiffening her jaws to smother a laugh at the pitiful picture he made. *He's nothing like his twin. When I was ten and six, I tried enticing Derrick by unbuttoning my dress hoping he'd seduce me, then because of his moral standards he'd insist on marrying and I would become a duchess. But he refused and...*

"Why are you so silent, my dear? You're frowning."

Eudora's reaction was swift. A deliberate smile materialized. *I must be careful as sometimes he isn't as obtuse as he appears.* Taking Delbert's hand, she began to walk under the spreading branches. She shivered; as the sun didn't penetrate through the leaves. It was chilly this April afternoon and that helped keep her devious mind in motion so she could hurry and be away. "Well… my darling," she cajoled, "I want to talk about an injustice that is being wielded against you. I truly believe," she held up her small gloved hand to rub her bogus tears, "that you are the son who should inherit Penumbra."

Delbert wished always that he were born first. He began laughing at her. His shoulders shook as he roared, the long feathers on his hat bouncing with his movements. "Eudora, I think our ride has rattled your beautiful, silly little head."

She was livid—not because he called her silly, but because he was laughing at her. Still, to follow through with her plotting, she must pretend to be perturbed, so stamping her foot on the rough ground and raising a powdery dust, she lightly scolded, "You should take what I am saying seriously."

In cold fury, he rebuked, "Really, Eudora, you know Derrick, that dastardly milksop, was born first. Unfortunately it was not me. We're wasting time," he reached for her. "I want to hold you in my arms."

She looked at Delbert thinking, *he* is the dastardly milksop, not his twin. Pausing to organize her line of attack and slightly stepping back, she said, "I've heard it said that there was a mix-up at the time of your births and the Staunton babies were switched."

That had never occurred to this twin. Delbert's features drew together in thought—disbelieving, yet holding a trace of hope. "That is wishful thinking, Eudora." He brushed at his rose-colored sleeve and his handkerchief fell to the ground. "Drat, that was one of my favorites." He kicked it away from him. "So tell me when and where you heard this preposterous tale."

Eudora didn't breathe, not wanting to break the spell of having Delbert's attention.

"Once when I was passing through the kitchen, Cook did not see me, I heard her talking to Father's valet, saying that Jeffers was the one that moved the cradles around when your mother was sleeping."

He was laughing again and then said, "I would like to believe that, my sweet, but that is ridiculous—impossible! You see, Mother always had old Vera with her at all times. Besides, Jeffers is a faithful servant and has been with Penumbra since before Father was born. He loves the place as we all do."

Removing her gloves, she slapped them in her hand. "Exactly! So why would he not do what he thought was expected of him? After all, you and Derrick are not identical twins and of the two of you, Derrick resembles the duke. You, my dear, except for the duke's same dark eyes, you have your mother's fine-looking features and are much more handsome than your brother."

He gave her a smug grin.

Eudora buried her disgust at his grandiose conceit. He was always preening, looking for confirmation of his handsomeness. It aggravated her so that it was all she could do to keep from loudly screaming her true feelings.

Delbert, pondering this news, said, "All I remember hearing is that Vera was old and slept half the time, but Mother loved her and wanted Vera with her. Vera was a trusted part of Penumbra. As for Jeffers, he always had the run of Penumbra with both Father and Mother's approval."

"Think, Delbert, think!"

"Do you know what you are implying, Eudora? Jeffers would…" He wanted to accept her words, yet… "I can't believe it."

"Believe it, Delbert."

"If this is true, I have been cheated and no one knows it, except Jeffers."

Pleased at how easy it was to instill these fraudulent thoughts in him, spitefully, she added, "I hate to have to tell you this, my darling, but I think the duke is well aware of what happened. In fact, it would not surprise me if Jeffers obeyed his orders."

Delbert stood in the cool afternoon shade, contemplating, digesting the startling possibility—Eudora observed Delbert's facial expression, he *was* considering her lies.

He twisted his mouth and charged, "I shall confront Father on this at once. I will force the truth from him. I shall get what is mine… that I'm entitled to." He pulled at Eudora's hand, taking long steps to hurry to the curricle.

You idiot, thought Eudora. *You are the most gullible man I have ever set eyes upon.* She had to stop him or else all her plotting would fail. The duke would laugh at his son's absurd accusations and throw him out. More than likely, should the duke learn who planted this seed of chicanery, he would disown Delbert just for giving one iota of consideration to these bizarre allegations. "Darling, wait," her voice was anxious, "you cannot do that."

He gaped at her. "Are you addled? Of course I can, I must have the truth."

She recognized his righteous determination and quickly cajoled him. "Don't you see, if your father is aware of this, why has he never corrected this disgraceful blunder? It had to have been done by his volition. He will be angry with you for your discovery and deny it all. If he allows you to expound your beliefs, he could disown you for it. Think, my darling, when has anyone ever forced the Duke of Grenfell and Penumbra to do anything against his will? He has tremendous power and that power can be yours if you proceed with diligence." Putting her arm around Delbert's waist and drawing him to her, she whispered, "I have an idea that will not only grant you your rightful heritage but ensure that the duke will be unable to cause a scintilla of trouble."

She led the man she could barely abide to the trunk of the oak. It was so huge it was like leaning against a wall. "You have to trust me, dearest."

Delbert took Eudora into his arms and kissed her roughly with one of his wet kisses. He first missed her mouth, catching her on her chin before seizing her pouted lips. Her mouth sealed, he pulled from her, panting. "Open for me." And she did, not daring to disobey his order. He slobbered her face as his hands slid to her breasts and squeezed them mercilessly. She would not cry out. She did one time and he had become more brutal; now, she gently pushed him away. "Let me catch my breath. We'll have plenty of time for that later." She desperately wanted to draw her hand across her mouth to rid his wetness, but again, she didn't dare. "Do you want to hear what I have in mind for you to become the Duke of Grenfell and command Penumbra?"

Filled with lust, he decided to let her have her way, just this once. "Of course I will listen, but I will tell you I can see no other solution."

Eudora gritted her teeth. There was no hope for him; she would have to do it all. "There is a way, but you must promise that this conversation will always remain just between the two of us. No one must ever know."

Delbert peered at her, his eyes narrowing. "Sometimes you surprise me, Eudora. I find this secret talk quite appealing." *Whatever she is scheming and I go along will give me control over her.* "You have my solemn promise—what is said here goes no further."

Believing revenge to be at hand she greedily accepted his words. "You mentioned last week that your father and Derrick were leaving for France to conduct business. What would you say if they met with an accident and never returned?"

Delbert froze in place. He stared at her all the while his brain began clicking. Then his mouth twisted into an ugly sneer, his eyes looked as if they belonged to the devil, even the sun couldn't warm them. The hatred he always carried within him expanded. He wanted it all— everything! No matter how or by what means he wanted it all and the very thought of making it happen, to enable his becoming the next

24

Grenfell heir, he'd do it. He grabbed Eudora's shoulders, eying her, his voice no longer whining, but intense. "How... how can it be done?" Suddenly, it seemed as if lightning struck, "You must be crazy, to kill a *duke*—even harm one is putting one's head in a noose." He shook his head. "Agree to kill an aristocrat? Never!"

Eudora hid her feelings of loathing—motivated to fulfill her goal, she said, "There are ways, but it will take blunt... lots of it." She lightly ordered, "Please release me, so I can breathe."

He wanted answers, so he dropped his hands allowing her to step away. "Who? Who in their right mind would kidnap and do away with the Duke of Grenfell and his son? No one would dare." He laughed, "They would have to be *out* of their mind to even think it."

You dolt! "Dearest, they would not know that they were kidnapping a duke and his heir. They will only know that they are doing away with a rich man and his spoiled son and being amply paid to do so."

Suddenly, the scheme penetrated, "Oh, I see... I see." He clapped his hands, "Do it, Eudora, if you can. I will have what I am entitled and you, my beautiful angel, will be the next Duchess of Grenfell."

She placed her hand over her mouth needing to hide her glee at how easily she had succeeded with her trickery—yet it still remained that she tie Delbert to the kidnapping for her own protection. It would give her something to hold over his head when he became duke. It would guarantee becoming Grenfell's duchess. "As I said, darling, they want a lot of money and also they will not deal only with me, but must deal with a man."

"I... I don't understand." Quaking inside, not wanting her to know he didn't want to be closely involved, he griped, "I cannot meet with these people, whoever they are," he became squeamish, "they might recognize me. How did you come in contact with *those* kinds?"

She wanted to smack him and shout, but again perseverance prevailed. "Who they are is no concern of ours. Two of them helped fix a wheel on my carriage when Cobble took me to the village. They told me they needed work—they'd do any kind if there was money paid and could be found at Pigwhistle. So I got in touch with them." She shuddered and imitated fear. "It was frightening, but I had to tell them I knew of someone who would pay well to do away if two men didn't reach their destination. All I could think of was of your being cheated since birth."

"But, Eudora…"

"I am but a woman and they do not trust doing business with a woman. But do not worry, for I'll be with you at the meeting. We can cover our faces and they'll not know our names."

"Well… I guess…" he looked at her, his eyes narrowing to slits, "then we do this together."

"Of course. I wouldn't think of not being with you. Can you get the money?"

"How much?"

"I'll have to let you know."

"All right, just don't be too generous."

Idiot! "Why, Delbert, you surprise me," she smiled, "you're going to be the Duke of Grenfell, the richest duke living—this isn't the time to deny someone being compensated for handling this situation with its predictable outcome."

He reached out and pinched her right breast. He knew he hurt her and dared her to say so.

Ever so careful, she playfully slapped his hand. "Stop that, we have many more things to resolve and not much time for your teasing."

After another hour of discussion, it was agreed his father and twin would leave for France and never be heard from again. Delbert must convince them to travel to the harbor in an unmarked coach. But before the duke and Derrick departed, Delbert would visit with Lord Weston and Eudora would see their banns posted for their forthcoming wedding.

Delbert helped Eudora into the curricle. As they settled in, both euphoric over their scheming, Eudora cunningly inquired, "Darling, will you permit me to wear the famous Grenfell jewels when we marry?"

"So, with all that we are about to do, your greedy little mind still wants more." He turned the horse and snapped the whip hard. "I will tell you something, my sweet, I have looked, hunted, and scoured the premises for them and have found nothing. I once mentioned them to Father and he laughed and thought it a joke. So, my future greedy little duchess, if you want to waste your time searching for them, you have my permission. But I assure you they don't exist. No doubt they have been sold off if they were real jewels."

"Oh, they were real. My father and others have seen them. Only the king has jewels and gems more famous than the Grenfell jewels. People talk, you know, and everyone says they have never seen anything as magnificent and costly—I want to wear them."

Dream on, Eudora. "Then we shall see, won't we?" He whipped the horses again and turned to take his love home to Sherbrooke Hall. *Let her think there are jewels to be had. She will find it is nothing but gossip.* He bided his time this long, he could wait. She would belong to him. He would not only have her but Sherbrooke, too. He hid his smile as all this time Eudora thought she was controlling him. She was in for one big surprise. Keeping his thoughts buried, he relaxed—content to wait. His future duchess was not going to enjoy her acquired status all that much if she didn't obey his every wish and command.

"Really, Delbert, must you constantly whip the horses?"

"You're right. Best I listen to you and leave the beasts be." *Don't get too comfortable giving me orders, Eudora, as you're going to have a lot to learn, but that will come later.* He put the whip in its sheath and slackened his hold on the reins. He smiled at his lady, turning the horses toward Sherbrooke Hall.

Chapter Four

Ten days later, after Eudora's planned revenge

The Duke of Grenfell sat with his twin sons in his study.

"Why don't you change your mind and come with us, Del?" Derrick urged.

Just as there's a chance of finding snow in the tropics is there a chance I'll join you and Father on this trip. "Thanks, Derr, but you know I despise ships."

The duke moved to place his hand on Delbert's shoulder. "Well then, Son, promise me you'll wait until we return before you wed—Eudora hasn't set a date—there's no rush."

"Really, Your Grace, I wish you would stop trying to discourage me. Eudora and I will be married and that is all there is to it. She hasn't set a date, but she will soon. We are committed to each other."

Derrick said nothing because the more he tried to convince Delbert marrying Eudora would be a grave mistake, it only strengthened his twin's determination.

The duke returned to his desk. "As you will. You understand that once you wed Eudora, you both will be welcome to visit Penumbra but your residence will be the dowager house on Penumbra's southlands. You may restore it to your liking—have the statements due sent to my solicitor. Eudora will be your wife and I will accept that if she makes you happy. At this time, it is impossible to recognize Eudora as a *close* daughter-in-law, but overtime, if you are content, we can mend our attitudes." His tone brooked no interference. "I stress to both of you that what is said in this room is to remain a private family affair and no one is to be aware of any disagreements. I won't have it any other way! This discussion is over."

Delbert's face turned a deep red to match his temper. "If Eudora had chosen Derrick, you would have accepted her. But because I am the winner, you will not."

Derrick stood. "You are a fool, Del. Eudora loves only Eudora. This is not a game. We are brothers... we are family and we are all Stauntons."

Delbert's mouth twisted, "That's easy for you to say—you have it all. Except Eudora and that gnaws on you, doesn't it?"

Derrick opened his hands, palms up. "Please believe me, Del, I have no interest in Lady Eudora Weston, whatsoever. She is a crafty little schemer." Impatient with his brother's blindness, he went on, "Why can't you believe I don't care for her? In fact, I don't think Eudora is good enough for *you!*" Seeing his twin sit in a sulk, Derrick realized Delbert didn't believe one word he'd spoken. He shrugged, "You're my brother and because of that, Eudora will be welcome as your wife." His voice softened, "I cannot help being the first-born, Del." He walked to stand in front of Delbert and held out his hand, "Brothers, right?"

Delbert slowly raised his hand; Derrick gripped it hard, offering a warm smile.

"Maybe when Father and I return, you and I can go off to London for a few weeks like we use to." He grinned, "That way we won't have to travel over water—what do you say?"

Inwardly, Delbert smoldered. *If he thinks he can fool me believing he cares, well, soon it'll be over and done with.* Adjusting his features, he answered, "That's a great idea, Derr. We can discuss if you... I mean, when you return." Shaken by his slip, he quickly explained, "I've been rather edgy. Sorry about that, I'm glad we're brothers. I'll think about London."

The Duke of Grenfell said nothing. He didn't trust his younger's son's apology. Something was amiss. Delbert's restless mannerisms and attempt at deceptive camaraderie toward Derrick made the duke suspicious. His gut told him something was going on—it raised the hair at his nape. *If only I could delay our departure, but this meeting took months to set up and Derrick must take part.* "We're running late, Derrick. I'm glad the trunks are loaded. We'll have to ride into the night to arrive at the harbor." He put his hand on Delbert's shoulder, "Take care, Son. We will see you in about three months. If anything should come up, Jeffers knows to contact Barslow."

"Do not worry, Father. Everything is going to be all right. I'm capable of looking after Penumbra."

Jeffers pulled open the big oak door where the coach waited.

The duke bellowed, "What is the meaning of this? Why is this not the coach with the Grenfell crest? Why have you loaded this unmarked one?"

The coachman stood next to the big wheel. He never saw his grace in this uproar, ever. Shaking, he said, "Yer Grace, tis upon orders from your son."

"*What?* You know better, Derrick."

"Twas yer younger son, yer Grace," the coachman corrected.

"How dare you countermand my orders?" He shook his cane at Delbert and spoke to Derrick. "We've no time to change coaches now." Going toward the open conveyance, he turned, "Delbert, hear me well… I want you to do absolutely nothing regarding Penumbra. You only look after yourself and nothing more. We'll discuss this matter when I return."

The duke became more suspicious of his son and almost called off their journey, but it would be difficult to explain when it had taken six months to arrange these clandestine meetings that also included the king's accords.

Delbert raised his hand to his mouth to cover his snicker as he watched his father and his twin drive away. When they were out of sight, he gloated, stepping back into Penumbra Manor humming a tune as he thought of becoming the next Duke of Grenfell. Being master of these lands and its people—he strutted into the drawing room and poured some of the duke's finest brandy—his hand shaking, he used deliberate care lifting the oversized snifter with both hands. Swirling the mahogany liquid before he gulped it to fortify himself knowing the time was near and he was scared, if there was a mishap and his father lived, he and Eudora would be sent to the colonies without a farthing.

Taking another swallow, he hurried to the stables to their covert meeting. Eudora would be waiting. His upper lip curled as he thought about the surprise he had for his future wife, but first things first. He had the blunt. It was time to act.

Chapter Five

Cold damp air with its thick hanging fog added to the uneasiness the duke couldn't shake as the black unmarked coach rolled along.

"If at all possible, I would cancel this journey." The duke fisted his hand, pounding the seat next to him.

"You're worried about Del, aren't you?"

"Yes. Something is not right. Lately his behavior is cause for concern. He's been overly patronizing and that is not consistent with his character—now switching to this coach is not to be dismissed. Damn, I wonder what that son of mine is up to."

"I agree, Father, though I hope we're wrong."

"Our crested coach would make someone think twice before stopping us. I no longer trust Delbert and I suggest you heed my warning and do likewise." Pounding one clenched hand into the palm of his other, he added, "He must have an ulterior motive—we best be alert."

Wanting to ease his father's worry, Derrick said, "You know Del, he seems to carry a chip on his shoulder for just about everything. His thinking I resent Eudora for choosing him, and my explaining only made him more belligerent. Perhaps our being apart will help."

"There's more to it, Derrick. I hope I'm wrong, but I think not. I cannot put my finger on it, yet I am unable to shake this feeling of trepidation. We're going to return to Penumbra."

The duke was about to knock on the coach roof to order the coachman to turn back when the coach lurched and tilted as a wheel broke from its axle, frightening the horses. They kept galloping, dragging and scraping on three wheels. The driver shouted at them to stop while pulling on the ribbons, just as suddenly it came to a halt. Both Staunton men were slammed against each other.

"What the blazes happened?" The duke called out, "Is anyone hurt?"

The door was pulled open. The duke, trying to raise himself, saw a monstrous man with a blunderbuss aimed at him. Behind the big man was a gathering of men all in ragged clothing with swords drawn. Their faces covered with dirty cloths. Some had stockings pulled over their heads with eyeholes cut in them. The nervous robbers couldn't keep their horses from prancing, causing more upheaval.

"Hurry up, Big Mike, get the job done so we can get our money."

"Shut up, you fool of a hare-head, now they know it's Big Mike. You sure are stupid, Rafferty."

Big Mike raised his voice, "Will you all just shut up. You ain't got no brains." There was an immediate hush. Only the horses' snorts disturbed the silence.

"Get out of there, you jelly livers," Big Mike yelled at the duke and his son. "You men watch the driver and his lackey. Billy Jig, you go find the other one that fell off back there and make sure he ain't going nowhere."

The duke made his way out of the tilted coach; it rocked as he tried to get a bit of balance. Derrick followed, causing it to tilt more and sway with force. Holding on to one of the broken lanterns, the duke whispered, "Are you all right, Son?"

"Yes… are you?"

"Stop gabbing," roared Big Mike.

Making their way to stand, the duke unafraid, straightening his waistcoat—having lost one glove pulled the other off. Thinking this was a robbery, ordered, "Hurry and take what you want and be off with you."

"Now ain't you acting like some big lord?"

"I am the—"

Without any warning, Big Mike took the blunderbuss swinging it hard against the older man's head, crushing his skull. The duke crumbled onto the ground with blood oozing from his head. His eyes were open wide, possibly in disbelief. One leg was bent underneath his immaculate tailored clothes now disheveled and muddy. His coat hung open and his white linen shirt covered in blood. The Duke of Grenfell did not know what hit him. He died in seconds.

Derrick jumped at the oversized man landing a punch, but it was futile; he was pulled away while Big Mike howled with laugher. Derrick landed on the wet ground and crawled next to his father. He could not hold back his tears as he picked up his father's crushed head and held it against his chest. He looked up at the men who had dismounted. "Why? What has this man ever done to you to deserve this? This is my father…" he choked on his sobs; he couldn't help it if he tried. He couldn't control the tremors racing through him, not for himself but for this man he loved. "He did nothing to you. Why?"

"We got us a rich little crybaby!" Big Mike crowed. "Why, I bet his hands are nice and tender like a baby. I bet he never lifted a barrel or a crate in his soft mushy life."

The men, laughing, slapped one another on their backs. "When are you going to kill him, Big Mike?"

Big Mike rubbed the dirty stubble on his face. "Did you take care of all the others?"

"Yeah, it was easy. They be singing with the angels."

Derrick heard their wretched bragging, he had to get away, yet how could he leave his father? He never felt so helpless in his life. His father dead and he could do nothing.

Horses' hooves could be heard in the distance. Derrick heard then— help is coming—until he heard the next words from one of the bandits. "Just like you said, here comes our pay. Hurry and get rid of the other one so we can collect."

But Big Mike had another idea, he grinned as he punched the side of the leaning coach, rocking it. "Listen, I'm going to knock this one out. He's already covered with the old man's blood, so they'll think he's dead. We can collect for the job and sell him to Zuber. I say let this rich one find out what work is. He'll learn what it's like to eat slop and pray for rain for his dry innards." He gloated, "That's what we'll do." Without care, he swung his fist and knocked Derrick unconscious. "Rafferty, come over here and keep your foot on his chest. Whatever you do, don't let him move or make a sound."

"Don't worry," Rafferty took a dirty rag from his pocket and stuffed it into Derrick's mouth. He rested his heavy, dirt covered boot on Derrick's chest. "All set."

Two horses trotted upon the scene. One horse carried a veiled female in a fancy red riding habit. She controlled her mount, it halted and she slipped from its side saddle. The other rider, dressed in dark stableman's clothes with a scarf exposing only his dark eyes, sat in his saddle trying to keep his horse still. Looking at the devastation—shivers ran up and down Delbert's spine. Terrified, he had to relieve himself in the worst way but knew it was impossible. So he gripped the reins, yanking on them and unsettling his horse.

Lady Eudora walked straight over and stared at two bloodied bodies lying in the muddied earth. She withheld the smile that wanted to burst. *Now I'll name our wedding day.* Her body tingled—she'll become the Duchess of Grenfell—she did it. Until seeing this carnage, she had no intention of marrying Delbert. "You have done well," she complimented Big Mike. "Are the others dead?"

"If you mean this rich man's lackeys… yeah. When I do a job, I do it like I say I would," he bragged. "We've did away with everybody. Now, where's our blunt?"

Derrick came to. His head ached, he wanted to move, but the pressure on his chest kept him in his prone position. Something was stuffed in his mouth; he needed to remove to breathe easier but he felt more pressure on his chest. He stayed as he was and listened.

Eudora called to Delbert without using his name. "Bring the money to these men. They have completed our agreement. It is done."

Delbert swung from his saddle bringing a heavy leather pouch, unhappy having to part with it. Yet consoling that there is more… much, much more and soon to be all his, he capitulated without a sound.

Big Mike eyed Delbert and laughed. "He's a weak sister, he is." He gave the man with the money a malicious grin. "I say, do you want to come over and feel for a heartbeat?"

Delbert took a closer look at his father and brother's bloodied bodies and shuddered. "Here... here take it." He pushed the promised payment toward Big Mike and stepped away, unable to take in anymore.

Big Mike taunted, "Where you going? I think I better count it." He recognized fear and saw it in the money man's eyes.

Eudora took over. "You don't have to count it, you clodpoll. It's all there. Now be sure you take these bodies out to sea. They are to be washed up on shore and found so they can be immediately reported to the local magistrate. Take what you want from them, but be sure you leave his papers in the waterproof packet on the old man's body. They must be found on him. Is that clear?"

Derrick heard Eudora. Her voice he'd never forget or his twin's whine. His eyes were closed, but tears escaped, rolling unnoticed by his captors. At first, Derrick thought he was part of a nightmare until he heard Eudora giving orders. His twin and Eudora were responsible for his father's death and the rest of this mayhem. *Father, you were so right.*

"What's in those papers, lady?" Big Mike asked.

Knowing Big Mike and his companions couldn't read, she answered smoothly, "They are necessary letters with his name on them. They will identify this man for the magistrate. Check them over if you want, but put them back as they are—to be kept dry."

Shrugging his shoulders, Big Mike nodded. "Right you are then. Take this blunt, Billy Jig," he tossed it over, "and guard it. You others, let's get a move on and get these bodies down to the sea."

Satisfied and not wanting to be found in these surroundings, she nudged Delbert and walked to her horse. "Give me a hand up," she ordered Big Mike.

He obeyed without thought and trod over, lifting her onto the side saddle with a plop, like she was a feather. Her veiled face covered her grimace as he squeezed her small waist with his dirty hands. His smell almost made her vomit; she swallowed her bile and thanked him graciously.

Big Mike grinned, exposing rotten teeth. "You be some kind of woman. Why, you didn't even flinch, not once when you looked at your dead friends." Looking over at Delbert, who was struggling to find the stirrup to mount up, while his horse wouldn't be still, Big Mike added, "That one's a weak pup. You want a real man—you know where to find me." He gave Eudora's thigh a couple of pinches. When Delbert was finally sitting his horse, Eudora kicked her mount and rode off in the same direction whence they came with Delbert following. The fog lifting, Big Mike and his men watched, their low laughter heard by the two conspirators until they disappeared into the early morning mist.

"All right, strip them of their worth. Bring the wagon around so we can load them up. Let the horses go. We must get rid of that coach."

Billy Jig piped up, "Can we trade off the horses?"

"You crazy? This is one rich man. Do you want to chance that someone could connect us to this?" He waved his arm. "We don't never take belongings we can't hide." Standing with his thumbs hooked on his rope knotted belt, he offered a sly grin, "You did good, Rafferty. I saw the rich milksop try to move. Get him loaded… Captain Zuber will be at the wharf tomorrow night."

Billy Jig cackled, "He won't last long with Zuber. That man is so mean everyone stays clear of even getting close to his ship."

Derrick heard Billy's words, he couldn't have said anything if he wanted to, his throat felt as if it was filled with sand. Grief ran silently all through his body, striking every nerve, and then was replaced by rage. He vowed to do all possible to stay alive and however long it took, he'd avenge his father's murderers and without question or doubt come back for Delbert and Eudora.

Chapter Six

Viscount Delbert Stephen Staunton faced the short, rotund magistrate and his two aides in Penumbra's drawing room. Delbert kept his eyes down concealing his overriding satisfaction at a job well done. His hands, clenched behind his back, he stood, nodding in agreement at the words championing the duke.

The magistrate, Hillery Bowles, continually shaking his balding head, went on, "It is too much a shock to find his grace dead, washing up on shore. My condolences."

Anxious to get this three-hour meeting over with, Delbert interrupted the talkative man. "Thank you… thank you all. This has stunned me more than I can say. My poor father—I only wish you had news of my brother. Are you sure you have no information as to what happened?"

"No, my lord. We know it's the duke because of his private papers being on him. He was a fine man, a fine, fine man." Taking in the viscount's sober character, the magistrate apologized having to continue his inquiry. "You said the duke and your brother were to sail to France. We heard nothing about a ship being in trouble. The sea can be pretty rough, but there's no word of a big blow." He shook his head confirming his words, "Nothing, not a word. Such a tragedy," he began twisting his hat, "such a tragedy. Such a tragedy."

Delbert said nothing, waiting for this man to end his telling.

"There must be some way to get in touch with your older brother. When did you say you expect him back, my lord?" He raised his eyebrows, his features coming alive. "Oh my, oh my, he might not know that he is now the new duke."

Furious that Derrick's body was not yet discovered and filled with resentment at having to pretend his twin will be the Duke of Grenfell, Delbert's voice turned snappish, "For the fourth time, Bowles, they were both to return in about three months." Thinking he better tone down his retort, explained again, "Please forgive me, but I can't believe this accident has happened. I'm concerned about my brother. I can only hope that nothing untoward has happened to him. This is very difficult to accept. Are you sure you have no more information?"

"I'm sorry, my lord. We do not." Bowing his head, he said, "It grieves me greatly to have to ask at this time, but what do you want us to do with the duke's body?"

Concealing his repressed rage because those clumsy oafs didn't follow through with Derrick's body, Delbert reached to grip the back of a chair.

Mistaking Delbert's silence for distress, Bowles lowered his voice. "I'm sorry; but I must know. I understand how worry can get to you at such times."

Before Delbert could make a decision, Jeffers knocked at the opened door, announcing, "The Earl of Sherbrooke and Lady Eudora Weston to see you, my lord."

Delbert breathed a sigh of relief, as his dear Eudora could talk to this garrulous magistrate. He had enough of listening to the continuous praise about the duke.

The Earl of Sherbrook strode into the room. He ignored the magistrate, speaking to Delbert, "My boy, I just heard of this terrible tragedy that has befallen you."

Eudora followed her father and could immediately recognize Delbert needing her help. "Dearest," she went to him, "we can't believe the duke is gone from us. Is it really true?"

The earl was totally aghast. "Are you sure it's his grace? Why, I saw his grace the other day as hale and hearty as one could hope to be. This is catastrophic. What happened? How? Where is your brother? Derrick should be here."

Hillery Bowles took two steps forward, bowing, "If you will allow me, my lord, I will tell what we know. First off, Jeffers, the duke's long-time butler identified the body even though it was quite beaten from the sea and rocks, Jeffers assured me it is the Duke of Grenfell. Jeffers also said that he must notify the duke's solicitor, a Mr. Barslow."

The earl waited.

Bowles kept twisting his hat before he spoke. "It was… it was early this morning and little Robbie Wickslee came running to my quarters. He said two fishermen found a body in the water. I hurried and Robbie took me to the spot where the fishermen were waiting. One handed me the packet that was on the body and when I found it belonged to the Duke of Grenfell, I couldn't believe it was the duke's battered body washed up against the rocks. It was bad, my lord. I never saw anyone that bad. We wrapped him in a blanket and brought him here. His lordship being quite upset—Jeffers made the identification. Now, I'm waiting for his lordship to tell me what to do."

"This is horrible. Where is Derrick, the Marquis? Lady Eudora said he was traveling with the duke. Was there any sign that the same thing could have happened to him?"

"I'm sorry, I can't say. We don't know how the duke landed in the water and drown. The sea can be rough," Bowles shook his head in a quandary, "could be the duke slipped and had fallen overboard. Though if that were so, it being the Duke of Grenfell, the *Silver Cloud's* captain would have returned to port to report it and his son would be here."

Delbert and Eudora said nothing all this time; they stood together listening as the earl questioned the magistrate.

"This is dreadfully upsetting—Derrick, the marquis, must be grieving over this tragedy. He will have many responsibilities now that he's the new Duke of Grenfell. Penumbra needs him. He may well be traveling back as we speak."

Eudora squeezed Delbert's arm, keeping him from saying anything. She didn't trust him not to blurt something to give anyone cause to think other than what they already knew.

"Delbert," she spoke softly, but loud enough for she wanted the others to hear, "would you permit Lord Weston to take charge of the duke's interment?"

The Earl of Sherbrooke straightened, knowing any connection with the esteemed Duke would bring him goodwill from his peers. "I would be honored."

Delbert's voice rang strong and proud. "Thank you, Weston, but I have decided that an expeditious burial must take place. There is no telling when Derrick will return. I will seek the cleric's help and inter my father immediately. He will rest next to my mother on Penumbra land."

"But Delbert... my lord," the surprised earl contended, "don't you want to wait a few days to hear from your brother? Why, there are many who value the Duke of Grenfell as a peer as well as with deep friendship. The King especially holds your father in high esteem. I'm sure that many of them would like to attend the service."

Keeping his wrath smothered and hating this man for trying to countermand his arrangements, especially in front of others, Delbert stood tall, looking down on the magistrate before eying the earl, and then said, using his most authoritative tone, "My father will be interred tomorrow. When Derrick returns, we will hold a service and anyone who wishes to attend will be welcome. I consider my decision to be observed. After all, it is only right that Derrick be part of our farewell to our esteemed Duke of Grenfell."

Presuming Delbert's decision and tone was to cover his grief—not wanting to upset him further, said, "You are right. I should have understood. Please accept my apology, and if there is something I can do to alleviate your pain, I am at your disposal."

Looking at the Earl of Sherbrooke, his eyes not blinking, Delbert said, "Just now I would like to be alone. There is nothing anyone can do. Jeffers will see you all out. Thank you for coming, Lord Weston." He eyed Eudora, "And thank you also, my dear Lady Eudora. And Bowles, thank you and your men for all that you have done. I must have time—accepting that my father is gone and not walking about Penumbra, well…"

Jeffers appeared. They all followed the old butler, but Eudora waited. Delbert nudged her along. "You'll attend the burial with me tomorrow, won't you?"

"But of course."

"I'm glad. I need you." He left and climbed the stairs. He heard Jeffers usher everyone out and Penumbra's heavy oak door clicked shut, its echo shaking the old butler as a tear escaped.

Reaching the second floor and heading for the duke's study, Delbert couldn't contain his self-satisfied grin. He sat in his father's desk chair. *Finally, I have what rightly belongs to me. I am the Duke of Grenfell and master of Penumbra and all its land and holdings. I am not like you, my munificent twin, I will use Grenfell power and rule it as it should be. Whatever they did with you, Derrick, matters not; for dead men tell no tales and I saw you dead. As the new duke I will demand the honor due me and no one can alter my station in life. As the Duke of Grenfell, I will be obeyed.*

He rose from the desk and strutted, taking his handkerchief from the cuff of his coat and twirling it around and around. A smile built until it exploded as he knew without a doubt in his mind everything now belonged to him and it would not be long until he could permanently move into the master's rooms that were always occupied only by the Dukes of Grenfell. *Grenfell Power!* Delbert was filled with elation and not one ounce of remorse.

Chapter Seven

Derrick knew the thugs that killed his father had finished their dirty work. He had no idea how much time had elapsed. He was at sea; hearing the water slap against the hull and feeling the roll of the waves as the ship cut its watery path. There was no light, it could be midnight, as all he remembered was being hauled and thrown on the ship's deck. When he landed, he must have hit his head; he recalled nothing until this moment.

His body aching along with his head pounding, his throat dry-wet clothes stuck to his body as putrid smells assaulted his senses. He tried to rise up on his elbow, only to slip on slime. *The gnawing and scratching must be rats.* He was sure one ran over his thigh.

Someone was outside his prison, struggling to lift a bar that must be levered across the door to prevent any escape. The door creaked on its rusted hinges and a boy held a lantern as high as he could over his scrawny head. Derrick squinted, blinded for a moment from the lantern's light.

"Mister?" the boy called out in a loud whisper. "Mister, are you awake? Can you hear me?" He panicked. "You gotta say something, you gotta…"

Derrick hesitated to answer, filled with trepidation but knew there was nothing he could so about his predicament, he'd do whatever it took to stay alive. The rage seething within him built a powerful strength. Hatred will be his friend and those involved will pay, but a particular *two* will feel his vengeance, no matter how long it takes, he will see his twin and Eudora pay for murdering his father.

"Please, Mister… if you can hear me, I'm not supposed to be here. If I get caught, I'll be in trouble. I got a message for you from Gully."

The pleading and fear in the boy's voice penetrated into Derrick's mind. When Derrick tried to speak, his mouth was dry and he could make himself heard. "I ah…"

The boy quickly set the lantern down and took a tin hanging around his neck and passed it to Derrick. "Here, Gully said you was gonna need this."

Gulping the tepid water, Derrick barely said, "Thanks."

The boy spoke so low, Derrick strained to hear. Trying to keep his balance as the ship cut its way through the rolling sea, he said, "Mister, Gully says to tell you to do everything the Captain says and to do what his mate, Kellowing, says. You're to say the guys who brought you here owed you money and this is how you got paid. That you know them from Pigwhistle where you gambled." Backing toward the opening, anxious to get away lest he get caught, he begged, "Do you understand, Mister? You can trust Gully. I gotta go."

"Wait," His throat raw, croaked, "Who is Gully? Who are you?"

Hanging the tin back around his neck and taking his lantern, he answered, "Me name is Muggs and Gully is me friend. He's the best one on this here ship. He mends the sails and cooks." The lantern's light lit the boy's eyes, "Gully can do anything… I gotta go, if they catch me here, I could get the whip. Remember, just do like Gully says." He closed the noisy door slowly to hide its noise and put the lever back in place.

Derrick did not move. His throat felt a bit better. He thought over Muggs' message and decided he had nothing to lose by following this Gully's advice. He would go along and take things as they transpired. For now, he had to get some life back in his muscles and began moving his arms. He could not stand—his head just barely cleared the top of the cramped compartment. Besides, he was sure that even if he could stand, he would slip in the slime. He stretched his arms as best he could, his fingers touching wet wood. He concentrated on working his mind and staying his energy for only one thing—to live.

The hinges screeched as the door was flung open on Derrick's prison. A callous voice yelled, "Crawl out of there, you scourge of a dog, the captain wants you topside."

Derrick moved toward the opening, crawling, his cramped legs forcing him to progress slowly, but he was not fast enough for the seaman, known to the crew as Knife. He pulled Derrick out of his cramped prison by his loose hair, now matted with grime. Pain shot through Derrick's already pounding head as Knife continued yanking him forward, not releasing his hold until he had him out of the lock-up. He then gave Derrick's hair one good yank and proceeded to swing back his foot and kick his ribs. "Stand up," he ordered. Derrick tried to stand, but his legs buckled, they would not hold his weight. "I ought to leave you down here with the rats and let 'em eats your bones, but I got orders."

Knife hauled Derrick and thrust him up one hatch and then another and another into waiting hands. From there, he was dragged and pushed onto the dirtiest deck he'd ever seen. It was a cloudy day, far from nighttime. He wondered how long he'd been at sea. The salty air was cold and he shivered, but its freshness helped revive him. He breathed deeply, taking in fresh air. Lying on his side, he was looking at a huge pair of crusted, unpolished black boots.

"Stand at attention!" The gruff voice snarled.

Derrick assumed it was coming from the owner of the dirty boots. He'd do as the unknown Gully had chanced to tell him. He made himself stand. Determined to survive and lifting up on his knees, pushing with his hands he rose, wobbling to stand upright. His nose crinkled at the pungent odor that hit his nostrils.

Derrick looked Captain Zuber in the eye and did not blink. They were the same height, but there the similarity ended. The captain's leather sun-lined, scarred face exhibited icy glaring blue eyes. His untrimmed beard was foul smelling with dried food. Derrick steeled himself not to step back from the captain's fetid breath; instead he inhaled as much salty sea air possible while keeping his head up, stayed put with his hands fisted, and kept his weakened legs spread to give him balance as the ship rode the waves.

The grubby crew of the *Shark Tooth* watching with their grins waiting with anticipation for the humiliation their captain was going to inflict on the fancy man—knowing Zuber always got his money's worth.

Captain Zuber stared at Derrick for several minutes, but to Derrick it seemed like hours. He felt his knees wanting to fold, but unwavering, he bit into his cheek and stifled a groan. The wind cut across his shoulders, turning his lips blue. They felt raw as he licked them and tasted salt.

Zuber recognized the defiant pride in this rich jellyfish Big Mike had sold him. *This one might need a little more breaking than the others. He may not be a jellyfish at all. I'll just have to show him what it's like to take orders.* Zuber's broad smile displayed unkempt crooked teeth. His crew knew what that smile implied and nudged one another, waiting. Zuber's eyes narrowed, *I hate these rich high-bobs. They took away my certification papers and command because of a few drunken sprees. Well, I showed them when I sailed off with their ship. I answer to no one. I take what I want, when I want, and I drink all I want. They can keep their bloody certificate. They'll never catch me.*

"I am Captain Zuber. The *Shark Tooth* is my ship. Welcome aboard, my lord," the captain taunted. "So tell me why you chose to join me and my reputable crew on this fine vessel?" His crew roared their approval. "Is it special learning you are seeking? I suppose you want to boast about being a pirate to the ladies or..." he jeered, "mayhap it's not the ladies you're interested in."

Derrick ignored his snide, absurd remarks. He raised his voice above the splash of the waves, "You asked, Captain Zuber... Sir, why I wanted to come on board your ship." His tone clear and steady, "It was not my choice. Know this, someday I will get my hands on Big Mike and I will kill him." He remembered what young Muggs had told him. "That cheating lowdown weasel owes me money and I intend to collect it and when I do, he will not live to ever gamble again." Derrick's features tightened, his voice filled with iron wrath and radiated hatred as he promised, "It may take a long time, but someday I will return to the Pigwhistle and Big Mike will not live to see another day. I don't forget and I don't forgive. I will personally beat him until he begs for mercy. He will pay; he will pay for everything. Never doubt that I will succeed." Derrick's body swayed, but his anger gave him energy to survive. *I'm a Staunton—we do not give-in or give-up.*

Captain Zuber sized up this man for whom he had paid Big Mike a minuscule sum. He always took what he could get, but this one was different. Though soiled, his shirt and pants were costly and he had never lacked for food. Zuber wordlessly admitted to a bit of respect for this high-bob, concluding he was no jellyfish Big Mike had believed him to be. Who he is will have no bearing. They were at sea and the *Shark Tooth* was his ship, his domain and he was the one that held the power.

Zuber didn't miss several of his crew backing off after hearing Derrick's violent threat of retribution, but there were some that would have their way. His men were a grungy lot, but they obeyed orders and accepted sharing the booty as he stipulated. That was all he expected from them.

Kellowing came over carrying a coiled lash. He was grinning, relishing what he had in mind. He snapped his whip; it caught one of Derrick's legs and as Kellowing pulled it back, Derrick fell as it ripped his skin, spinning him like a twig.

The crew, silent, but their juices were flowing. Now they were going to be treated to some brutality. It was a normal way of life for them. They thrived on it as long as it was the other guy.

"Hold on, Kellowing," the captain's smug tone carried out to his men, "I think we have a *gentleman* here." Standing with his scabbard hanging against his leg with his hand on the hilt of his rapier, said,

"Before you give him a good talking to with your enforcer, don't you agree we should let some of the crew have a say?"

Kellowing didn't understand class, he only judged a man by the size of his purse. The bigger the purse, the more significance he gave to the man. Big Mike said this one was rich; no doubt his purse was big but Big Mike got it. Kellowing showed a vile toothless smirk, but Derrick pretended not to take notice. "Well now, you scummy land lover, how does it feel getting your pretty face and hands dirty? How do you like your stink?"

The crew, some standing, some leaning against the ship's rail, others were loitering nearby waiting for the coming assault.

Derrick scoffed at his would-be tormentor even as the burning gash hurt from his whip, said, "My clothes and I stink, but that only matches what you're used to. Right?"

The verbal comeback was unexpected and it infuriated the first mate, especially in front of his captain and crew. It took a split second for Kellowing to raise his hand to wind the whip up, but expecting it this time; Derrick used all his strength and butted into Kellowing, knocking him off balance. He was tired and weak, his body freezing when he became cognizant of someone grabbing him. His fingers numb, his legs like rubber, he thought of why he was on this filthy boat and blood surged, his fortitude intensifying, he had to live to get back to Penumbra.

Kellowing was roaring as the biggest black man Derrick could ever recollect seeing, with large black eyes, flared nostrils and rosy cheeks against his ebony skin, lifted Derrick as if he weighted nothing at all. The crew watched, waiting.

"Put him down, Gully," the captain ordered.

Derrick was dropped on the deck, standing. He was panting as he held his head up. Blue and shivering from the cold wind with Gully grasping the back of his shirt to give him support, he couldn't stop trembling while trying unsuccessfully to keep his teeth from chattering. He would have collapsed but the black man kept him on his feet.

"I won't have my crew attacking one another unless I give them permission. I warn you this one time, do that again and you'll be fully punished. My first mate has a temper; you might do well to remember that."

Regaining his breath and some stamina, Derrick looked at Kellowing who stood one step behind Captain Zuber. "Mr. Kellowing misunderstood, Sir, I meant no disrespect."

"I think you're going to find trouble if you go around opening that arrogant mouth of yours. You mistake Kellowing, he really didn't want your answer."

"Yes, Sir!"

"That's the first sensible words you've said. You'll take orders from me and Kellowing if I so wish. Is that clear?"

"Yes, Sir."

"That settled, now what name do you want to go by?"

Derrick was taken aback; unaware he could select a new identity just like that. His only preoccupation was not to divulge his real name.

"Well?"

"I don't know. What would you suggest?"

The crew gasped. No one talked back to the captain.

Zuber grunted, "What the devil's deep do I care what you call yourself."

Deliberating, Derrick said, "I think *Wolf* will suit me."

The captain bellowed, his laugh carrying out to sea. His crew following his lead did the same. But Gully did not, nor did Kellowing or the small skinny lad who was hiding behind a water barrel. It was obvious to Derrick the boy was trying to be as inconspicuous as possible.

"I do not know if it is courage or audacity, but to name yourself after an animal is something my crew has never done."

Kellowing snickered, "Yeah, why would you call yourself Wolf?"

Derrick didn't want to mistakenly antagonize this man again, he asked, "May I have your permission to explain?"

Kellowing's chest puffed, *this one knows I'm boss.* "Yeah."

Derrick knew to carefully word his answer so that any idiot could understand. "As you probably know, Mr. Kellowing, a *wolf* is always on the lookout for something it wants. When it makes up its mind, it never gives up. A wolf will trail its prey for miles if it has to and is malicious and sly. Sometimes it will go right out into the open and be seen, but just as suddenly disappear only to show itself again if it wants to. When a wolf sets its mind on getting something, it hunts until it's successful." Derrick was calculating, he softened his voice to sound savage forcing the crew to strain to hear. "I'm going to be like a wolf for I'm going to get Big Mike even if it takes me years. I will trail him; I will find him. I will kill him. I will be successful just like a wolf."

Kellowing's insides knotted, coward without his whip, he did know this one was not to be fooled with unless the captain gave the nod to use his whip. The safest way to go would be to kill him and be done with it.

"From this day, you are *Wolf*." Then the captain sneered, "Now's the time for you to show if you are all talk. Let's see what you're made of." Raising his voice, he asked, "Which one of you sea bums wants to take on Wolf?"

"I ain't afraid of him," came a voice from up in the rigging. Sliding down as if he were on a brass pole, Knife strutted over to stand in front of the captain and Derrick.

"Oh no!" someone loudly whispered.

Another voice said, "Shut your trap, he's got it coming."

Everyone moved back, forming a circle on the dirty slippery deck. The captain nodded to Knife, then turned to Wolf. "Knife here wants to show you his mettle and see if you have any." Enjoying the situation, he grinned, "You're on your own, no one interferes."

Gully speedily thrust a dagger into Wolf's hand as he spoke into his ear, "Watch his left arm; when he swings it back, he's going to strike with his right."

Tired, cold, and not without terror, sweat breaking on his brow even with cold air chilling his salty body, Wolf prepared to do his best, telling himself he had to live… he had to live for his father and for Penumbra.

Knife heckled verbal threats to frighten the new man. He and Wolf circled one another, round and round, both waiting for the opportunity to strike. Wolf, a master with a sword, had no intention of becoming Knife's casualty. Wanting to be first, Knife misjudged his light-footed opponent and tried to close in on him fast. Wolf watched Knife's left arm and swiftly jumped away by a margin of a second. *That was close*, Wolf thought, but now he was able to judge his opponent's knife swing. Both men slashed and jabbed at air, missing each other. Knife reluctantly owned to himself that this man was better than he thought, but the Wolf was tiring and no one ever beat Knife in a knifing contest, that was how he got his name. He wickedly grinned with satisfaction as he lunged one way, anticipating Wolf to move in the other direction, when instead Knife jerked his step and followed Wolf's stance, plunging into Wolf's side, near his rib.

Stunned, having felt the deep thrust, Wolf slipped on the scummy deck, fell and lay still, panting. Knife thinking it was over, pulled out his dirty knife from Wolf's chest and raised his hand for his victory and proceeded to wipe the bloody blade on his pants. But it was not over; Wolf used one last burst of energy as he gripped Knife's legs. Caught off balance, Knife's knife flew from his hand as he fell flat on his face. Bleeding profusely and weak, Wolf rolled on top of Knife and held his dagger below Knife's earlobe, gasping for air and aching, Wolf growled, "As I said, a wolf always gets his prey." He was about to pass out when Gully went over and snatched Wolf's shirt, pulling him off Knife. "It all right for me to look after him, Captain?"

Tired of it all, Captain Zuber nodded. "Let me know when he stops bleeding. This is no passenger ship."

Gully carried Wolf to his small cabin that he shared with Muggs and Bender, the navigator. There was an extra bunk in the cabin because no one would share with a black man. It looked like they had found a fourth bunk mate.

Wolf came to as he lay in pain, but said nothing; resolved more than ever to seek revenge.

Gully spoke, his touch light as he examined the wound. "Tch! Is going to hurt you, Wolfman. You're probably going to get some infection from the dirty blade. I hope you're strong enough to beat it."

Wolf grimaced, "Thanks for your help. I'll beat this and it'll *never* happen to me again."

The tall black man looked at him, no pity. "If you're waiting for me to tell you that you did well, forget it. You're alive for now. Seeing as Knife always carries a dirty blade, the worse is yet to come, you can still die." Turning to the young boy who stood near the door watching, Gully said in a kind voice, "Go back to your duties, Muggs, before the captain and Kellowing look for you and cause trouble."

"Is he gonna be all right, Gully?"

"Yeah, I think so. Now go."

Muggs left without another word, closing the door. Gully pulled out a leather pouch and began to set his healing methods in motion. He moved to stuff a piece of white canvas cloth in Wolf's mouth.

Eying the man that helped him, Wolf whispered, yet with force, "I will not die!"

"We'll see." Pleased that this Wolfman would fight to live was encouraging to Gully.

"When I pour this on the cut, bite down, do not yell out for if you do, you will never make it to live on this ship. They're waiting to hear you yell your fool head off."

Waiting for a greater pain than he was already experiencing, Wolf did not see the blow coming, but felt a jolt and remembered nothing else.

While tending Wolf's wound and bruises, Gully became aware of the tiny mark under the upper part of Wolf's arm. He knew it meant something being hidden like that when Bender leaned over to see what held Gully's attention, he gave a soft whistle, then suggested to Gully to just forget about it and never mention it to anyone.

"It's important, ain't it?"

Bender barely nodded his head. "Yes. It would be best if no one knew about it."

"Whatever you say. It might seem foolish, but I like this man and I'll help him any way I can."

"Maybe someday he'll tell us what happened and why he was thrown on this filthy boat. But for now, we leave things are they are."

Gully nodded. Grinning, he said, "It looks almost like the one you got, Mr. Bender."

Bender's eyes twinkled. "There isn't much you miss, is there, Gully?"

"No Sir, I sure don't miss much and I keeps my mouth shut too."

"Thanks, Gully. I appreciate it and I'm sure our new bunk mate will too." With that, Bender left their cabin.

Chapter Eight

Gully and Muggs tended Wolf's body for three days-Wolf would toss and mumble.

Gully lifted him at his shoulders, keeping Wolf's head, up to spoon-feed him a liquid he concocted from seeds secreted in his leather pouch. Then he'd cover Wolf's face with an odd smelling cloth that put him into a deep sleep. The wound festered as Gully predicted and the best he could do was apply his special poultice and hope this stranger had the will to ride out the fever.

Cutting its own swath, the *Tooth* withstood the pounding sea. Although a dirty ship, it was seaworthy plowing through waves slinging seawater across its deck.

Gully, oblivious to the roll of the ship, did his best to stay awake long hours caring for the fearless unknown man. Soon the captain would demand Wolf appear on deck. Wolf would work or be thrown overboard as shark food. Though the captain had paid coin for a man, he had to be useful or he was gone.

Gully was thinking of when he first saw Wolf's bruised and bloodied body tossed on the *Tooth's* deck. He had a gut feeling that this was not a typical shanghai. The captain had argued price with Big Mike. Finally taking Zuber's offer, Big Mike gave the inert body lying on the deck a hard kick before climbing over the rail, never revealing to Zuber that he had to get rid of the evidence that he'd already been paid for. And Zuber yelling after him, "Bring me another sort like this one and I'll keep you on board in his place."

Gully knew that Big Mike's prospects were usually drunk. He'd have the poor soul tied and gagged so he couldn't yell his head off. This stranger was the complete opposite. Although unconscious and obviously battered, through the grime there was tidiness to his person, and he was not tied, gagged, nor drunk. Just as Gully took Muggs under his protection, he felt compelled to do the same for this bloodied stranger.

No one on board ship paid much attention to Gully—even the overeager brawlers left him alone. Perhaps it was his seven-foot height, his muscled torso or his deep dark color that kept them at bay. They were cowards and wouldn't risk their necks confronting him.

The first day Gully was shoved on board the Shark Tooth at Kingstown wharf, his hands were shackled at his waist and tied to his ankles while being prodded at the point of a sword. He was avoided by the crew and that never changed. When the Tooth had sailed away, the sun about to set, the captain had Gully's shackles removed but warned Gully that he would become shark food if at any time he did not obey orders or caused trouble. Much to Gully's surprise, he liked sailing and easily adapted to sea life. He obeyed orders, did his share of the work, if not more, and kept to himself.

The sugar plantation owner had been glad to be rid of Gully as all the beatings did not change Gully's belief that he was just as good as anyone—regardless of skin color. Gully had been taught on the sly to read and write by the plantation's overseer, Dreeco. Gully did Dreeco's work while the overseer was in a habitually drunken stupor. When the plantation owner returned unexpectedly and discovered Gully was running his plantation, he had Gully whipped. Then he fired his overseer, tossing him in the swamp. But Gully, proud of his abilities, bore his knowledge proudly and no punishment could change his manner or way of thinking. His attitude caused disruption among the other slaves and the owner knew he had to get to get rid of his problem. It was against the law for any black person to read, write, or do sums. Not wanting anyone to know of his lax in maintaining his plantation, especially that a black man was capable of doing a white man's work, the owner made arrangements to sell Gully to Captain Zuber, never revealing Gully's educated abilities. Gully kept it his secret, never telling anyone.

Time passed and Gully loved the sea. It was his paradise. He could endure the captain because in his own way, the captain was a fair man, nothing like slave owners.

Gully sailed on the *Tooth* for two years when Muggs, not more than eight years old, was pitched over the rail as good riddance from a drunken father. When Gully declared skinny little Muggs as his own, no one offered to fight him for ownership. Muggs was a small and bony and took verbal abuse from the crew, but no one dare touch him.

Now, Gully studied the sleeping man. He held respect for any man that stood up against odds, especially when there wasn't a chance in this wide ocean of escaping alive. Gully saw Wolf mask his qualms as he stood and faced them all. The captain ran a tight pirate ship because he had the *power—Shark Tooth* belonged to him. Kellowing with his whip and Knife with his blade were a brutal pair, delighted at inflicting pain, and Zuber tolerated it, but only with his consent.

"How do you think he's doing, Gully?"

Looking up, he said, "I don't know for sure, Muggs. He talks a lot, but I can't understand all that he says," lied Gully. "He's not as hot and he's sweating, that's a good sign; the worse part of it might be over."

"Do you want me to do something?"

"No," Gully smiled, his white teeth bright against his dark mouth. "You better get some sleep. When I have to leave, you can check on him."

Muggs yawned and was soon asleep.

Bender turned over on his bunk. "You get some rest, Gully. I'll keep an eye out. I think you're right, the worst is over."

"Yeah." Gully was not surprised that Bender was awake and listening. He knew that nothing escaped the soft-spoken, tidy white man; there wasn't any doubt that Bender understood what Wolf was saying during his restless moments. Still it didn't tell them very much about their bunkmate. Both realized he was an educated man and in his delirious state vowed to kill his brother.

Exhausted, Gully stretched out and fell asleep.

Chapter Nine

Captain Zuber ordered Wolf to report to him on the forecastle. But it was Bender, his adept navigator, that was standing before him.

Appearing before the foul-smelling master of the *Shark Tooth* and not intimidated, Bender respectfully declared, "Captain Zuber, I ask your indulgence, if you allow… Gully another three days with the new man, I think you can look forward to having a good extra hand. He is strong. He survived Knife's infectious wound and needs but a few days to heal. He is weak and cannot stand on his own."

Zuber shook his head; his tone filled with amazement and a bit of admiration. "You know, Bender, you volunteered your services on my ship. You came well-fed, muscled, and wearing expertly tailored clothes. I recognize quality." He offered a wily grin. "Simply because I know this vessel is nothing but a wooden crate and no one in their right mind would willingly want to join my crew, you struck my curiosity. And then you were the only one agreeing to share a cabin with a black man." He waved his dirty hand, his fingernails filled with grime, "and with Muggs; it mattered not." He scoffed, "That skinny little stick thinks he protects Gully," laughing at the ridiculousness of it. "I didn't mind for it keeps things running around here as slick as a greasy pole. You see, I never miss what is happening on *my ship* and that is why there is no fighting among the crew unless I say so." Zuber pointed his index finger at Bender, "Now getting back to you… you speak the king's English, something I never hear from my cutthroats."

Bender couldn't help but smile because he was well aware of Zuber's shrewd handling of his men and his ship. He nodded.

Zuber went on, "These last three years, you've proved to be an excellent navigator leaving me free to oversee incidences that can be troublesome. You've asked for no special deals or favors and you mind your own business. The crew chooses to ignore you and I find no fault with that. It is for that reason I have let you be." His voice became ominous, "I question no one aboard my ship as to who they are or where they hail from as long as they obey my orders. Am I making myself clear, *Mr.* Bender?"

"I would say so, Captain."

Shouting, "Then where in the devil's deep do you take it upon yourself to stand here in place of my new man? I will not have my orders disobeyed by you, Wolf, or anyone."

Being not the least disrespectful, his voice full of entreaty, said, "Captain Zuber, I would not disobey any of your orders without good reason. You have been fair with me and I ask nothing else. As you say, Wolf is your new man and I believe that he can become a remarkable member of your crew. However, *not* if you insist that he be dragged up here before his strength has returned. He is totally unaware of your orders to report to you."

"If it were anyone but you, Bender, I would have you and he flogged. I do not take kindly at having my orders countermanded." His tone became aggressive, "You and Gully have exactly two sunsets to get this wounded Wolf on his feet. I expect to see him standing before me at sunrise the following morn." Adding with sarcasm, said, "Have I made myself clear, Mr. Navigator?"

Bender saluted. "That you have, Sir. May I have your permission to leave?"

Satisfied with his reprimand, Zuber answered, "Yeah… go. And Bender, don't do it again. My orders are to be followed just as you are obeying them by heading us southwest toward the tropics."

Bender couldn't withhold his grin. "Still checking on my navigational skills, Captain?" Giving his head a slight shake, not using the steps, he slid down the ladder and went to give Gully the news of Wolf's two-day reprieve.

Chapter Ten

With stamina inherited from his father, Derrick Grayson Staunton, now known to those aboard *Shark Tooth* only as Wolf, stood in the cold gray dawn on the forecastle, waiting for Captain Zuber. The sea was rough and Wolf barely kept his balance, but did so despite his weak condition. He knew some of the crew watched and he would not permit his mind to cave and do his body's longing to drop. Wolf had refused Bender's clothes, but now, because Bender insisted, the jacket was protection on his wounded body against the wind and sea spray that cut across his gaunt face. Unaware that he looked eerie to the seamen because his eyes came across as hauntingly spooky as he stood, moving only to keep his balance, a struggle while waiting… waiting… waiting.

Zuber purposely let Wolf wait, standing for one hour, testing his mettle. *Bender was right*, he thought, *this new fish is going to work out all right. He might be worth the trouble.*

Zuber came out on the forecastle and roared, "I see those dirty riffraff got you out of your warm bunk to obey my orders."

Pulling his shoulders back, Wolf looked into the eyes of the slovenly *Shark Tooth's* captain, and boldly said, "Yes, Sir."

"It's good that you show respect. Good for scum like you."

Wolf said nothing. He continued to stand erect, his eyelids half closed to block the glare on the water from the sun rising. The ship lurched and he lost his balance slipping on the wet deck. Using every ounce of energy that he could conjure from his sore body, Wolf stood again. He could feel his wound open and begin to seep against his clammy skin, but said nothing.

"You will work with each man on this ship and learn how I want things done. Whatever each of the scourge of a man tells you, that is what you will do until I tell you different. Understood?"

Though in pain, his eyes blurring, Wolf kept on his feet anchored to the rolling deck and again said in a bold voice, "Yes, sir."

Captain Zuber snorted as he moved away, half turned and grunted, "See that you obey orders from now on. I can see you're a weakling, but I'll make a man out of you." He wanted to demean Wolf so that he could control him. He did not need another Bender. He would make sure this high bob could earn his way knowing Gully fed him enough of his voodoo medicine to get him well. "Tomorrow morning you will start your day alongside Gully. He can teach you what he puts into all that slop he feeds us." Yelling, "Gully… get this scum out of my sight."

Wolf nudged Gully aside as he weaved back to his bunk. Other than some leers and sickening remarks, no one came near him.

Captain Julius Zuber sneered outwardly, but within himself he was pleased. He knew about everything that went on his ship. That was why he had control and no man would defy him. As captain and master of this wooden tub, his plan was to mold Wolf the best way to fill gaps among his crew—there wasn't any doubt Wolf would take nothing from his cutthroats. Zuber wondered how Big Mike came to kidnap this rank of a man and why.

Just as Bender was an excellent navigator and swordsman, this Wolf carried similar qualities. But the captain's curiosity didn't dwell, time would tell what this Wolf man had in him to survive. Zuber smiled, then muttered, "I will sail the sea for my personal gain going wherever I choose and those high bobs in London can keep my *certificate*. I'm showing them and they'll continue to pay for ruining my life. Kellowing," he shouted, "stay the course." Then he went to his cabin to take a look at his charts. Perhaps a touch of brandy would warm his innards.

Chapter Eleven

"Time to hit the deck. Captain said you're to work with me in the galley." Gully knew Wolf was still weak. The trip up to the forecastle had opened his wound. Gully was able to stop the seepage letting Wolf sleep through the night, but orders are orders. "I'll keep your workload light so you can regain some strength, but you have to get moving."

Wolf opened his eyes, started to rise too quickly when Gully grabbed his shoulder. "Easy, don't do nothing to start that cut to bleed again. It's healing fine."

Wolf felt pain stab as he swung his feet onto the cold deck. The cabin was damp and frosty, but clean. It made Wolf wonder if he had only dreamed he was on a filthy boat. His mind cleared and he knew better, it was dirty everywhere but here.

"Here," Gully tossed some clean clothes at him, "put these on, they're from Bender. He said to share with you until we hit land and you can get your own."

"Thanks. Who is Bender, anyway?" To himself he wondered where he'd get the money to buy anything.

"Never mind the thanks. Bender, Muggs, and I share this cabin. Now you do too. But if you want, you can choose to bunk with the rest of the crew."

Grimacing at the black man's taunt, Wolf said, "Thanks, I can't wait."

Grinning, Gully shot back, "Well, for now better get yourself to the galley as fast as you can." He turned to leave, "Muggs will be here to show you the way."

Wolf began to diss. "This is the only clean place I've seen since I was shanghaied onto this dirty boat. Why does the captain allow such filth?"

"Don't let the captain hear you; he's mighty proud of it. Remember one thing: the captain runs this ship and every man on it." Then Gully disappeared.

Muggs was panting, "You awright?" He gasped for more air. "You gotta hurry. I had to run down from top deck. I'm supposed to take you to the galley and I don't want Gully to get in trouble so hurry as fast as you can."

Wolf shoved the shirt into his pants careful not to start his side bleeding. "I never got a chance to thank you, Muggs, for giving me that message."

Muggs scratched the back of his head. "You mean when they pitched you down in the orlop? That was a long time ago that I sneaked down to see you—seven sunsets ago. Gully said you wouldn't survive down there long, the bilge always floods that deck and the captain just leaves it."

Astounded, Wolf shook his head. "Are you sure it was that long ago, Muggs? I have no idea how long I've been laid up."

"You were real sick." Boasting, Muggs added, "Gully mostly took care of you with his own medicine he makes by hisself. I helped too and so did Mr. Bender."

Wolf knew he had to get to the galley and picked up a sweater. "Well, if you hadn't been there to give me that good advice, I might not be alive. I appreciate what you did."

Smiling broadly, displaying crooked teeth, proud of getting Mr. Wolf's praise, Muggs said, "Aw, it weren't much. I just did what Gully said."

The galley was just that, a tight space. A scrubbed plank served as the work table. A smoky stove was attached to the deck near the outer planks with its smoke pipe stuck through a hatch. There were some casks and crates shoved to one side. Some shelves were built above with racks nailed across to keep everything stored as stationary as possible. The galley was as clean as one could possibly keep it.

"Sit down before you fall down. You eat a couple of my biscuits with some of the captain's sweet honey and in no time you'll feel like a new man."

Wolf sat on one of the crates, gripped the table with one hand as the ship pitched while reaching for the mug of coffee Gully held out to him.

"This coffee is from the captain's private stock. Enjoy it 'cause it'll be the last you will get. After you'll be drinking whatever I can find to grind up for the rest of us."

Wolf was not surprised over the separation of rations. He read enough to know every captain ran his ship under his own laws. Still he couldn't resist teasing Gully, "You mean the captain and the crew don't eat the same food?"

Gully let out a roar, laughing. "You got a lot to learn, Mr. Wolfman. On this ship, the captain is the boss, king, and even god. That makes him mighty powerful. He tells me what grub is his and what is ours."

"I don't think that's right."

Not laughing now, Gully's voice hardened, "Right is what the captain says it is and if you want to stay alive and get along, you follow his orders and you eat what he says you eat." Turning back to the stove, he said, "This smelly smoke pipe is called Charlie Nobel. We cook a lot of biscuits and store them for when we can't use old Charlie in rough weather. You can help me make up some batches of hardtack."

Wolf grinned. "I heard about those, they're sea biscuits… the staple on all ships. And Gully, don't worry, I know how to follow orders."

Glad to hear the resolute tone from his bunkmate, Gully ordered, "Then ties that towel around you and let's get busy. There's more to do around here than making biscuits."

The captain's hot coffee, sweetened with the captain's brown sugar from the captain's private stock along with the captain's honey spread on biscuits, gave Wolf renewed energy. His first work day began with uncommon friendliness. He'd keep his unfinished business stored inside his mind and heart. His memory of the carnage his twin helped perpetuate burned in his soul. But for now his most important objective was to live; he'd give it his all. He had no choice.

Chapter Twelve

Ten weeks on board the *Tooth*, Wolf adapted to his daily responsibilities. He worked in the galley beside Gully and learned not only how to cook with short rations, but to clean and scrub. He never complained and followed orders.

Early one morning, Muggs appeared in the galley. He twisted his tanned little face into a puckered brow as he wiped his hands on his shirt, back and forth. "Mr. Wolf, Captain say you're to report to Knife and learn to handle the halyard. Captain say *right away.*"

Wolf pulled the towel from his waist and tossed it on one of the crates. Gully continued kneading dough. Wolf had progressed fully over this last week, his strength built and Gully recognized his unforgiving attitude when he would often stare off without blinking. A hard shell covered any gentleness that had been part of his nature. Pounding the gray-colored dough, Gully watched Wolf's unyielding demeanor take hold.

Wolf's color—once again tawny, his hair clean was tied back with a leather strip and his height along with his lean body—made him someone to reckon with. He knew he had three friends on this ship and he revered his close association with them Still, he never spoke to them of his life before Big Mike dumped him on the deck and no one asked.

"Looks like I have a new partner, Gully. Think you can run this place without me?"

Gully didn't smile and ignored Wolf's banter. "Better get yourself on deck and you watch yourself."

Wolf nodded, slapped Gully's shoulder, and headed out the opening.

Wolf squeezed through the companionway with ease. He attuned himself to the roll of the sea as the ship continually cut its way through the waves. He had regained staying power; thanks to Gully's medicine he no longer felt weak from Knife's hit. He listened and learned from everyone and stored it away. The *Shark Tooth* was a dirty ship with a tough relentless crew. There was no self-esteem among them except when it came to cruelty. Wolf was determined to meet each man equally and prove himself. He had to or he wouldn't survive. Survival, to seek revenge is what fed his soul and he was steadfast that no one would deter him from that obligation.

In borrowed clothes, standing with legs apart, his arms dropped leisurely beside his body, his broad shoulders squared, Wolf was unaware of the vitality he portrayed as he asked Knife, his tone flat, "What do you want me to do?"

Knife sat on a dirty coil of rope as he tapped his honed blade against his filthy britches. He leered as he looked up at the man he hated, not because he survived from the knife fight, but because Wolf ignored Knife and no amount of verbal abuse seemed to get to him. "The captain says you're to learn about the lines and I get to teach you. That be okay with me because you might as well know that when I get you up there," he pointed with his shiny knife to the ropes leading to the upper part of the mast, "you're gonna have a sort of accident and fall." Grinning from ear to ear, his dirty stubble-bearded face blended with his mouth of bad teeth. "Probably break your neck and the captain won't be able to blame me. No way, see… the Wolf just ain't no good at climbing them lines."

Wolf had no intention of letting Knife play him a fool. No more, he had enough. He would not be bullied by him or anyone. With others nearby listening and with Knife puffed up with his usual overrated overconfidence, Wolf took a step toward him. Looking down at the villainous man, Wolf narrowed his eyes, his lips barely moving, said, "No, you listen to me, Knife, the captain ordered you to teach me about the halyards that run up these sails. I have every intention of obeying his orders. Do not for one second think I will cower and shake around you.

I am not afraid of you. If you want to get along, good; if you don't, I suggest you be very careful when you are up there with *me*." Wolf raised his eyes upward to the tops of the sails, "For it might be you that takes a dive."

Angered at being shown up in front of the others and being called out, Knife viciously spit out, "Then follow me up those lines, jellyfish, let's see if you can do the job you're supposed to." He leapt off the coil of rope with ease and was halfway up the footropes before Wolf took two steps.

Wolf made it to the footropes with little trouble, but Knife was already climbing the ratlines, higher up. Giving no quarter, Wolf followed up the ratlines; it became easier as they were tarred and crossed one another at intervals and used as a ladder. Knife climbed like a monkey in a tree, whereas Wolf was struggling with the wind and the roll of the ship to get to the top.

It was when Wolf reached the ratline just below Knife that he felt the pressure of Knife's foot on his knuckles. Unused to climbing ropes, Wolf's hands were sore and burning from the tar and gripping the salty lines.

Straight away he knew this was the beginning of Knife's challenge. Knife was going to follow through with his threat and show the men watching he meant what he said.

Wolf also knew that he had to prove himself now; there would be no other time. He was going to have to let go of the line because Knife's foot was grinding down on his knuckles and he could no longer sustain the crushing pressure. Wolf used his other hand to tighten his hold on another rope. He was prepared to swing, then grab hold of a line and climb back up. His plan was to climb beneath Knife, but this time he would surprise Knife by grabbing his pant leg and pulling with all his strength.

Just as Wolf was going to execute his plan the *Shark Tooth* ascended a wave that pitched Wolf from one side to the other. He hung on for his life as he was sprayed with seawater. He was wheezing for air as he struggled to get away from Knife's feet. The wind carried Knife's roar to the men below energizing Knife's purpose. Wolf was dealing with a sadist, forcing Wolf to seek vengeance. He settled himself against the lines and the roll of the sea; he was not going to tolerate Knife's spite. Incensed, an extra surge of power burst; not willing to lose he scrambled up the ratlines against the blowing wind- filled sails with unexpected agility.

Knife was ready to pull the same stunt on Wolf again, but this time Wolf was ready and yanked hard at Knife's pants. The unexpected pull cause Knife to lose his balance, but not for long. Knife, accustomed to the rolling sea regained his balance immediately, but not before Wolf was up beside him hanging on the opposite line.

"I'll get you for that," Knife shouted over the wind. "The only way you'll touch deck is head first."

Wolf's dark eyes stared at his adversary. "You call it," he shouted back against the noise from the wind and the billowing sails.

Knife realized he had met his match. Jitters ran through him as if lightning were to strike as it did another time when he was up high working the lines. Still, he wouldn't stop his assault, he couldn't. "One of us is going to die and it ain't gonna be me." Quicker than a serpent's tongue and as deadly, Knife held his sharpened shiny blade in his hand. His evil grin would make a devil wince.

Holding his arm out with his hand clutching his blade, Knife waved down at his shipmates. They offered him the courage he needed to fight this man. Knife was totally at ease high in the riggings. That's what made him so valuable to Zuber. This was his territory and no one had lasted up here with him if he didn't want them to.

The fairness instilled in Wolf's rearing spilled out. He found himself yelling to Knife, "I'm offering you one last chance to end this war you're bent on having with me. I have no intention of losing."

"You must have seashells for a brain, liver-belly. I'm gonna slice you up and feed you to the fish."

Just as Knife spoke and before he could make his next move, Wolf set his planned strategy in motion; first, he had to get Knife to release his blade. Holding onto the lines with both hands, Wolf swung his body with all his weight and kicked Knife in the stomach, but Knife still hung on to his blade as he swung loose for a few seconds. He didn't expect Wolf to be on the attack so soon. Wolf scrambled above Knife and this time wasn't in the same position when Knife stood on his knuckles. The problem remained—Knife still held his blade and was reaching up to strike. Wolf was waiting for Knife's reach and as the ship ascended another wave and rocked them both back and forth, Wolf thought they'd hang on and wait for the ship to heel, but Knife was not waiting-he swung and caught Wolf on his calf, the gash soaked his pants with blood and dripped down from Wolf's leg onto Knife's face. "I'll get you for that."

Wolf's temper exploded, yet it being essential he control his anger to overcome this cold-blooded stupidity. Wolf raised his body and with both feet jammed them on top of Knife's head. He saw Knife bounce against the mast and the blade fell from his hand. Knife began to slip, but his hand was caught on a twisted line and he hung free swinging like a ragdoll. The ship continued to ride the waves and it was all Wolf could do to hang on, but he knew he couldn't leave Knife tangled and hanging. As much as Wolf despised what the man stood for, killing him was not going to happen. Decency still argued deep inside of him.

Wolf's body was pummeled against the mast and the sails were pressing him further out over the deck. The creaking and rocking caused him to wobble-it took all his strength and common sense to ease down alongside of Knife. There was a loose line hanging close by that Wolf later learned was called a preventer line, used as a temporary replacement for when a main line breaks. Carefully he wound the loose line under Knife's arms, struggling against the elements, weighed down at his task. His aim was to get the line around Knife's chest so gradually he could pull the unconscious man up easing his body weight off the rope that had tangled around Knife's fingers and wrist. It was a hairy process and seemed to take an eternity before he was able to free Knife's hand that had turned blue from lack of circulation.

Wolf rested; inhaling the cold sea air that was stinging his body. Hanging on to Knife and one of the ratlines, with his feet anchored around the line, he rode the squalls with thrashing winds showing no mercy. Talking to the unconscious man, Wolf grumbled, "I don't know how I'm going to get you down or why I'm even bothering, but if I don't then I'll become as demented as you."

No one below, offered to come up and give Wolf any help as he looked to see where the preventer line was attached to be able to get enough of it to lower Knife. He heard someone shout from below. Peering over Knife's body, he should have known who would come to their rescue. Gully was climbing with ease up the ratline with a coil of rope resting on his shoulder.

Together they tied Knife with the new line and lowered him as they descended down the lines. Upon reaching the deck, an angry Captain Zuber was there, watching.

Zuber's voice carried around the deck. He wanted to be sure that every man on board heard him. "Tell me," he roared at Wolf, "what is the meaning of this?" Not waiting for an answer, "Get Knife below and fix him," he yelled over his shoulder to any one of his crew. Looking at Wolf, Zuber's mangy beard hid part of his flushed face, "I will not tolerate fighting among my men unless I say so. Kellowing, give this man ten lashes for disobeying orders."

All smiles, Kellowing stood with his whip coiled in his right hand.

Captain Zuber continued roaring at Wolf, "If Knife is unable to perform his duties, I will hold you responsible and there will be twenty-five extra lashes waiting for you. Do you understand?"

Wolf smoldered; he sucked in his cheeks and when angered, narrowed his eyes.

Having learned from Gully, one did not reply or *ever* explain to the captain.

The blood on Wolf's leg had coagulated, only the dry blood was plainly visible on his pants. The cut didn't hurt, there was only minor discomfort. Wolf could only hope that the seawater had cleansed Knife's blade so as not to infect him again. Standing erect, returning stare for stare, knowing Zuber knew exactly what took place, Wolf nodded his head just enough to acknowledge this demonized captain.

The rest of the crew were about to explode with delight over the flogging to come.

Once more, Wolf was to witness how they thrived on brutality.

Kellowing swaggered over to Wolf and started to reach for his shirt to rip it off.

Wolf raised his hand and pulled the shirt over his head and tossed it to Muggs. "It belongs to Mr. Bender."

Captain Zuber heard the exchange, without showing admiration at Wolf's acting.

Now he imposed the most excruciating test on the man who called himself Wolf. Kellowing's whip was thin, smooth and had five well-worn tails on its end. The captain was aware Kellowing used it with relish and a harsh unforgiving nature. Puffed up like a peacock, Kellowing could wield the long leather strap with precision at the flick of his wrist. The damage he created cut not only into the body but the soul as well.

Kellowing's voice was boastful as well as filled with mockery, "What's the matter, Wolfman, don't want to get your shirt bloody?"

Wolf refused to be goaded. He ignored the First Mate.

Kellowing snickered, "Tie him to the mizzen, Louie, and then see how brave he is."

Wolf's arms and wrists were stretched high and bound to the mast. His toes barely touching the deck as his long muscled torso hung free feeling the cold wind; he kept his face pressed hard against the mast figuring it would help him keep his head from bucking when the leather cut into his skin. Wolf tried to spread his legs to brace himself, terror, fear and hatred building inside of him while waiting for the first strike to make its mark. He closed his eyes making his mind revert to Delbert and Eudora and his need to survive to personally take care of them, he had to live, he had to keep his head and never give in. *I've got to get back to Penumbra... think of beautiful Penumbra.*

Wolf heard the whistle of the whip as it first sailed through the air; it was at that instant that he tried to block his mind, but nothing prepared his for the sensation of pain. It *happened...* ahhh... the leather cut into his skin, the strike so fierce-something no one could ever contemplate. He couldn't describe the pain, but he would never forget it.

Somewhere in the back of his mind, he heard the crew counting, it went on and on and on, he couldn't comprehend the number, only the chant. He would not utter a sound; he choked back the horrendous burning, his body on fire as he bit down on his lip feeling its blood, but drawing on all his Staunton heritage, needing it as never before. Somehow, the count of seven registered, *three more... oh god.* Suddenly, incredible and unexplainable reaching into the depth of his soul, he heard his ancestors repeating over and over again, *You can do it... you will survive... we are Stauntons... live... keep Penumbra safe... you will survive this.*

Derrick George Staunton now Wolf, lifted his head with Staunton pride, determined not to lose consciousness. It was on strike number nine that he heard nothing but the wind and the water swishing, no other sounds, the crew silent. *What happened? Do they think I am dead, then why aren't they rejoicing... why?* Later Wolf found out it was because he didn't cry out, beg for mercy, or pass out. His silence had stunned them—it was usually on the count of four or five that bellowing would begin from the very strongest man.

The last lash, Kellowing ignited with rage at not bringing Wolf to his knees, he poured all his built-up malice into the tenth and final strike. Number ten sailed through the air and cut across Wolf's bleeding-burning flesh. His bloody back raw with crisscrossing gashes of open flesh, many on top of others.

When the bonds were cut, Wolf wobbled, grasping the mast with one arm, he stayed on his feet, barely… but made himself do it as he looked at Captain Zuber, through a haze, hoarse voice, unable to disguise the pain, he dug deep to speak, "May I have your permission to go, Sir?"

Zuber was astonished and for the first time in his life, ashamed. He knew Knife had caused the trouble and Wolf had saved Knife's life. "Go, get out of my sight."

Faltering, but determined to stay on his feet as long as possible, grasping at any of the clutter. Still on his feet yet almost crawling he made his way past the crew to the hatch. When Gully offered to give him a hand, he said, "I'll make it." The crew broke out with cheers for the Wolfman. This was beyond anything they had ever experienced and if they hadn't seen it, they would not believe it possible.

The *Tooth* continued to plow through the blue-green seas humongous waves, then fall into its deep swales and then bound forward to ride the crests again. Unaffected, the crew was astounded that Wolf never said a word about saving Knife's life; he was a kind they never knew existed. Unknowingly, Wolf had just accomplished what no one on the *Shark Tooth* ever did, along with their admiration, he gained their respect.

Knife recovered in two days with a headache, a bruised ego, and his customary ugly disposition.

Wolf lay on his stomach with Gully's creative poultice quickening his healing. This time Wolf remained conscious keeping the hurt and soreness inside of him, never forgetting Gully's gentle touch or the care he received from Bender and Muggs.

The healing process on his back and shoulders surprised everyone at the speed Wolf was recovering. During his mending, some of the crew stopped Gully asking how the Wolfman was doing. But not once did Zuber inquire, though everyone knew their captain didn't miss a thing. Surprisingly, he left Wolf be and after a week assigned him back in the galley. Unable to wear a shirt as the long red puffed scabs crossed his back, it didn't stop Wolf from carrying on with his duties, regaining his vitality. "It was your medicine, Gully... my thanks."

Gully's wide smile displaying his white teeth dragged his hand over his head. "You're strong-willed and it's in you to get well. That is what's needed—the mind cures the body."

The day Wolf came out on deck without a shirt for the first time; the crew gawked at his wounds, still in awe over Wolf's strange power to withstand the brutal beating. It was hard to believe but they'd seen it happen. Wolf noticed the nods and smiles imparted to him; not realizing what had attributed this sudden change in hostilities. He'd ask Gully or Bender, but right now just to breathe fresh salt air raised his spirit.

The weather was chilly, but not as cold as it had been. Wolf looked forward to the warm air and waters everyone talked about. They told of the huge playful gray dolphins that followed the ship for miles and actually breathed air. They spoke of water so blue and clear that looking into its depth and its unknown bottom added a strange fear in some of them. Best of all, they said, was the air that was so warm all day and all night; you could wear practically nothing.

Wolf went back to functioning with his duties as the captain ordered. Working alongside the men, he listened to their tales of the sea and the different ports they anchored at and then the places they dared not show themselves. They embellished about the beautiful women waiting for them on shore and how they'd make them happy. "You won't have trouble keepin' any of the lovelies happy," they joked.

All the while, Wolf was a fast learner and showed great respect to his teachers, finding that each man really excelled when doing what he knew best.

Gully taught Wolf about mending sails using a complicated zig zag lacing. Gully would shake his head at Wolf's work, telling him it would do in a pinch. Louie taught Wolf how to splice the ends of two roped together by interweaving the strands of each into the other so they could pass through a hole in the ship's block. Wolf became adept at this chore and his splices would pass through the block with perfect thickness at the joint. Louie would throw out his chest and flex his arms while showing a spliced rope for all to see. Proud of himself and his protegee; he boasted to everyone that Wolf mastered the splicing because of his teaching.

Wolf learned about deadeyes, dunnage, fids and nettings. These were some of the words used describing parts of the ship. They were all everyday words to the seamen and Wolf discovered that learning about them filled him with satisfaction. He took in the detail in the ship's workings; absorbing it all like a sponge. He held a bit of respect for Captain Zuber knowing what had to be done in keeping the *Shark Tooth* afloat.

Everyone gladly taught Wolfman what they knew. They liked his company and for all his educated manners, he never made them feel less worthy than him. Wolf asked them so many questions that they had to reach back into their old experiences to expound on what they knew.

Still, there were times when Wolf would stare out at sea, not seeing the white on the waves crest or the endless blue sky meet the horizon, for he was lost in thought thinking about his heritage. The waves slapping against the side of the ship lulled one's senses.

Wolf felt so small; it was like being in a corked bottle bouncing around in a mammoth pond. He was alone upon this vast sea, yet finding it so commonly serene. He wondered if other Staunton men went to sea. He looked around narrowing his eyes reminding that his present circumstances prevented him from following his ancestors' footsteps at Penumbra. He liked the sea finding an uncanny excitement sailing into the unknown and not knowing if the weather would cooperate. However Penumbra with its green lands and farm lands, its forest and lakes… he wanted to go home. *And I will.*

Kellowing and Knife stayed away from Wolf. They held a grudging respect for him but wouldn't admit it. Still, they couldn't forget their humiliation the Wolfman caused them and together they agreed to wait for their first chance to get even. When the time came, Wolfman would no longer be part of *Shark Tooth's* crew.

Chapter Thirteen

The *Shark Tooth's* men, some half-dressed, eased from their tasks as they sailed in warm, clear blue tropical waters. The sea glittered like diamonds as the sun flickered over gentle ripples, less than a foot high.

Mokes, a short, wiry, muscled, bow-legged dark-skinned man; wore his long black oil hair plaited-tied with a fat leather strip. He kept his mustache trimmed and turned up on its ends, oiled, matching his hair. His duty was to man the cannonade, a short four-foot gun used for close-in fighting. Mokes, not only expert in handling the cannonade, he was fearless when performing his job, no one dared bother him. Mokes, well aware the captain depended on him, leaving him to his own devices.

This day Mokes, smoking a short stump of a cigarillo, was determined to. fence with the Wolfman. Brash, he approached Wolf and handed him a sword. "Are you interested in a little disport, *Friend?*"

Wolf took the sword, examined it, and smiled. He handed it back to Mokes. "I might be interested if you allow me to use the one you have strapped in your scabbard."

The crew knew the sword Mokes had given Wolf was a reblade. Any knowledgeable swordsman would never use it because as soon as the nailhead tip is broken from the blade it loses its flexibility to be a formidable weapon.

Of course, Mokes refused to give up his highly prized sword. "How you know?"

"I think you're testing me, Mokes. But I warn you I can handle a blade well enough. Do you still want to try?"

Very confident, Mokes boasted, "Aye."

"Then, before we begin judging our skills, I need an equally good weapon. And I think we better get permission from our captain."

Mokes yelled, "Kellowing, quit standing there like a plank and ask the captain if I can cut up Wolfman." It was an order and coming from Mokes, it was acceptable.

Kellowing listened to words exchanged between Mokes and Wolf. He hoped they'd start their duel without permission so he could flog Wolf again. Now enraged because Wolf was wise enough not to act without the captain's say-so, he grumbled, "You don't have to tell me what to do, Mokes. I'll ask when I'm good and ready."

Captain Zuber, standing on the forecastle, watching and listening, called down to Kellowing, "Tell them to go ahead." Grinning, he added, "Let Wolf try."

Kellowing became exhilarated. Mokes, being the best swordsman on board, even better than the captain and the captain was better than good. No one ever bested Mokes. At one time or other, each had felt the tip of Mokes sword somewhere on their body knowing they were at Mokes' mercy.

Hearing the captain sanction their match, Wolf looked around for another weapon. "What's wrong?" Zuber goaded, "you're not going to turn jellyfish, are you?"

Wolf knew he was being set up by the captain. He could feel the anticipation running through the crew. Wolf kept his smile hidden for what they didn't know was that he and his twin were taught by the best fencing master in England. Suddenly being reminded of his brother, Wolf cringed. This being mistaken by the crew to be a sign of fear, they couldn't have been more wrong.

Wolf saw Bender leaning against the bulwark. He blinked and slightly moved his shoulder trying to caution Wolf.

But Wolf wouldn't heed Bender's warning. He was a Staunton and a Staunton would never turn from a challenge. Speaking up to the shirtless captain, his voice courteous, "No Sir, I have no intention of backing down. Though I wonder, Captain Zuber, *Sir*..." he raised his hand to shade his eyes as he peered up at the forecastle. "If you would consider letting me borrow your sword for a few minutes? I promise to return it in its excellent condition."

The crew, flabbergasted, fell silent. It was so quiet you could hear the water lapping at the ship's planks. *No one* ever asked the captain for the use of his weapons.

Zuber, taken by Wolf's audacity, roared with laughter. "I will say this for you, High-bob; you got more entrails than a black devil whale." He loosened his well-cared for sword and literally pitched it down to Wolf. "See that you return it to me in its same condition, or else…"

As quick as he could move, Wolf caught the sharp sword at its hilt. He visibly looked it over, checked the heavy pommel that lightened the balance, tested the steel, then raised it up and saluted Captain Zuber.

Zuber recognized Wolf's actions for what they were, an experienced swordsman. No jellyfish after all. *This is going to be quite a match.*

Mokes was the best swordsman Zuber had ever come across; now anxious to view the forthcoming battle, he called out with relish, "I'll have no killing, but you can draw all the blood you want. Go to it!"

Wolf was about to salute his opponent and ready his position to defend, but Mokes was not of that caliber of meeting eye to eye and returning a salute.

Mokes had learned to fight and cross swords from living on the streets. He learned the hard way from brawls in ale houses, on wharfs and on board ships. Most important he learned that to win he needed a good balanced weapon and to know when to retreat.

Mokes also discovered he liked the stimulation and the sound when steel blades clashed; sometimes it was better than being with a woman. The steel blade gave a small person like him power that he perpetually longed for. Fearless because he believed he would never die from another man's sword. Mokes lived by his wits all his life and felt immortal when holding his treasured sword.

Completely at ease and feeling the power from his sword, Mokes manipulated the point of his blade with utmost precision and quickly advanced on Wolf. Wolf, alert, noticing immediately that though Mokes held his weapon with an extended arm and properly controlled it with his thumb and index finger; yet he did not keep his body upright but arched his back. Mokes balanced himself on both his feet without using his knee to point straight ahead toward his adversary. Wolf knew how important this was when taking a simple step forward toward your opponent.

Steel clashed; its singing carrying through the air and out over the ship's rails into the sea. The crew watched with enthusiasm, staying clear of both men. None were willing to bet against Mokes, they knew he was the best.

Wolf had to retreat, in doing so he measured the distance backward. He found that Mokes fenced to win without regard to timing and attacked with ferocity and gave no quarter. Keeping in mind the first defense is to retreat before the point of the opponent's blade reaches you—Wolf was in retreat constantly as Mokes continued to push forward.

Wolf and Mokes parried. First Mokes parried to protect his high inside. Wolf would parry to defend high outside the area of Mokes' target.

Mokes' eyes glistened, his shirt becoming saturated with sweat, he was in his glory.

Usually, Mokes could quickly get a feeling of how to handle his opponent, but this Wolfman was of another breed. "I like you, Wolfman, so I will be gentle with you," he mocked, "you make one misstep and I will cut you."

Wolf held his arm out for balance, his knee aimed at Mokes and before Mokes could say another word, Wolf moved his blade counter clockwise and pointed it for the attack. But Mokes was not taken in by Wolf's tactics, he leaped up onto a coil of rope, laughing. "I don't think that was very smart, Wolfman." Mokes lunged forward as Wolf had backed himself against the main mast. The crew was shouting cheers and some were pounding each other on their backs, but Wolf whirled away just as Mokes make a lightning thrust and missed.

Wolf's shirt, plastered to his chest and perspiration glistening on his forehead, taunted Mokes, "You forgot to lunge out, Mokes. Tut-tut... never down, Mokes, you lost your momentum." Now Mokes was in retreat. Unbelievable... the crew turned silent, other than the clashing steel, the sea continued to beat against the *Shark Tooth* creating its own musical chorus.

With his arm fully extended, Wolf counter attacked, knowing Mokes was in a vulnerable position because he had spent himself in that last lunge and was busy recovering. Wolf's attack was swift and accurate; he drew blood on Mokes' shoulder.

The crew couldn't believe Wolf was the first to draw blood.

Mokes was not discouraged, he aimed his blade at Wolf's body, aiming to provoke him into doing something stupid. Covering the deck quickly, Mokes jump-lunged at Wolf and with precision and surprise caught Wolf unguarded. This factor was what Mokes was waiting for; it had always worked for him. It was the perfect move that disengaged Wolf's sword leaving him without any defense.

But Wolf wasn't going to be defeated. He must retreat to the mizzen mast before Mokes could recover. Backing away with Mokes coming toward him, Wolf could only hope he could make it, for near the mizzen was the greatest heap of slime for when the waves washed over the deck, usually missed this area. Wolf had to get Mokes in it, without getting caught in it too. Leering and filled with confidence, Mokes came forward making his movements look casual, but Wolf knew better. He was being stalked by a worthy opponent.

Wolf continued to concentrate on retreating safely and getting to the mizzen, he needed just the right moment... it came! Mokes took a precise thrust at Wolf, not realizing he had stepped in the heap of slime. As quick as a shot, Mokes lost his balance and slid down on the deck. Still holding onto his sword, Mokes yelled like a wounded banshee, words spewed that would even make the devil quiver. Wolf did not watch but circled forward and searched for his sword. He did not see it anywhere and Mokes, his clothes covered with green and black slime, advanced.

Someone had picked up Wolf's weapon. Wolf knew whoever took it had no intention of giving it to him. He looked around, took one leap and swung his body up, grabbing hold of the mainstay. He climbed hand over hand until he was out of Mokes' reach.

Taking a few deep breaths, he looked below and saw the exuberance of the crew and how they thrived on violence. Knowing he could not hang on the main stay much longer and knowing he was giving Mokes time to rest, Wolf spied Bender just below the forecastle. Bender was holding a sword, but it was not the captain's. Without hesitation, Wolf shouted, "There's a frigate on starboard." The crew, including Mokes, turned and moved starboard as Wolf slid down and just reached Bender's side when someone yelled, "It's a trick." But it was too late, Wolf held Bender's sword, his brow furrowed, his jaws clamped shut and his eyes seemed blacker than ever before. "I'll not lose this one and then I'll find the other one."

Wolf realized Mokes fought to win at any cost. There were no rules in fencing with Mokes… this was a duel to the finish. This was more than just a game to the short, confident muscled man; it had to have a deadly outcome to consider it successful, it was his way of proving he was better than anyone. He would thrust, lunge and strike. *So*, thought Wolf, *I'll play by your rules.*

Mokes moved his head from side to side. "Very good, Wolfman, but it is over for I shall make fast work of you now."

Wolf spoke in his usual unruffled manner. "I like a confident opponent, Mr. Mokes; it gives me an edge to prove him wrong."

Wolf crossed blades with Mokes and retreated, but this time he would give no right of way. Wolf was sensitive to Mokes' methods and parried to the inside of Mokes' blade in a low clockwise arc.

Mokes was taken off-guard as Wolf switched his position. The Wolfman was now on the attack, remaining cool and in control.

Mokes instantly put himself on guard. Never had he experienced such drive as this man. Again they parried, but there were no more smiles or snide words. Both gasped for air to fill their lungs. Not only were there shirts soaked, their pants were also. Perspiration caused them to blink the sweat from their eyes. Both men knew they had met their equal in this match.

Captain Zuber was also aware of it. He saw Knife pick up *his* sword and stow it under the canvas leaving Wolf defenseless. He was not surprised when Bender came to Wolf's rescue. Captain Zuber reminded himself how right he was when he said Wolf was someone to be reckoned with. He privately admired the man and wondered who he was, but he lived by his own code, he would never ask.

Wolf again tested the distance of his new weapon with one of his thrusts. He had to become familiar with the striking distance. Slowly and deliberately he retreated from Mokes attacks.

The crew no longer yelling or slapping each other with joy as steel against steel rang out, scowling with their mouths hanging open that Mokes had yet to put Wolf down.

Mokes tried to cut over on Wolf, but Wolf was ready for him and Mokes could not disengage the blade; his timing was off to implement his surprise planned attack, it was no longer an option. The loss of assault that he was certain should have worked shook his confidence and for the first time he was laboring hard and sweating profusely. This was a battle overflowing with embarrassing tension.

For Wolf, the opportunity came at this moment, it was exactly what he'd been waiting for. *I've got to flee him now.* Wolf, an expert at this fencing move, rapidly closed the distance on Mokes, giving him no time to recover in retreat. With total concentration on the point of his blade, sure of the exact distance for his thrust, he leaned his body weight forward and touched his blade into Mokes upper arm. With a twist of his wrist, Wolf's blade was under the forte of Mokes' sword near the hilt. It happened so unexpectedly and shook Mokes' focus that he couldn't help but drop his sword.

Stunned, Mokes stared at Wolf, his eyes as big as the cannon balls he handled, not believing he'd been bested. He had no weapon to go on with their duel. The stain was too much for him. He slid down on the deck with the crew ranting at no one in particular. The Wolfman had done something no one dared, he bested Mokes.

Wolf stood, unmoving. The crew waiting, expecting him to slash Mokes. He saw Gully, Bender, and Muggs off to one side, their faces covered with smiles. Wolf knew Captain Zuber was watching. Using his left arm, he dragged it across his brow to blot the sweat before more it could leak into his eyes.

Wolf looked up to the forecastle. "As you said, Captain, I can draw blood." He nicked Mokes' skin and left a mark that would heal without any danger of infection.

"Is that it?" roared Zuber.

"I assume, Sir, that you will want Mokes to be able to handle the cannonade when the time comes and also to use his sword to the best of his ability. I see no reason to cripple him. Mokes is very experienced with his sword. He is the best I have ever dueled with. I am surprised I had the luck to end standing." He turned to Mokes, grabbed his hand, and pulled him up from the dirty deck. "What do you say, Mokes, don't you agree that *we* are the best?"

Mokes nodded. Hearing Wolfman's praise in front of everyone and not shaming him, he couldn't be mad. "You're right; we are the best… today I let you win."

Both men laughed when Louie shouted, "Ship on the starboard, Captain, and it ain't no trick this time."

"Bender," Zuber shouted, "can you tell what it is?"

"Aye, Captain, it's a merchantman. It has no gun ports and is riding high."

"Damn," grumbled the captain.

Gully standing next to Wolf, said, "That means it's carrying no cargo and we get no booty, unless…"

"Unless there are passengers on board and they got some rich belongings." Mokes, grinning, always looked forward to confrontation. "You ready, Wolfman? Now we're gonna have some real fun."

"Whose flag is it flying?"

"It's English, Captain," answered Bender, his voice lacked spirit.

"Don't worry, Bender," Kellowing sarcastically yelled, "we'll be careful how we handle you lily-white Brits."

Kellowing could not stand the fact that Captain Zuber left Bender alone most of the time. It irked him that Bender was content to be on the *Tooth* and keeping to himself with the exception of the captain, Gully, and Muggs. Kellowing hated that Bender seemed to be watching, though he never bothered anyone. True… no one on board this ship was mates, but still they were from the same crowd. Unschooled and looking out for themselves first, that was how they survived. Bender didn't belong and now this Wolf was part of the crew and he didn't belong either. Some snickered when they heard Kellowing ridicule Bender. Bender ignored Kellowing without as much as a blink. That caused the first mate's temper and hatred to swell.

"Hove-to," ordered the captain, "remove the shutters on two gunports and send a blow across the bow." He shook his head, muttering to Bender, "This is too easy."

Without another word, the crew scattered to their stations and waited for the captain's next command.

The blast from the *Tooth's* cannon vibrated the ship. Wolf was next to Gully and grabbed hold of the rail.

"Loud, isn't it?" Gully added, "You'll get used to it. We have no choice."

The merchantman raised a white flag and Zuber ordered to heave-to. There was no resistance as the men on the merchant ship stood on deck.

Zuber was suspicious. What were they carrying on board? Riding high on the water would give them the opportunity to pick up speed and take off. Something wasn't right. It was an eerie situation and he was going to investigate.

The sea had a slight roll so rather than using gaffing hooks and board directly, Zuber ordered, "We'll board her from the accommodation ladder. Kellowing, you stay on board. Mokes, Knife, Louie… you come with me on the first boat. The others are to follow in the second." Getting ready to go over the rail, Zuber looked back and saw Wolf. "I think, *Mr. Wolf*, you will join me and see how this is done." Not waiting for a reply, the captain went over the side. No one would dare disobey his orders.

Gully warned, "You watch your back."

Bender walked over and handed Wolf his belted scabbard. "You should have a sword with you." Nodding, Wolf buckled it on and went over the side to join Zuber.

Chapter Fourteen

The first thing Wolf noticed when he jumped over the rail of the merchantman behind Captain Zuber was its cleanliness. Its teak deck was devoid of grime.

Zuber, his stained uniform along with his long beard, began yelling orders to his men. The people standing in a huddle gaping at the seamen climbing over the rail wearing only cut off pants, sun browned bodies, unshaven faces-stirring fear into them. Petrified, silence held them in place.

"Who captains this ship?" Zuber's voice carried across to them and out to sea.

Receiving no answer, he stepped forward, his chest expanded in his once white shirt now marked with food stains with his belly protruding over his waist band, he waved his sword. "Answer now or I shall cut out your tongues and give you cause to not talk."

There was shoving in their midst and a young man was pushed forward.

He was not one of the merchantman's crew for he wore civilian clothes, though no longer pressed and dapper, yet they were clean. He couldn't seem to get his words together... he stuttered, his body trembling, "We... we are without a captain and... and crew, Si... Sir. We... we'd be privileged to have you help... give us aid."

"Aid?" roared Zuber. "We did not come on board to aid you; we came to take your cargo and valuables." He sneered, "Perhaps I will decide to kill you and take this ship."

The young man's trembling increased, "But… but Sir, our captain became ill and… and died when we… we were six and eighty days out. We… we have nothing. Why… why would you think… think to kill us? We… we have done… done you no harm."

Wolf, completely taken aback by their plight, without thinking asked, "What happened to the crew? Surely there is a first mate?"

Zuber glared at Wolf. "I don't care about them or the crew. What I want is their cargo and everything of value. Get on with it."

Wolf moved next to Zuber and spoke for only his ears, "Sir, they are in need of our help. We can't steal from them and leave them out here. It's a wonder they haven't lost control of the sails."

Enraged, Zuber shouted, "How dare you speak and disobey my command. Step aside or I will have you thrown overboard."

Wolf would not back down. "Sir?"

"Did you not hear my order, *Mr.* Wolf?"

Wolf moved to the other side of the captain. He saw eight men and no women. He was sure there were women on board; no doubt they were hiding below. Wolf was also sure the captain surmised the same.

The young man didn't move. "Captain… Sir, we… we were bound for the Virginia coast but… but the *Hampton* was to stop first… first at Somers Island to pick… pick up the captain's wife. We… we are only passengers and have nothing. The… the crew stole from us and… and abandoned us when we… we neared land and left us to… to ourselves. They took the… the cargo with them. They left water and food fearing it was… was contaminated. They took… took what valuables we had. They said our captain was… was diseased and we will die too. None… of us can sail this ship."

When the men from the *Shark Tooth* heard about disease, they shuddered and headed to the rail wanting to flee. "He sounds like he knows what he's talking about, Captain," Knife pleaded, "let's scuttle this tub and be gone. We can't get diseased, Captain, we can't chance it."

"Shut up, Knife."

Wolf noticed an older man standing alone, off to one side, seeming to want to be as inconspicuous as possible. Wolf slid his foot over to move to his right to enable him to see the man better and when he did, he quickly looked away. He knew the man. He was James Barslow, his father's friend and solicitor. Wolf felt certain Barslow recognized him as his eyes widened, his mouth hung open, staring.

Unaware of Wolf's attention being elsewhere, Zuber shouted orders to the passengers, "I want everyone to come forward and stand so I can count all of you. That includes the women you're hiding."

Gasps burst from the abandoned travelers. "Oh no!" Their whispers carried. "How did he know? It can't be."

Wolf offered, "Captain, your permission to go below and see that everyone comes on deck."

"Now you're talking like a true pirate. Think you need help?"

That was the last thing Wolf wanted, holding his sword, he grinned, "I think I can handle it, Captain." He hurried past Barslow, his eyes in recognition, and jumped down through the open hatch. He could only hope Barslow would remain still and say nothing.

Below deck, Wolf found a young boy standing guard at one door. He looked to be about ten and six years. "You cannot enter. Leave... go... before I have to kill you."

Wolf understood the boy's fright. "I mean no harm," he postured, "I'm only here to see if you need help."

"That's a lie. I heard what was said up..."

Before the boy could finish his words, Wolf's wrist turned so swiftly and with his sword slashed down, frightening the boy so that he dropped his weapon. Wolf grasped his neck and pushed him into the cabin. A young girl whimpered. And elderly, elegant attired lady, along with a plain dressed woman, whom Wolf presumed to be her maid, remained astonishingly calm.

Wolf's voice was low. "Listen to me and do exactly what I tell you. I will help you all I can, but you must not question me for there is no time."

The elderly lady, her eyes so blue they gleamed in the darkened cabin, peered at Wolf. "Believe me, my lady, time is of the essence."

She spoke without preamble. "Robert, do as the man tells you. Regina, cease your crying." Holding her head high, asked, "What are we to do?"

"Do you have any powder or chalk that women sometimes use?"

The woman nodded.

"Use it and do whatever you can to make yourselves look sick and ailing. Cover your skin to look ashen, not from mal de mar, but a diseased appearance. Spread some black around your eyes and on your neck. Also put some on him," he pointed to the youngster. "Get yourselves in as horrible shape as possible. Get into your bunks and cover yourselves. I want you to shiver and shake as best you can. You must prove yourselves too sick to come up on deck. The captain will be down here to check you out." Wolf looked about the small cabin, spying the chamber pot he kicked it over. The cover fell off and as he expected, the smell was offensive.

The maid yelled, "Oh, how dare you? We can't stay in here now."

"Hush, Maude," ordered the elderly blue-eyed woman. "I suggest we get busy and make ourselves look sick." Undeterred, she added, "I think it will be considerable effortless now because of the pervasive stench surrounding us."

Wolf moved to the door. "I'll do what I can to give you time. Whatever you do, do not talk. Perhaps you might try a moan, that might help but don't overdo." About to leave, he said, "It would be better if you unrolled your hair and made yourself look disheveled. I'll try to hold the captain on deck and if possible, I'll come back."

"Sir? Whoever you are," the blue-eyed woman said, "we thank you and we'll do our best to hurry. Is there anything else?"

Wolf's demeanor was solemn, "Perhaps a prayer might help." He left them to face Zuber.

Coming up on deck, Mokes was heading down. "Checking on me, Mokes?"

"Just obeying orders."

They reached topside and as Wolf expected found Zuber suspicious. "What the devil took you so long? Where are the women?" He mocked, "You weren't enjoying yourself while we were up here waiting, were you? Mokes?"

Mokes shrugged his shoulders.

Wolf knew the captain was no fool, but he hoped he could strike some fear in the *Tooth's* slow-witted crew. Whispering, but intentionally speaking loud enough for the crew to pick up some of his words, he said, "Captain, god knows what they caught on this ship. There are three women and one boy down there. They are wasting away. I would have to drag them up here. I'd rather not touch them and they cannot stand, let alone walk. Their smell is putrid."

"What the devil deep is going on?" Zuber was mad. "I want everyone up on this deck *now!*" Rubbing his beard, then taking off his hat and putting it back on pulling in down to shade his eyes, "If you can't obey my orders, I'll send someone who can... Mokes," he yelled, "go with Knife and bring anyone that's below up here at once."

Wolf gritted his teeth to keep from saying anything further to antagonize the captain.

He thought Zuber wasn't all that sure about the sickness and decided not to chance it by going himself. Wolf could only hope his plan would work and Mokes and Knife wouldn't get too close to the bunks.

It wasn't long before Knife and Mokes raced up on deck. Knife was babbling, fear filling his voice. "Captain, we got to get off this tub. It's full of sickness. You can't believe the smell from them sick ones." He was shaking his head as he looked over at Mokes to agree. "Ain't that right, Mokes? Ain't it?"

Swarthy, wiry Mokes nodded his agreement, only he was not upset as Knife. "I think we better get off. It don't look good at all. I sure don't want to *have* one of those women. They be diseased, Captain."

Zuber was not convinced. "You there," he called out to the young man who was the spokesman for the others. "Go down and bring those women up here and anyone else that might be hiding their skin. And I mean *right now!"*

Whispering loudly, needing the crew to hear, Wolf added, "Captain, they could be contagious and it could move through the air. I don't feel that good myself."

That was all Knife had to hear. "Please, Captain, let's just scuttle this tub and go."

"You yellow-livered coward," bellowed Zuber.

Wolf, aware that Zuber had every intention of having the women hauled up on deck, had no choice if he was going to save everyone on board from this vile man. Zuber would see through the disguise he had permeated. He knew what they would do to the women.

Wolf took a step behind Zuber, reached into his boot, coming up with the knife Gully had given him. Before anyone knew what was happening, Wolf grabbed Zuber's neck with his left arm and using his right hand aimed the sharp point of the knife just below Zuber's ear.

"I have no choice, Captain. You would not let the matter rest."

"I knew it... you were lying." His voice hardened ruthlessly, "You will die for this, Wolf, make no mistake, I will kill you myself."

Squeezing his arm tighter around Zuber's neck, Wolf warned, "I'm dead serious about what I'm doing, Captain... tell your men to surrender their weapons and stand starboard."

Zuber remained silent.

Wolf pierced Zuber's skin. "I swear I'll follow through. I had only my life to lose since I was thrown on the filthy bucket you call a ship—I have nothing else to lose now."

Choking out his words, Zuber asked, "What do you want?"

"Send Knife and the other men back to the *Shark Tooth.* Have them tell what I'm doing. If Bender, Gully, or Muggs or anyone else wants to join me on this ship, they are welcome. They are to return within a half-hour."

"What about Mokes?"

Wolf laughed, "Really, Captain, you expect me to send Mokes over the side so he can aim one of your cannons at us?"

"I swear you will regret this."

"I'm giving the orders and I have no fear of you. I never did. You prey on the poor, homeless, defenseless souls and turn them into worse human beings for your pleasure."

"I treated you fair."

"Did you? You had Kellowing whip me for no reason and you knew it. Is that what you call *fair*? Enough… order your men!"

Fear blossomed in Zuber as never before. He struggled and Wolf drew blood. Everyone watched and listened. The waves rocking the boat, but no one noticed. Sweat reeked through Zuber's clothes. "All right… all right."

"I also want a fresh barrel of water, along with some of Gully's hardtack."

Zuber, blistering mad, wanted to shout, but mumbled, "Are you crazy? We don't have that much water left."

"Quite right, but you know these waters and can easily find fresh water." Giving Zuber another squeeze and then releasing the pressure so he could speak, Wolf voiced, "I will not ask again… give the order."

Captain Zuber did as he was told.

Less than thirty minutes, still holding Zuber around his neck, Wolf grinned, "Welcome aboard. Are you certain you want to join me?"

Bender, the first over the rail, and then Gully was next pulling little Muggs with him.

Most surprising was that Louie came up over the rail, too. "Where are the provisions I asked for?"

Bender answered, "The water barrel and some kegs are on the way up."

"Glad you're willing to join me."

"We wouldn't have it any other way," grinned Bender. "Would we, Gully?"

"Not a chance." Gully looking at Zuber and said, "I'm sorry about this, Captain."

His voice hoarse, the captain glared at the big black giant. "I treated you right, Gully. You'll be sorry for this."

"I paid my debt to you, Captain; you never shared the booty with me like you did with the others."

The provisions Wolf had demanded came over the side along with several other different sized kegs tied together. Zuber had a fit. "Those were in my cabin," he croaked, "they belong to me."

Eying Gully, Wolf knew what he had done. He winked and then said to Zuber, "I know they belonged only to you, however, we will need what's left of the fruit and nuts. Gully, crack open a couple of those barrels and make sure I'm getting what I asked for."

Gully's big smile showed his white teeth as he used Mokes' dagger to open the lids. "It's all here, Wolf." He laughed. "They didn't have sense enough to try to outfox you."

With the provisions on board, Knife and Kellowing hung over the *Tooth's* rail not knowing what to do. Bender spoke softly to Wolf and Gully, "Look at their dim-witted expressions; it'd be comical if this wasn't serious."

Zuber heard and glared at Bender.

Wolf, standing with his feet apart for balance, keeping his arm around Zuber's neck and the dagger in his right hand, issued his first order, "Leave one boat with one oar tied to this ship."

Mokes' mouth fell open. "What you gonna do with me and the captain?"

Wolf couldn't let his guard down or Mokes would pounce on him straight away with his sword. He would be unable to handle both of them at the same time. Wolf had Bender's sword and Gully's dagger. He had had enough, becoming infuriated. "Mokes, you didn't think I'd send you and the Captain back now? Just as I know fish can swim, that's how sure I am that as soon as you got on board the *Tooth,* you'd blow us out of the water."

Zuber grasped at Wolf's arm at his neck, "I can't breathe. What the devil deep are you planning?"

"I'm not choking you, yet… but keep it up and you'll find you won't have to worry about breathing at all. Now I'll say this just once, so listen… *you* and Mokes will stay with us until I deem it safe to put you overboard."

"Are you out of your mind? No man can handle a small boat in this sea with one oar. Why, that's crazy."

"And I would be equally mad to let you go back to your ship this soon." Wolf ordered Mokes, "Yell to Kellowing to keep us in sight, but to keep far away from this ship. They are to watch for you and your captain in the boat and can pick you up when I decide to send you overboard."

Mokes sneered. "I'll get you for this if the captain don't." Then he called out to Kellowing. "Now what?"

The *Shark Tooth* moved away from the *Hampton*. Still holding Zuber, Wolf said, "All right, Mokes, now it's your turn. Lay your sword on the deck and go stand next to Gully."

"NO! My sword stays with me."

"Sorry, Mokes, not now. But I give you my word that when you leave this ship, I'll see that it goes with you."

"Do it," grunted Zuber. "I don't trust him."

"I said *do it*… that's an order."

Strangely, Mokes, still in awe of Zuber, obeyed. He laid his sword down and went to stand by Gully.

"Tie him, Gully, and when you're done with Mokes I want you to tie our esteemed captain good and tight. Then give them a few drops of water. Until I find out how much water we have and where we are and what course we'll have to take, we'll be on rations."

Mokes securely bound, Wolf released his hold on Zuber.

Zuber did not hold his tongue. "You will rue this day, Wolf, I will kill you."

Wolf stood over the seamy captain with disgust. "Be grateful that I do not feed you to the fish as you have so often and so willingly done to others. I'll let you return to your ship, but don't push me further." Wolf's eyes darkened and with his hair slipping out of its leather tie and blowing in the breeze appeared ominous, "I do not forget my enemies, Captain Zuber. Consider yourself lucky that I do not kill you here and now. I warn you not to threaten me again."

Zuber stared at Wolf hearing the venom and felt the vibrations reach him from what he measured to be Wolf's soul. He said no more. *When I get my hands on Big Mike, I'll kill him before Wolf does.*

Wolf asked all *Hampton's* passengers to gather and then explained their precarious situation. "I know that if I didn't take the captain hostage, he would have killed the men and taken the women back to his ship."

Most nodded their understanding. The spokesman for the group asked Wolf to become their captain. "We'll do whatever you say."

Smiling, Bender seconded their request.

"I'll do my best to captain this ship, but I am not *captain,* my name is Wolf and you are to refer to me by that name. Also, we are fortunate to have Mr. Bender," he nodded toward Bender, "as he is knowledgeable in navigation. This is Gully," he brought Gully to the forefront; "he will be my First Mate. Make no mistake; whatever he tells you to do, *do it exactly* as he says. We are all going to have to work together to survive."

"Louie and Muggs, you will be Gully's all-around helpers. You are to put the men to work to keep this ship on an even keel. If anyone refuses to do their share, they will not receive their share of food or water."

Zuber snorted and laughed. "There is more to sailing than raising a sail or two."

"Don't worry about it, Captain, I've had good teachers, thanks to you, and I paid attention to my lessons. We'll find land." Wolf didn't add his thought that only if the weather cooperated and they had enough water.

"Why, you no-good thieving scum."

"If you don't want to be gagged, Zuber, I suggest you keep your mouth shut."

Wolf left to inspect the merchantman from bottom to top. He discovered the curve between the side of the hull and the bottom, otherwise known as the bilge, reeked with smelly liquid and ran with rats. Wolf discussed it with Gully.

"I think, Wolf, we should think about finding land and not worry about those rats. We keep the hatches closed." Gully spoke with assurance. "We got trouble coming if we don't find water."

The *Hampton* wasn't much of a ship. It carried cargo with a few passengers for extra money if the captain was so inclined. There was no galley, the passengers provided and cooked their own food on the deck. If it rained or the seas were too rough, Wolf learned they did without. It was a rough crossing and Wolf held respect for those that managed as best they could.

Slowly, the *Hampton* got underway with the *Shark Tooth* trailing a good distance behind, following Zuber's orders.

Wolf had just climbed down from the foremast when Muggs approached him with a big smile. Muggs was happy. He was glad to get away from Zuber and that he was with Gully. "Mr. Wolf?"

"What is it, Muggs?"

"Am I really going to be one of the crew? I mean, not like on the *Shark Tooth.*"

"I want you to call me *Wolf,* Muggs… after all, we're all shipmates, aren't we?"

Beaming, Muggs eyed Wolf, "You really mean that? Like everybody else?"

"I do. On this ship, we are all equals."

Turning to leave, Muggs said in a broken whisper, "I never was before."

An unexpected reaction riveted though Wolf, *Little Muggs grateful for being treated as a person like everyone else.* Wolf swallowed, and then said, "Just carry out your duties, you'll do fine."

"Yes, Sir, Mr.—I mean, yes sir, Wolf." Wolf smiled as Muggs hurried off.

Wolf welcomed this sudden unforeseen burden realizing its advantage in nearing him to his final destination—Penumbra, his twin, and Eldora. *Father, their last day staying with him...* fury expanded within him, his entire torso tightened and his eyes darkened with ferocity. *I am coming for you, Del, and for your duchess. Though dressed in finery, you two belong with the Tooth's crew, Del. You and Eudora would do well in their company.* Unclenching his fists, taking a gulp of sea air, he went to find Bender, hoping *Hampton's* charts, maps, and log were left on board. After, he'd talk privately with Barslow—anxious to learn what had transpired since his father's murder. Rage hung in his mind thinking of that last day. *I'm returning to Penumbra. No matter how long it takes, I'm coming back for you both.*

Chapter Fifteen

When Bender asked to sign on the *Shark Tooth* years ago, he hadn't been aware of its filth or reprehensible crew. Needing to learn more about the stars and heavens, what better place than sailing the oceans; his father's power prohibited him being accepted on any ship and so, with determination, he had approached Zuber. Unfortunately, he was stuck and, having no other choice, minded his business and stuck to the captain's routine.

The *Shark Tooth* captain never questioned the well-mannered man about his reason, but finding him good at navigation, agreed. Bender obeyed orders and with his free time studied the stars, keeping a journal and jotting descriptions and his theories.

Now on board the *Hampton* Bender will be challenged to put his knowledge to test.

There would be no Zuber rechecking the course. Working on the compass card, he marked the lubber line on the compass case to show the center line of the ship-he repeated the names of the points in order, clear around the card as N (north) and so on. He did this to maintain the compass bearing. Wolf watched Bender subdivide the points for determining direction by comparison with the constant needle.

"You're very good."

Bender didn't look up but continued with his work. "You were getting pretty good with this yourself."

"You're the genius, my friend."

Picking up his head, Bender looked about making sure they were alone. "Seeing as we are friends, I think it is time you called me Reggie, my lord."

Wolf leaned back on his heels, his mouth gaping as his eyes widened. Thinking that Bender and Barslow had talked, he said, "I trust this will go no further. I had hoped that Barslow would not have disclosed my identity."

"Barslow? Who's that?"

"If you don't know Barslow, then how do you know?"

Bender's tone was just above a whisper, "You carry a small identification mark on your body. Gully and I saw it when you were sick. Of course, Gully doesn't know the meaning of it."

Wolf raised an eyebrow. "You wouldn't know that mark has any meaning unless you also carry one." He looked hard at the man standing next to him. "I think I'm beginning to understand… Reggie, is it? There is a Duke of Tayford, better known as Reginald Carson, late of London and Shropenshire. Is that not so?"

"That would be my father." He smiled. "I'm glad we have something we can share."

"But why? Why would you willingly be part of Zuber's sadistic team?"

Bender shrugged, "The Duke of Tayford and me disagreed. When I lost respect, I had to disappear and Zuber was the only one to accept my offer. I never realized how horrible the crew is and him despicable, but once on board and sailing away, I made the best of it. Gully and little Muggs helped."

"I can't imagine being under Zuber's command is better than Tayford's."

"The Duke of Tayford is a greedy tyrant. When my mother died, I picked up and left knowing my father would look for me but only if there was no cost to him. I left him a note telling him I've gone sailing. I've been on that dirty bucket for seven months plus four years. I've been waiting to for the right time to jump ship."

"I can't believe you went from a spark into a fireball—greed to murder."

"Whether I was on board the *Tooth,* matters not. Zuber would still roam and scrounge. I took no part in it except to protect myself. I shared none of the so-called booty. In one prospect, my father and Zuber have a lot in common. They take and think nothing of the harm they cause. Tell me, Wolf, when does one have enough gold? Is it when one dies? If so, perhaps justice prevails as one cannot take it with them when they turn to dust."

Wolf said nothing. His father cared not only for Penumbra but also people No one went hungry under the Duke of Grenfell's stewardship.

"So tell me, Wolf, how did you get waylaid by Big Mike and thrown on *Shark Tooth?* The duke must be frantic."

Tall, strong, and standing with his legs apart, wearing black pants that were now tight because of the muscles he had developed, along with Bender's borrowed white shirt partially open, exposing black hair on his tanned chest, Wolf stared out to sea, his soul interconnecting with his father, seeing him clearly. Tears clouded his eyes but they did not fall. He spoke softly, his voice in contest with the wind that Bender had to strain to hear with the waves rocking the *Hampton.* "My father was murdered and I was supposed to be too, but Big Mike's greed got the best of him. Zuber needed men and anchored nearby at the right time for Big Mike."

Bender's mouth fell open, and then he said, "Murdering a *duke?* They are insane."

"True, but you've seen Big Mike… that says it all. So, if I have your word, I'll tell you who I am."

He lifted his hand. "You can trust me, my lord."

Wolf trusted Bender just as he trusted Gully. "I prefer that you didn't recognize me with that title. I am known only as Wolf. Agreed?"

"Of course… say no more."

Wolf showed no emotion, no boast, just truth. "My name is Derrick Grayson Staunton."

Bender whistled. "You're a *Staunton?* The Duke of Grenfell's heir… my god, are you saying the duke was murdered and you were there?" Completely thunderstruck, Bender's eyes bugged, he shook his head. "But why? The Duke of Grenfell is the most revered man in all of London and just about everywhere." Taking a deep breath, realizing the catastrophe in his friend's life, Bender quickly said, "I'm so sorry, your gra—Wolf."

"Thank you." Wolf looked out at the water's continuous movements, he ran his hand over his brow, confessing, "Talking about this brings to mind that my father and I will never sit and talk with one another again. We had so many pleasant conversations." Wolf remembered their last conversation and turned to hide his distress.

"The Duke of Grenfell was most respected and well liked. His beliefs and work in Parliament were exemplary and well known." Bender smiled, "The ladies were quite taken by him, yet his decorum was above reproach and he never showed any interest."

Wolf's voice softened. "I asked him why he never remarried and he said he married the woman he loved and my mother was irreplaceable."

"We should be so lucky."

"That's what he wished for me."

"Well, who can tell?"

"Nay, Bender, that will be a long way off, I have unfinished business first." Then he smiled, "Just think of all the mamas that are going to be parading their daughters not for *us,* but for our title. I dread to even think about it."

Bender knocked on Wolf's shoulder, laughing. "I bet you get shackled before me."

Wolf joined his laugher. "I don't want to take your money." Wolf turned serious. "A surprising coincidence—one of the men on board is the Duke of Grenfell's solicitor and more importantly, a trusted friend. He is escorting Lady Amelia Thomas and her granddaughter. Later, I'll introduce you. We can trust him. Hopefully, he will have good news of England."

"Let's hope for the best." To lighten their conversation, Bender patted his hip and then thigh, "Are you going to return my sword?"

"Feel naked, do you?" Wolf unbuckled the scabbard and held it out. "Here and thank you. It's saved my life twice. But now I have a far better one."

"That'll be the day."

"That day has come, I'm going to confiscate Zuber's sword."

They both began laughing as *Hampton's* passengers looked up, wondering what was so funny. As far as they were concerned, their situation wasn't the least amusing.

Wolf and Bender descended to the main deck.

Wolf, nearing Zuber, said, "As soon as the sun sets, I'll release you and Mokes."

Zuber, spitting mad, glared, "Are you crazy to put us off at night?"

"It won't be night and if your men are paying attention, they will pick you up before dark. It's the best I can do, Captain. You know as well as I that we have to make our escape. You'd do the same."

"The devil… I'll send you all down with the fish and have my ship ride over you."

"I think you've just given me a grand idea."

Mokes grunted at his captain. "We should stay quiet."

Wolf said, "Worry not, Mokes. I will set you both free to join your mates. As your captain knows, my word is honorable."

"And my sword?" Zuber snarled.

"I almost forgot to mention that. I plan to keep it as a souvenir. I want to remember you and my welcome on the *Shark Tooth*. But Mokes keeps his."

"Like hell…"

"I agree, Captain, that's what it was like on board your ship. Now, I have other matters to attend." Wolf walked away and didn't look back.

Mokes couldn't contain his smile. "Too bad for you, but you know that my sword is part of me. You can always get another."

"Watch your tongue, Mokes, if you plan on staying on my ship."

Suddenly brave, having taken cues from Wolf, he said, "That's true, Captain, but I also know that what I do, no one else can do it better. You need me as much as I need you."

Zuber scowled.

Mokes didn't want to rile the captain too much. He added, "You've been a fair man and you're a smart captain. I like being on the *Tooth*, you'll have no trouble from me."

Zuber looked at the man he took for granted. Said nothing, only nodded.

Chapter Sixteen

Three men sat almost knee to knee in the small cabin that once belonged to *Hampton's* missing captain. Bender sat on the narrow bunk. Barslow, usually an immaculate man, his ruffled shirt no longer in pristine condition, sat in a chair at a table that also served as a desk. Wolf sat across from him with a map, some charts, and the ship's log pushed to one end of the table.

They shared wine found stashed under the captain's bunk.

Wolf, leaning with his elbows on the table, holding his head in his hands as anger surged through him.

"I'm sorry to have to give you this bad news, Derrick. As the former solicitor for the Staunton family—"

"What do you mean *former*?"

"Delbert has withdrawn my services. I no longer represent Grenfell, its properties and that of course includes Penumbra. I regret having to enlighten you when our situation here is dire, but it is imperative that you know."

Wolf felt sick—his father had given crucial attention to the care of his dukedom.

"Penumbra needs your attention anon." He stopped talking—benumbed and staring at Wolf, the Duke of Grenfell...right here in the middle of the Atlantic Ocean dressed almost like a pirate. "Even though there is no definite proof, except for the lapse of time and no one heard from you, it is assumed that you also died with the duke." Barstow wrung his hands, "How providential it is, Your Grace, that our paths cross, but most central is you're alive."

"No one is to know who I am. Please refer to me only as Wolf."

Barstow heard the command in Wolf's tone; he sounded as his father. "As you wish, your," Barstow slightly shrugged, "Wolf."

Knowing the forthcoming conversation between the two men should be confidential, Bender moved to leave. "I'm going to relieve Gully. I'm pleased to have met you, Barstow. Thank you for the news about Shopenshire. It is time I returned home." To Wolf, he said, "I'll take first watch. You get some rest. The weather seems to be holding steady if we're lucky." Grinning, her added, "Though with the clouds covering the moon it will cause Zuber to cuss at the heavens."

Wolf shifted his weight and hid a yawn. "Giving us time to make our move before Zuber can open his gun ports at us." Pointing to the rolled charts, "Didn't you say you thought it's possible that we may be about three days away from one of the big islands?"

"Yes. Zuber was going to weight anchor there. Surely, you're not thinking of going there?"

"That's what Zuber will think if you whisper it loud enough to Gully so he can catch a few of your words."

"But if we don't put in there, I don't think we'll have enough water to carry us to another island. As you know we are far from any other shore."

"We have no choice, Bender. Zuber will surely sink this ship but first he'll play with us by aiming at our masts and deck. He would like nothing better than to see us scramble for our life boats so he can torture us further. And think of the women." Wolf stood, his muscled body appeared more massive in the confines of the small cabin.

"You're right. Consider it done. I'll go tell Gully our plan and let Zuber think he overheard them."

"Good. I'll see you in a couple of hours and we'll plot our course. In the meantime all food and water is on ration. Put Muggs in charge."

"Agreed." Bender nodded to Barstow and left.

Wolf moved back to his chair and stretched his legs while resting his feet on the bunk. "I'm glad you're here," he said to Barstow, "but not under these circumstances."

"I still can believe you're here...alive."

Wolf snorted, "These many months have taught me about survival. Since kidnapped my main objective has been to endure and return to England. I will not permit Delbert to lay blemish on the Staunton name. To hear my twin trashing what the duke always meticulously tended," Wolfs voice hardened, "he will be stopped." *No one will know, dear brother, what that I plan to do to you for murdering our father. As the Duke of Grenfell did in the past—I will continue to keep Staunton family business private.*

Barstow drummed his fingers on the table. "Bender seems like a good man. I can't come to grips with the future Duke of Tayford electing to give up an easy life to become a sort of pirate."

"Bender has his reasons. I respect him for doing what he believes to be right for him. If it weren't for him and Gully, I doubt I would be among the living." Wolf dragged his hand across his brow as Barstow drank the rest of his wine from a dented pewter mug. Wolfs anger apparent, said, "First, you are to represent me, Grenfell properties and Penumbra. In fact, when I return, we'll go over the Grenfell's assets. You will continue as you did for my father. Understood?"

"I do. I'm honored to serve you, my," he almost said grace, saw Wolf's frown, and added, "I'm honored."

"Tell me what you know of Penumbra."

"Will you first enlighten me how you came to be on that pirate's ship? I swear when I saw you, I thought I was hallucinating."

"It's a good thing you said nothing. Zuber would have done away with us all if he knew my identity or too, he might have tried for ransom. I doubt if that would have been paid."

"Of course it would, but that's beside the point as it's blessing to find you alive and able to return to England."

You'd lose a bundle if you placed a wager at White's that Del would pay the ransom. "I am alive not from the good will of the duke's murderers, but because of their greed. They kicked, clubbed and gagged me before pitching me onto the deck of the SHARK TOOTH to sell me to Captain Zuber." Wolf cleared his throat, "How was my father discovered?"

The barrister's mouth fell open and he remained silent before saying, "His Grace's body was found by fishermen. He carried papers on him and was identified. Because your body was not found it was assumed that you drown and the current carried you away. The duke was interred next to his duchess and we were informed that a Service for the Duke of Grenfell would be held upon your return."

Wolf slammed his fist on the table rocking the empty wine bottle— it fell over and rolled on to the floor. The rolled maps bounced and rolled off the table too. No one tried to catch them. Doubly angered and outraged, Wolf asked, "What is Delbert doing? Has he married? I remember he was considering marriage."

"Your twin married Lady Eudora, the Earl of Sherbrook's daughter. The last I heard he has not been recognized as the next Duke of Grenfell."

Wolf yanked at his shirt and pulled on it to expose the family *mark.* "Father said you know of this."

"Yes. It is because of that mark that your twin has been unable to lay claim as duke. He doesn't understand why the Crown has ignored his three requests for an audience. There are many of the king's associates waiting to lay claim and share Penumbra lands if it is not protected. His Grace entrusted me with knowledge of keeping his dukedom safe. Under my watch it will remain so."

Vengeance ablaze in his soul, Wolf said nothing.

"Wolf?" Barstow broke the silence, "I must get news to the Crown that Derrick Grayson Staunton, the first-born son of George Richard Staunton, Duke of Grenfell, is alive. We must get back to London as quickly as possible."

"That is easier said than can be done. We have difficulties ahead and it is imperative that we all pull together. As for getting to London, let's hope we can find land and that it has fresh water. If you believe in prayer, Barstow, I suggest you start now."

Barstow got up to leave. *This man Wolf will fill the duke's shoes.* "Let me know what I can do." Wolfs features softened, "Thanks, Barstow."

Chapter Seventeen

"You will regret this, Wolf. You will never live to see land again," shouted a fuming Captain Zuber. He yanked his hat down on his forehead. "You'll never make it!" Zuber clutched the side of *Hampton's* rail. Mokes, already in the small boat, was grasping the side fearing waves would pitch him in the sea.

Wolf stood at the rail. "I'm being quite magnanimous with you, Zuber, considering how you first welcomed me on board your ship and then having me whipped for no reason; it stays in my memory. Even so I've shared water here with you and Mokes and I'm allowing you to take one of our lanterns; consider that payment for your sword."

The sun was fast sinking below the horizon. The orange ball aglow spreading its color upon the sea, but the two men paid no attention. Wolf saw Zuber's fierce glare plastered across his face; he shrugged it off.

"Stand by," yelled Gully. "Down you go, Captain, and good luck."

"You're the one that's going to need the luck, you double-crossing scum. I was good to you, Gully."

Leaning over the side of the ship as Zuber climbed down the accommodation ladder with surprising agility, Gully retorted, "You were a lot better than the plantation owner, but Captain, I was still your slave." The captain sat in the rocking boat, Gully let the line loose as the small boat rolled with the sea, and Mokes put the oar to work.

Wolf couldn't help but grin. Gully was standing there wearing clean clothes and the biggest smile. His heightened spirit seemed to swell and reach everyone.

"What you want us to do now, Wolf?"

Wolf reached to shake the tall black man's hand. "I'm proud to have you as my friend, Gully. We proceed with our plan."

Gully, his pulse pounding, choked back his heartfelt feelings—he had never had a white man call him *friend*. He knew this white man meant every word, or he'd never have said it. "It turned out to be my good day when Big Mike dropped you on the *Tooth*. You can always count on me, Mr. Wolfman, ask anytime."

"I appreciate that, Gully." He put his arm around Gully's shoulder. "Seeing as the sail is set, let's go up and see if Bender knows what he's doing."

"That Mr. Bender knows what he's doing, but I got this feeling there's a lot of trouble to come."

Bender chuckled as the two men approached. "I presume that Zuber was delighted to be leaving our company."

They could hear Zuber calling out to his men but they could barely see the lantern he had with him. The waves would lift the small boat and then plunge it down in its trough, concealing his location.

It was beyond dusk now as the men on *Hampton* waited; they needed the dark of night to make their move.

Wolf told everyone on board about the *Shark Tooth's* cannons; reminding them that Captain Zuber would relish using them. Hereafter, there were to be no lanterns lighted, no flint struck, and no smoking for those who had any. Most important, no one and Wolf stressed *no one* was to talk or make a sound, as a precaution that the wind might carry their voices. Wolf added, "We will all share equally with food and water. It will be our only chance of making it out of this alive. If you will trust us, we'll do our best. For now, take your places you've been assigned and stay put."

All lanterns were extinguished. Everyone followed Wolf's orders.

It will take stealth, cunning, and a run of luck to succeed in outmaneuvering Zuber.

The turbulent sea gave no quarter, it was difficult to keep one's balance, but they situated themselves to do just that. The wind filled the sails—looking back they spied light emanating from Zuber's ship. There was no doubt the captain and Mokes would survive.

Bender in charge of navigation and steering; Gully, Louie, and Wolf were ready to do the rest with help from the passengers.

Whispering into Bender's ear, Wolf said, "Get ready, we're boxhauling as soon as I get up to the tophamper. Wish me luck that we can manage the sails and keep them in place."

Bender touched Wolf's arm and Wolf was gone.

They all understood the plan. They were going to change the tack by going down wind and executing a controlled tricky stunt. They were going to sail in the opposite direction and away from the island Zuber was headed. What they were depending on was for the quarter moon to stay hidden in the cloud laden sky.

It all took time and they could hear the *Shark Tooth's* crew yelling. It was eerie. It seemed they were sailing alongside, but it was evident their voices carried across the water.

Waves rolled and slapped against the sides of the ship as Gully and Wolf maneuvered the big sails with Louis handling the short lashings. It was tricky, but they had no choice. They had to get away and out of sight by dawn.

The night was so black one had to feel his way around. The night air chilled their dampened clothes. Tension so thick none would barely breathe for fear of causing a mishap and have their adversary discover them and open fire.

Zuber wisely doused any light on his ship and the crew quieted. Only the sea could be heard. Neither ship's crew knew where the other was. It was a game of one hiding and the other seeking. Zuber, sailing toward the island for water thinking the *Hampton* was doing the same and when the sun rose, he would turn Wolf and his gang into fish food. Zuber had no inkling that as he ordered the clews tightened to hold the sails against the pull of the wind, he helped put distance between his ship and the one he wanted to destroy.

Hours passed as Wolf and Bender made their way further out to sea, away from land. The warm water and cool air aided them further. A heavy morning mist hung over the sea building a cloak around them to prolong their possible discovery. They had no way of knowing exactly where Zuber would be. He was smart and he was sly and those who knew him respected his expertise with sailing.

By the time the sun ate up the fog, the *Hampton* was well distanced from the *Shark Tooth.* If noticed at all, they would appear a speck on the horizon.

The *Hampton* passengers were euphoric. Wolf, Bender, and Gully did not share their elation. They had accomplished their feat to lose Zuber but now they had just as great an ordeal. They were far from land and they were in need of water.

Chapter Eighteen

Bender was worried. "There is a bank of islands somewhere off to the west, Wolf, but I don't think we have enough food, let alone water to see us there."

"We're existing with only spoonfuls now. *We have to try!* If we show any weakness to the others, they'll give up."

At that moment, Lady Amelia Thomas knocked on the cabin door. She called out her voice just above a whisper but with dominance. "I should like to enter, if I may?"

Gully opened the door. "Please come in, Mrs. Thomas."

Barslow corrected, "It's *Lady* Thomas."

"Oh faddle," she scolded. "Let us not stand on protocol when we are trying to successfully survive. I have formed good friendships that I admire." Peering at the huge black man, she said, "I am also proud to think of you as a friend... Gully, is it not?"

Gully's wide smile lit up the cabin, "Yes, Ma'am."

She looked at Barslow. "Pay that old man no mind, Gully." Then she looked at the men, who were surprised at her visit. "I have come with an important matter to discuss."

They were all standing and Wolf offered Lady Thomas his chair.

"Thank you, Mr. Wolf, I am a little tired." Though Wolf knew the lack of food and water had made everyone weak and lightheaded.

"What can we do for you, Lady Thomas?"

Before she could answer, Gully said it was time he got to the forecastle. "I'll stay our course, right?"

Bender nodded. Gully left.

The graceful, blue-eyed woman looked at the three men. Though her gown needed a wash and pressing, she appeared as elegant as ever. Her mannerisms and carriage evolved about her. There was no fear as she spoke without platitudes. "I am aware that we are short of water to survive, therefore, I speak only for myself... I no longer want any portion of the rations that we are all sharing. If you ask for a vote, I'm sure some of the others will feel the same. It is better that half of us make land than none."

Wolf viewed the petite, gray-haired woman. He remembered her doing as he asked without question. She had stamina and good judgment, but this time he disagreed with her. Without preamble, he said, "What you say is true, my lady, however, we are all in this together. To speak your views to others will take away whatever hope there is of our reaching land. We share the rations that we have equally. My answer to you is *no.*"

She looked at Wolf and did not blink. "I thought you were wiser than that, young man. We will all perish... equally, is that it?"

Wolf's eyes narrowed, his voice was noticeably hostile. "Whatever you wish to believe is no concern of mine. If you do not want to share the rations, yours will be tossed overboard. No one on this ship will be treated any differently from the other."

She stood, keeping hold of the chair while facing Wolf and having to look up at him. "You don't understand."

Wolf's nerves were on edge. If he let this lady start suggesting ways to survive, others would come up with their ideas and soon a selfish attitude would prevail. Self-preservation would rule. Well, not on the *Hampton* and not while he was in charge. "Lady Thomas, my decision is final. We continue to divide what we have; under no circumstances are you to voice your outlook to others."

"I admire your tenacity, Mr. Wolf, but permit me to tell you that I think you are wrong."

"I care not what you think, my lady. Unless all of you vote to put someone else in command, do not come here again with your foolish notions."

"I see."

"It pleases me that you do." Wolf intentionally turned to Bender, "See that Muggs waits for you before dispensing our rations. Everyone is to accept their portion; swallow it in your presence. There will be no exceptions. Now, if you will excuse me, I have duties to attend." Wolf bowed his head to Lady Thomas, nodded to Barslow, and left.

Barslow choked back his angst at Wolf's attitude—yet wondering what Lady Thomas would say if she knew she was debating with the Duke of Grenfell.

"Your offer is very generous, Lady Thomas, but if Wolf did as you suggested, there would soon be divisiveness among us."

"I disagree, Mr. Bender." She would not back down.

"Of course, that is your prerogative, my lady. Hear me well; do not even contemplate going against Wolf's orders."

"I can follow orders if I must, even though I am in disagreement with them." Holding her head high, her back straight, she stepped through the door.

Barslow glared at Bender, hiding his bluster, "Grenfell has changed from the young man I knew. There was a time when he would never have spoken to any lady as he just did to Lady Thomas. I do not approve... I do not approve at all."

Bender was in no mood to treat Barslow with soft gloves. He was revolted, not at Wolf, but at the ignorant London solicitor. "You expect Wolf to kowtow to the upper class because of who they are. What Lady Thomas said is true; none of us may survive this voyage. However, she is not in command. Wolf believes that if there is a chance, we will all have that same opportunity."

Bender was smoldering. "Wolf is a noble and consummate man and it vexes me that I have to point that out to *you,* of all people. Any other person that was kidnapped, tied, beaten, and literally dropped on a

117

stinking filthy deck to live with a bunch of masochistic thugs would have given up, begged for his life, or become fish food, but Wolf *did not!* He stood and faced that wretched Captain Zuber and the cold-blooded, pitiless crew. He survived a flogging that he did not deserve, where others would have pleaded for any kind of mercy."

"The man you are incensed over has courage that even Zuber had never seen, yet he never complained or asked for special treatment. Wolf is commanding this ship and is doing his best to keep us alive. He is treating everyone with the same degree of respect and offering them his strength to endure. You may be thirsty and hungry, but if Wolf had not saved you and the rest of the passengers you would've been fish bait long ago. And think of the ladies, they would not have been so fortunate; what they would have had to endure—being tossed into the sea would be a godsend."

"I... I... didn't know. I didn't understand."

"You don't understand anything, Barslow, unless it's written on those long sheets of parchment." Bender shook his head. "So until you walk in Wolf's shoes, keep your upper-class beliefs to yourself."

"I apologize. I have many shortcomings and I shall look to improve them."

"We all have our blind sides."

Barslow nodded and held out his hand. "Friends?" Bender accepted his handshake.

"Just one thing really mystifies me: how did he beget the name Wolf?"

Bender leaned against the cabin door. "I don't think it's a secret. Still, I think Wolf should tell you. I'm sure he would if you asked."

"He is not the man I once knew. Yet I know that his father would be proud of him."

Bender nodded and left.

118

Chapter Nineteen

A brisk wind filled the sails as the *Hampton* rode six-foot waves.

Rain showers blessed the passengers for two days and whatever could be found to collect water was used. There were happy faces as everyone remained on deck to feel the rain wash over their skin and soak their clothes.

Today the blue sky was hidden above a layer of dormant gray clouds. Even with its reflection upon the sea, the ocean waters stayed an imposing deep blue.

Regina, the fair young granddaughter of Lady Amelia Thomas, sitting under a makeshift canvas cover for protection from the elements, spoke in a pitiful voice, "I look out at the water and I used to think it was beautiful and how I wished to have a gown in its exact color… now I hate it. I shall never want to see blue again as long as I live."

Wolf heard as he was passing. He stopped, peering at the forlorn young girl who was trying to retain her milk-white complexion. Even wearing a floppy hat her skin was turning into what he thought a healthy skin tone He purposely spoke with a tinge of mockery, "If you continue to natter like that, Lady Regina, I promise when I next speak with your father, I shall insist that all your gowns be only deep blue in color."

Wolf, aware of gloom and despair among the passengers, did his best to discourage negativity, especially their voicing of not finding land. He taunted them and they became angry and wanted to vote command to someone else. But it was Lady Thomas that now understood why he pretended to be arrogant, vociferous, demanding, and most always rude.

Had he encouraged their self-pity, they would have given up. He wasn't going to allow that to happen.

"You need not bother to inform my father of anything, Sir. It is I who will tell him."

Wolf walked away hiding his smile; Regina's words were music to his ears as *she* expected to see her father again. *Keep believing, little lady.*

Gully's voice carried to Wolf. He was up on the forecastle in a flash and saw Gully and Bender, grinning, staring out across the water. Wolf followed their gaze.

"Tell me, Wolf, are my eyes betraying me? In this great big ocean is that land straight ahead?" Bender's grin was growing wider.

Shading his eyes, Wolf saw the darker speck on the horizon. "No question about it… I do believe you and Gully have sighted terra firma."

Wolf's loose shirt continued billowing in the breeze against his sun-browned haired chest with his glossy raven hair tied back picked up the breeze blowing against his neck and shirt, balanced his lean body against the roll of the ship. Some of his worry lines lifted. "Good work, Bender, I knew you could bring us to land. Isn't that right, Gully?"

"Yes Sir, Wolfman," Gully grinning with them, "Mr. Bender, he did it!"

Wolf's face and body were lean from lack of food, but the sinewy muscle remained. He was no longer the person tossed on the *Shark Tooth* nearly fourteen months ago. No longer did he dispense a gentle manner that used to be so prevalent in his personality. Now he was a man exuding power and a will that no one dare oppose.

"It wasn't me, Wolf. Gully spied the break on the horizon."

"So then, I thank you both. Let's hope it's a friendly place with fresh water."

"Do you think we should alert the others?"

"It would be best. It will give them hope as it's doing for us. Though, Bender, you might explain that finding land doesn't necessarily assure us that our troubles are over. The island may be deserted with no drinking water. We don't want to encourage them overmuch and have them doubly disappointed. Gully, will you fly up the *Hampton* banner?"

Bender punched Wolf's arm. "With you as our chief, we have succeeded so far." He slid down the rail rather than take the steps. He was happy to finally relay some good news.

Chapter Twenty

The gigantic banyan tree spread its exposed elephant size roots across the sand. Its big and bulky limbs extended fifty to sixty feet out around the jungle seashore. Marvalea Durand and Tishee, her black companion, viewed this tree as their own. Their private hideaway—their sanctuary. Its monstrous branches with shiny; thick waxy leaves were dense easily concealing the women high above the sandy soil. Occasionally, someone unknown would stray on this isolated side of the island— finding nothing around but banyan trees, palms and abundant undergrowth of nettles with their thorny flowers, they would quickly retreat back to the busy side of Port Charles.

The two eighteen-year-olds made their own trails from their plantation home. They had to climb various overgrown sandy hills, circle around briars and prickly plants, but were not deterred. Well aware of fire-ant mounds, they were careful for if attacked the ants infected the skin with burning welts that itched for days—often swelling the feet and ankles. So they made their own secret paths stepping over thorny vines and avoiding the fire-ants' domains.

Marvalea was fortunate as she was allowed to roam on Lady Slipper Plantation, so Tishee became inseparable with genuine camaraderie between them.

Neal Durand, adamant about his daughter remaining on Lady Slipper acres, stressed that she was not to go near Port Charles. He never knew that when Marvalea was eight years old, she talked her sixteen-year-old brother, Marshall, into taking her and Tishee into Port Charles with him. The girls soon discovered there was nothing exciting about the place.

There were sheds with roofs made from palm fronds. Things being sold didn't draw their interest. One noisy place had two girls with painted faces and bright clothes leaning against a palm tree next to its door. Terrified by the different kinds of men walking around, they wanted to go back to the Slipper. Marvalea never told her father and though Marshall threatened to wring her and Tishee's neck, she'd never go back on her word. She told him their secret was safe forever.

Thereafter, Marvalea and Tishee preferred to travel their own secluded route, spending their free hours in the banyan tree. The giant-sized limbs allowed them to stretch out comfortably as the sea breeze cooled them while the leaves hid them from the sun.

"Tishee," Marvalea lay upon the banyan limb high above the ground, "if you could choose a place to visit anywhere in the world, where would you go?"

"Oh Val," Tishee, drowsy after their swim in their private cove near shore, "you always ask and you know I can't go anywhere."

Tishee knew there were countries people traveled to—Marvalea cried until her father permitted Tishee to sit with his daughter and tutor.

Disgruntled, Marvalea said, "Well, I can't go anywhere either. Marshall is the one allowed to leave the Slipper and go off to school. But still, Tish, we can think about places." Stretching on the limb with one hand resting under her head, she stared up at the thick foliage. Rubbing her nose with her other hand, said, "I think I would like see Australia."

Tishee picked up her head and stared over at her companion. "Remember, Mr. Twolaney said that Australia is where they send bad people."

"He's only a tutor, where has he ever traveled," she exclaimed. "I can't believe everyone living there is bad. Look at what goes on over at Big Star Plantation. Medwill Starwell is always punishing his slaves for no good reason. You know as well as I that they can't all be bad."

Tishee lowered her voice, "That white man is evil and mean to black folks."

Marvalea's voice softened, "I know… I know. How I wish Father could do something about it. Maybe someday someone will come along and buy Big Star-then things will change for the better."

"It sure would be something and it sure would be good if someone would do away with mean old Starwell."

"Tish, you be careful when you say those things."

"I know, *I'm a slave* and I'm not supposed to say things about any white master."

Marvalea sat up with force. "Tish, I can't help that you're a slave. I have always treated you as my friend and father has given you every opportunity to have a good life. He has gone against a lot of island beliefs where you're concerned. So stop it! I can't change the color of your skin; I do my best for you as my good friend."

Sitting and swinging her shapely brown legs down over the limb, Tishee repented. "I'm sorry, Val. Will you forgive me? I just get so frustrated. We do so many things together and yet we don' t. You're my best friend and always will be."

Marvalea smiled. "Come on, best friend, I think we better get going. I'm getting hungry."

Mollified, Tishee responded, "Do you want some fruit?"

"What did you do with it?"

"I left the basket over by our granddaddy root. I'll go get it."

"Never mind, I will." Marvalea began to scoot down and moved some of the leaves.

"Tishee… look… a ship and it's coming this way."

"Let me see."

"Good lordy-forty, *Tish… pirates… don't* tell me it's going to try to come ashore here."

"It is… it is! Oh Val, do you think they're really pirates trying to sneak onto the island?"

"I don't know. Look! They're dropping anchor. They *are* coming here."

"What should we do?"

Whispering, even though the waves lapping the shoreline and the distance would keep their voices from being heard, Marvalea prodded, "Let's stay and see what they're up to. Are you in for some spying?"

"Lordy-forty… how can you suggest doing something like that?"

Marvalea, heady with intrigue, encouraged, "Let's stay right up here and watch and listen. It will be the only way we can find out what is happening. Who they are and what they plan to do. They won't stay around-there's nothing here to loot."

"I'm scared."

"You are not, I know you better than that."

"Well, what happens if they decide to camp right here and we have to stay here all night? You don't call that a predicament?"

"Like I said, there's nothing here for them. No water or food. They'll have to go into Port Charles."

"Then why didn't they sail to the other side of the island?"

"How should I know? They must have an idiot for a captain."

"Val, look… look! They're putting over small boats. They really are coming ashore. Ohhh look, there's a pink dress. They have women on board."

"Shhh, here's what we'll do. They can't see us up here. Besides, no one had ever looked up into the trees. So we stay quiet. You take this limb and I'll go up higher. Be sure you have enough foliage to cover you. Just sit and listen and when they leave, we can go home. We can tell Marshall about this, but we must not let Father know. He will make sure old Blossom watches us all the time and we'll never be able to do as we please."

The two young women settled in to wait for the intrusive captain and others to invade their sanctuary.

Chapter Twenty-One

Bender, the last to leave the ship, splashing in the warm clear aquamarine water, climbed into the small boat, smiling.

They slowly climbed from boat to shore. Gully, with Lady Thomas's permission, carried her to the sandy beach and gently sat her down. Wolf followed with Regina.

The warm sand lifting their spirits, they sighed.

Young Robert spoke, "It seems funny not to have to brace myself against the roll of the sea. I feel dizzy."

"Me too," someone else added, "yet the sand feels like heaven."

Wolf surveyed the area. His torso lean, yet muscled-his raven hair blowing in the breeze and his black beard and bronzed body made an astonishing picture to the two women hiding in the tree.

"Gully, will you walk around and check for water or berries that are edible?"

He nodded. "I'll take Louie with me."

Wolf turned to Bender. "We have to get the ladies in the shade. Let's hope there's water somewhere near."

Tishee, peeking through the leaves, heard Wolf *ask* the big black man to look around. No one asked a slave to do anything; they ordered him to do it. She was taken by the fact that the black man agreed as though it was natural to be asked and then said *he* would take the smaller man with him. This was the first time she heard of a slave treated as an equal with the exception, of course, of her and Val.

Tishee continued to peek and listen. The tall pirate must be the captain from the way he was giving orders. Val was wrong, he was no idiot. As far as she was concerned, he was a white master with a polite iron voice.

Wolf was tired and thirsty too and knew he couldn't show his needs. They were depending on him. "Barslow," his voice deep, dry from thirst, "you and Robert see to Lady Thomas and her granddaughter's comfort. Bender and I will explore this island to get our bearings."

Unexpected, Louie came hurrying, shouting, "Wolf… Wolf; wait 'til you see what Gully found."

Gully followed Louie, his big stride and a smile that warmed the hearts of everyone. "Will you all look at this?" He was carrying the wicker basket of fruit that Marvalea and Tishee had brought with them. There were two large white linen napkins folded neatly inside the basket along with two bottles of lemonade.

Bender, grinning, said, "This means there is fresh water around here and this is a picnic basket of sorts. But who?"

"What's in there, Gully? We'll share and explain to the basket's owner later."

Gully brought out four oranges, two bananas, and two mangos. Using his knife he began to divide the oranges.

With pieces of orange sweetening their mouths and dry throats, they glowed as though some god had taken them to heaven—never had anything tasted so delicious.

Next, Gully lifted out two heavy, round, hard, red fruits. Wolf stared at them. "What are those? Certainly not apples."

Gully laughed. "Pomegranates… come from my home. But they must grow here too."

"How the devil do you eat them? They look rock hard."

Smiling at Bender, Gully took his knife and cut away the hard leathery skin, exposing small red berries. "These are ripe and ready for eating. They're very tasty. Don't they just make your mouth water? It's been a long time since I've seen one."

"Then you shall have the first taste." Wolf grinned at the astonished man. "Gully, you and Bender cut up whatever is left of the fruit in as many pieces as you can. We will each choose one piece at a time until it is gone. Start with Lady Thomas. After, we will try to find the owner and express our appreciation."

Wolf didn't mention that the basket was made for *two* with linen napkins. This wasn't ordinary contents, there was quality in it. The basket well cared for didn't belong to drifters. *So where are they?*

Marvalea and Tishee sat quietly listening, moving only a leaf or two trying to see below.

After all, the fruit was eaten and all shared the lemonade, Louie said, "Wolf, this island has people on it. I'm going to head along the shore and see where it goes. I've been to a lot of places and this island has a port. I'm going to find it." He held out his hand, "You did a mighty fine job getting us here."

"I can't stop you, Louie. I thank you as without your help, it would have been a lot tougher. Be safe. I wish you well."

Mr. Shropp, a middle-aged man that did all that was asked of him and rarely expressed his thoughts, now spoke with surprising audacity, "I say that those of us who want to leave with Louie, should be able to do so."

Amazed, Wolf emphasized, "I cannot stop you from doing as you choose. I have accepted responsibility for all of you as well as the *Hampton.* Hear me well, if you walk away now, you will be on your own. I will no longer offer you my protection."

"Suits me," boasted Mr. Shropp. "Those coming, I say let's get on with it. Are you coming with me, Robert?"

Bender cautioned, "Think, after all we've been through, don't be hasty."

For the first time, Muggs, his wiry little body that bore well-earned muscles, offered his thinking. "I say we listen to Mr. Wolf. He knows best, right, Gully?"

Gully patted Muggs' shoulder.

Shropp ignored Muggs totally and began moving down the beach. Others followed.

Robert moved to Lady Thomas. "I would like to go with them, my lady. I traveled this far alone and I do want to get to Virginia."

She smiled. "Of course. Thank you very much for offering us your protection while on board the ship. It means a lot to us. Good luck. Take care."

Robert made a hasty departure to follow Shropp.

Louie turned to Wolf, shaking his head. "Seems to me, Wolfman, what little brains they have—not too smart, so they learn the hard way, like me."

Louie saluted to the three men. He turned to Muggs, "You' re a good sailor, Muggs. I'm proud to have gone to sea with you." He lifted his small canvas bag, slung it on his shoulder, and headed on down the beach.

Muggs grinned from ear to ear.

The only ones left were Lady Thomas, her granddaughter, Barslow and those from the *Shark Tooth*. No one said anything, they were strangely subdued.

Tishee was so intent on taking in the goings on below that she forgot herself and let out a groan when her leg cramped and she began slipping from her perch and on down toward the ground. Letting out a yelp as she grabbed on to a branch swinging back and forth in the air, she couldn't let go or she'd land on one of the cement-like roots.

Before anyone realized what was happening, Wolf had his sword drawn in the direction of the screech. Gully was right behind him with his knife. When they saw the shapely young woman swinging in the air, they were astounded. Without thought, Gully rushed over, reached up, and clasped her thighs, thinking that she would release her hold and let him help her to the ground. Tishee had no such thoughts. She hung on for dear life and tried to kick at the assailant trying to capture her.

"Here, here… little one," Gully temperately called up to her. "You best let me help you down from up there."

She shrieked, "You let go of me, you pirate, or you'll be sorry." She tried again to give a kick, but by then Gully had tightened his hold and she was unable to do anything as he began to pull her down. Her only hope being that Val would come to her rescue.

Wolf stood there, amused. He glanced up into the tree to see who else might be hiding.

Marvalea was up high enough and well hidden. She was not going to expose herself unless she felt Tishee was going to be hurt. From the looks of things, it seemed that they were sea travelers having gotten off course.

Gully, no longer in a jovial mood, tired and thirsty, said, "Listen, little spitfire, you either let go of that branch and let me help you down or so help me I will yank you down so hard it will pull your arms from your shoulder. Make up your mind, *now.*" Tishee let go and Gully almost lost his balance, except that Wolf grabbed to steady him.

Gully didn't release his hold on his captive. She was sitting on his right shoulder with her hand holding on to his ear while he continued to grasp her legs to his chest. He started to walk back a few yards as Tishee bobbed her head to miss hitting the lower limbs.

Just before reaching the end of the spread of shade from the banyan's branches, trying to flaunt some bravado, Tishee yelled, "Where are you taking me? Put me down, you Amazon." She began pounding on Gully's head. She was scared but was counting on Val to help her. Val would get away and get help.

No one spoke as the Amazon eased her off his shoulder and gently set her on the ground. "I'll let you go, Spitfire, but don't try to run. Understand?"

Gully smiled.

Wolf took a step toward her and she moved backward, afraid. "Who are you? Where do you live?" She was nervous. *What did he ask me? Everyone called him Wolf and he keeps staring at me. He's waiting for an answer but I don't know what he said.* She shivered.

Wolf's tone, resonant and abrasive, thirst adding to his deep tone, "I will ask you once again, young lady, who are you and where do you live? You have a name, do you not? You do understand English?"

Tishee's usual obstinate manner no longer evident, gulped a couple of times and then uttered, "My name is Tishee. This is Port Charles Island."

Marvalea up in the tree realized that they were not pirates. *The idiot captain doesn't know where he is. He's an arrogant surly kind of man, just the kind to stay away from.* Looking at Bender, Marvalea thought he was quite handsome, his hair bleached white from the sun, spoke much nicer. But he listened to the captain as if that brute was some kind of God. Marvalea couldn't figure the man called Barslow. His clothes messy, but he still held himself straight; he reminded her of her father's accountant. As for the big black man they called Gully, she wasn't afraid of his size, they had big men like that on Slipper. He seemed nice, he treated Tishee okay. *But Gully is black yet well-spoken and is treated like an equal.* He was also holding on to Tishee.

Wolf didn't realize what a powerful picture he made to the woman in the tree. Standing with his legs spread and his one hand resting on the hilt of his sword, he turned to Gully, his voice purposely harsh, "I think we had better get some straight answers from this healthy young lady or we put her on the boat and send her out to sea. What do you say?"

Gully's eyes twinkled, but his voice was cutting. "Sounds like the right thing to do, Mr. Wolfman. That okay with you, Bender?"

Bender pretended to hem and haw. "I guess… you know those sharks out there are pretty hungry. Maybe we could just tie her to that big tree." Bender removed his sword from its scabbard. "We could have a little fun to pass the time until she decides to cooperate."

Tishee pushed out her chin as far as she could and snapped, "Don't think I'm taken in with your threats." Trying to pull her wrist free from Gully's hold, she went on, "Now if you will excuse me, I must return home. Port Charles is that way—you can follow your friends' footprints."

Wolf had had enough; they were all in need of food and drink. "You speak well, young lady. We are impressed; however, these two ladies are in need of attention. Perhaps you do not wish to extend any hospitality to them, but let me tell you that you're going nowhere until you show us the way to your home and I do not mean Port Charles. Those linen napkins in your basket with the silver corked bottles tells me someone is comfortably situated. Also, the basket was made up for two people. We'll wait for the other to show himself. And make no mistake: the longer we wait, my rage will not be contained."

Tishee heard his anger and believed him. She didn't like this Wolfman and she didn't know what to do. It wasn't her place to take them to the Slipper.

Wolf wandered back to the banyan tree and looked up. Within seconds, he was easily climbing the elephant size limbs. Above he spied white pants with another pair of shapely tanned legs straddling a limb. *So she's not protecting a boyfriend.* Tishee froze. Gully watched her eyes grow bigger by the minute.

Bender walked to the trunk of the tree. He saw Wolf sitting on a limb. "What have you got up there, Wolf? Another tree nymph?"

Wolf called down, knowing the other spy listened. "I believe we have someone that has been watching us. I say, Bender, this is a most inhospitable island I've ever had the misfortune to visit."

Marvalea moved a branch and saw the dark-haired captain. She didn't think she and Tishee were in any danger, but she was in a position that was going to get her into a lot of trouble with her father. Besides, she had to go to Tishee's aid.

Wolf looked at the leg dangling above and noticed the feet were shoeless. Maybe if he promised not to report them to their boss for pilfering someone's picnic basket, they would be more cooperative.

His voice hoarse, he did his best to soften it, calling out, "Come, little one, if you come down and tell us where you live or work, we promise not to tell anyone that we found the basket you finagled from someone's kitchen."

Marvalea wanted to laugh, the audacity of him climbing their tree and accuse them of stealing; Lacy had prepared the basket for her just as she had asked. The nerve and arrogance of this pirate.

Marvalea thought it best to play along and do her best to extricate themselves from this unforeseen ambush. In her best innocent behavior, she said, "Sir, if you will climb down, I will follow and answer your questions."

"Do I have your word? That means… can I trust you?"

How dare he, thought Marvalea. Now she was really piqued, but she maintained her self-control, a bit childlike, answered, "Yes sir, you can trust me."

Without another word, Wolf swung down and was on the ground in seconds. Much to his surprise, the young lady was right behind him, agile and light-footed. As she dropped to the ground, Wolf barely managed to keep from gasping. She was positively the loveliest wild thing he'd ever seen. Her honey blond hair was askew. It was tied haphazardly on the top of her head with loose ends flying every which way. Her sparkling green eyes matched the deep shiny leaves of this giant tree. Her skin—clear, smooth and brown. She was so suntanned, he thought she must do garden work and not care a fig for her complexion. It didn't matter, she was gorgeous.

These were two odd companions. Tishee's hair soft, black and cut short with her big brown eyes ready to pop out of her head. Wolf noticed that Tishee said nothing but a tormented gaze was easily read from her features.

Both women wore white pants that had been cut off at the knees. They had on white shirts knotted at their waist. The shirts were stained from the tree limbs but they didn't seem to care about their clothes or their looks.

Marvalea was not to be bullied. After all, she was the one who knew where they were and how to get them to Lady Slipper Plantation. She knew that her father would welcome these lost strangers. She'd have to take control of this situation.

"Well, Sir," she brazenly attacked, "if you'll stop gawking, I might be willing to offer you some help."

Taken aback at her cognizance, embarrassed at his lapse of command, Wolf's tone was sharp, "At this moment, I don't think you have much choice."

Not backing off, Marvalea was about to retort when Tishee popped up saying, "Please, Val, help them so we can get home. We're going to be in big trouble as we have overstayed our time."

Wolf stretched one arm against the banyan and leaned his weight with it. He grinned, but it did not reach his eyes. "Now, Val," he mocked, "your friend Tishee is a very smart young lady. I suggest you help us," looking at Lady Thomas and Regina, "these ladies are in dire need of care. I *mean* for you to guide us to your home."

Marvalea would not back down so easily. "I will, on one condition."
"WHAT?"

Gully jumped in. "It's getting late, Wolf, what the heck, let's listen to her."

Exasperated as never before, with those green eyes staring him down and the rosiest mouth he could recall seeing; Wolf had to manage his wits. She was throwing him off balance; it must be his need for water and he wanted to lie on the warm sand and sleep. Glaring, he said, "Very well, what is your condition?"

Marvalea stood straight, not realizing as she pulled her shoulders back, she drew her white shirt snuggly over her small round breasts. She held her head up as a breeze moved her tangled hair covering her face. Her hand moved the hair away and Wolf, quick to notice, saw that her hand didn't look like it labored much.

At the same moment, Wolf wished he could slide his hand across her smooth tanned cheek and touch her luscious lips with his fingertips.

Bender eyed Gully with a glimmer of a smile. Gully turned, he didn't want Wolf to see him grinning.

Marvalea struggled to keep her composure as Wolf's eyes seemed to see inside of her. With as clear a voice as she could muster, she said, "All I ask is that you do not tell the owner or anyone on Lady Slipper

Plantation that it was Tishee and me that led you to its door. Also, that you do not mention the basket you *stole* from us."

Wolf, Bender, and Gully were completely dumfounded. They couldn't imagine what her condition would be, but this… they wanted to laugh, but didn't. Instead, Wolf raised his eyebrow, "Did you say *stole? We* are not the thieves."

Putting her hands on her hips, Marvalea blasted, "How dare you?"

"I dare, young lady. Now you listen, and I mean hear me well. I've been more than patient with you and your friend. I've no reason to think that you didn't pilfer the basket with its exquisite linen napkins and silver corks. You have not denied it, have you?"

"Why you—"

"Please Val," cried Tishee, "we've got to get back."

Marvalea, looking at her worried friend, turned to Wolf, "Do you accept my condition?"

"I must confer with my shipmates." Turning to hide his smile that this time did reach his eyes, he stepped toward Marvalea. "We do."

Not flinching, she peered at the dark arrogant man, "Do I have your *word*, pirate?"

This time Wolf let her see his warm smile. "You are a sassy one, I'll give you that. I don't know how your boss lets you run free. You must cause him a good headache."

She considered his insult; then beamed him a radiant smile exposing perfect white teeth, "Fortunately, that is not your concern."

All three men couldn't help but gape at the beguiling wench. Gully mumbled, "You got your hands full."

Marvalea had no idea the picture she presented. She was without conceit and quite innocent when it came to thinking of herself as a beauty. "One thing more—"

"Oh no you don't," Bender interrupted, but still smiling, "you named your condition."

"I know and I'll keep my word, I just want to ask one question of your tyrant captain."

Muggs, who had been silent for so long wanted to impress the beautiful lady, blurted, "He ain't a captain, Miss, he's Wolf."

She gave Muggs her biggest smile. Flushed by her attention, he turned strawberry through his deeply tan. "Well, I just thought because he was giving all the orders."

"He's just like a captain, Miss, but Wolf said not to call him captain."

"It would be nice to continue this tête-à-tête, but it's getting late. Suppose you ask your question so we can get started. You and your friend must be late getting back to your work."

Marvalea withheld her retort at Wolf's overbearing mind-set. *Late for work, am I,* she kept her smile; *I'll get even another way.* "My question is that I'd like to know how you discovered me hiding in this tree."

Wolf actually laughed. It was a warm sounding laugh; it softened his features and made him all the more handsome. "While everyone thought about consuming the fruit, I assumed there were two persons to share it. When your friend fell and joined us, I knew for certain she was not alone." He smiled. "I saw your legs dangling from the limb, the rest you know." He grabbed Marvalea's arm. "Look, how you got the basket is no concern of mine and none of us will mention it. Now, lead the way. Do we have far to go?"

"Let go of me and I'll show you the way." Wolf released his hold. "It is not too far. You must be sure to step where I do, otherwise the nettles and fire-ants are painful." She grinned mischievously, making her look lovelier. "I'm not worried for you, I don't want the ladies to suffer needlessly. You will have to help them as they won't be able to make it by themselves."

"Val?" Tishee called. "Please tell them to let me walk with you."

Marvalea looked at Wolf, asking softly, "Will that be all right?" He hesitated only a moment and then nodded. "Thanks." With Tishee right behind her, she led the way. Wolf was behind Tishee, Muggs followed, Gully offering to carry Lady Thomas with Barslow holding Regina's hand. Bender last in line of the weary sea travelers off the *Hampton.*

The hike from the banyan to the top of the hill was arduous.

Wolf prodded, "Are you certain you're taking us the shortest way?"

Without stopping, Marvalea said, "If I used our usual path, it would have been too much of a strain. Believe it or not, I'm trying to conserve your energy by taking this trail."

They finally reached the top of the last hill and were now walking on a wide sandy path on level ground. Marvalea still led the way, walking slower with Tishee at her side. Wolf, relieving Gully, carried Lady Thomas. Bender right behind carried Regina.

They were all tired. Barslow and Muggs trudged up the rear, toting a few of their belongings. Gully having gone back for Lady Thomas' trunk was far behind but he noticed what Marvalea did to save Wolf from stepping in an oversized ant hill. He continued to eye Tishee's beauty and saw how the blond beauty and her friend were trying to conceal her swollen leg. He said nothing.

Marvalea turned on the path and was out of sight for a few seconds. She leaned against a tree taking her weight off her leg.

Tishee worried, whispered, "Val, you're going to be sick. I can tell. Look at your leg, it's swelling faster than a pot of rice. It's going to fester."

"Shush!"

Wolf came and stopped, waiting for Bender and the rest to come along.

"We turn at the bend up there," she pointed to an opening that was arched with trees.

To Wolf, in the dimming light, his thoughts quickly reverted to Penumbra. He choked back a gasp and took a deep breath. The sun was setting. The tree branches reached over to one another forming an arbor that darkened the lane, yet on the other side of the opening-light and a green lawn with trimmed hedges in the background.

"Is this Lady Slipper Plantation? Do you know if the owner will be receptive to help strangers?"

Still leaning against the tree for support with Tishee standing on the side of her aching leg to shield it from being observed, Marvalea said, "I'm certain. Neal Durand is very nice and will welcome you."

"I'm impressed."

"The Slipper is a magnificent place, like having a corner of heaven." She was silent for a moment, and continued, "When we get to the arbor, Tishee and I will turn to the left and you go on through. It will take you to the front drive and once there, you'll be looked after."

The yearning for Penumbra buried inside of him, Wolf said, "That means, you won't be coming with us?"

Turning hostile, mostly from her leg pain, and resenting him for reasons she couldn't fathom, she snapped, "That was not part of my condition."

Wolf was tired. Still holding Lady Thomas, her head resting on his shoulder with her eyes closed—and with the others now waiting, he tempered his voice, "I gave you my word. I will say nothing about your helping us or about the stolen basket." Looking at Muggs, "Give them their basket."

Tishee took it.

"You better go ahead. Tishee and I will wait until you round the comer."

Bender spoke, "Thank you, Ladies. If we can put in a good word for you, we would be happy—"

Marvalea quickly moved from the tree. "No… no thank you. We will manage."

Wolf nodded to the two women. The weary travelers began to walk in the direction with hope that the owner was congenial as the blond declared.

When Wolf and the others were out of sight, Marvalea slid to the ground. Her leg was almost twice its size, burning and beginning to blister.

Tishee was scared. "I'm going to go get Horseshoe to carry you. You can't even stand on that leg anymore." Shaking her head, she said with disgust, "I don't know why you had to jump in front of that Wolfman and save him from stepping on those fire-ants."

"I couldn't let him, Tish. He was carrying that old woman and couldn't see where he was walking. The poor woman is just about dead. If the ants ever got on her or her clothing, you know what would have happened. They bite in seconds. He might have dropped her without thinking. She could die and I couldn't let that happen."

"Oh no, you just couldn't let that pirate get bitten, but now look at you!" Tishee was kneeling and staring at her friend's indescribable leg. "We need help... oh Val, your mother is going to be mad, but that's nothing compared to Connie's blathering."

"Just don't tell them why or how I got bitten. Now go get Horseshoe, I need Connie's doctoring."

Tears covered Marvalea's cheeks. "What have I done? I get this feeling I'm going to be in a lot of trouble and it isn't going to be from fire-ants. Be right back. Don't move."

Marvalea would have laughed, but the pain was excruciating. "Hurry."

Chapter Twenty-Two

When Jefferson, Lady Slipper's butler, summoned Neal Durand to his front entrance, his wife Marcella and son, Marshall, were there with him. Amazed seeing lost, straggling sea travelers, he welcomed them into his home and before long heard of their journey. He graciously offered them the comforts of Lady Slipper Plantation.

Now having enjoyed a full meal of snapper, wild rice, and tender greens, they sat in silence, smoking Cuban cigars. The nights hushed sounds rickets chirping to one another and far off dogs barking. The moon shadowed the palms and banyans. Brandy poured in clear crystal snifters, yet not touched.

Wolf explained how they had anchored on the far side of the island.

Neal Durand studied the tall, suntanned man, along with his friend. Both spoke well, fine table manners... no doubt gentlemen. Neal wondered how they found their way through the brambles and bug-infested jungle to the Slipper. The climb leading to his door seemed more than a coincidence, yet it could also be luck. "However did you find your way to the Slipper? Don't misunderstand, but we are a distance from the beach and it's almost an impossible climb, especially with the women. You're lucky you made it without coming in contact with those ferocious fire-ants that are everywhere."

Wolf wouldn't lie, but he would omit telling some of the details. He'd keep his word to the two servants. "When we spotted land, we didn't know if it was inhabited. In fact, it appeared deserted. Our only thought to make landfall and hope to locate water. Reaching shore, the others from the ship hurried off to begin searching on their own. I had

140

two ladies in my care so my consideration was first for them. Not knowing how long it would be to follow the shoreline, we opted to climb not knowing it would be tedious; arriving at the top we followed a path and saw your arbor and hoped for the best." Wolf rubbed his bearded jaw, "Especially our being a ragged bunch."

"It's fortunate that you made it to the Slipper, in Port Charles there are no accommodations for ladies and not much for yourselves either. We hope in the future, our town will prosper into a busy port for shipping."

"Your hospitality is treasured, Neal, our energy being in its last stages, we can't thank you enough."

"Please, it is the least I can do. Marcella is happy having guests. Having the ladies to look after and visit is an unexpected gift. She insisted having supper with them in their room. Marcella lived all her life in England until we married. I know she misses hearing news—now she'll have it direct, not from old newspapers."

"Again, our thanks."

"Jefferson has taken charge of Austen Barslow, you have no worries there. He requested water, food, a bath, and bed." Neal smiled. "We'll see him tomorrow. If there is anything you require, just tell Jefferson and he'll see to your needs."

"I recognize that you have slaves, Neal, so this may be an imposition. I would like to make sleeping arrangements for our black friend, Gully."

"I could tell you considered him a friend when you introduce him to me. Although it is highly improper, you understand. Please don't misinterpret what I'm about to say or do, but we have laws on this island. The blacks have places and we have ours. I obey those laws and consequently, there is no friction among the population."

Wolf said, "We don't want to put you in any danger. I might add that with food and water, Gully can stay on the *Hampton* until we get our bearings."

"Right now, your black friend and your other small friend," Neal grinned, "he said to call him *Muggs,* are in the cookhouse devouring

Darcey's best cooking. After, there is a cottage at the end of our back road, a short walk from. here. It was used as the schoolhouse for my daughter and has facilities used by her tutor. It has been abandoned and your black friend is welcome to stay there as long as need be. But I must insist that this not be made known."

Wolf grasped Neal's hand with his big brown one; it dwarfed his host's. "My sincere thanks. You're right, Gully is my friend. He is a loyal friend to both Bender and me. He saved my life. His skin may be black, but he is a gentleman too."

"As long as we have this understanding, I see no problem."

Bender added, "Gully took Muggs under his wing and looks after him. Muggs has no family and has adopted Gully. They'll stay together."

Darkness ascended, but the moon lighted the landscape. The men sat on the lanai in silence, both Wolf and Bender smothering their yawns.

Bender reached for his brandy, sipped while deciding to sail to England with Wolf. He'd try to encourage his father to understand that greed does harm to Tayford tenants.

Wolf stood and walked to the end of lanai staring at the shadows. He tightened the cigar between his fingers without realizing as his thoughts turned to Penumbra—he had to get home.

Unknowing of Wolf's turmoil, Neal went to stand beside Wolf. "It's nights like this that reminds me of my daughter loving this place."

Barslow appeared. "Excuse me, Neal, I can't help but worry about taking Lady Thomas and Lady Regina to their destination. Will it be long before we can find a ship, do you know?"

Neal offered Barslow a brandy that he refused. "We have many ships coming to port, mostly because we have an abundance of fresh water. If you like, I will take you to Port Charles and we can seek the possibility of finding you transportation."

Barslow thanked his host, agreeing to go to town, said good night again, and left. Wolf insisted that Barslow act as a passenger only and not know Wolf personally.

Neal puffed on his cigar, the smoke spiraling upward with a light breeze taking it away. Then he turned to Wolf. "I'm curious why you haven't revealed your true name—there's a mystery for sure."

Wolf said, his voice not hiding his anger, "No mystery. I was shanghaied and my family must believe me dead. Until I can return to them in person, I do not want my name known."

Bender offered, not mentioning how he was on *Shark Tooth,* leaving Neal to think the same of him. "Luckily, Wolf and I were bunkmates with Gully and Muggs. It was close quarters but loyalty prevailed between the four of us. As we explained, the *Hampton* gave us the opportunity to jump ship... so to speak."

"I'd like to go into town with you also. The soonest I can get back, the better."

Neal heard the anxiety in Wolf's voice. He said, "Of course."

Wolf's posture stiffened, his tone grated harshly, "I've got to get to England without delay."

"If possible, Wolf, I'd like to return to London with you."

"Thanks, Bender, I'd like that. Gully and Muggs will be traveling with me."

"Then we'll continue to be a foursome."

Neal interrupted, "You know you'll have trouble bringing Gully on board with you. I mean—"

Wolf didn't hold back his annoyance, "Gully goes with us; no one will prevent him from boarding a ship. If that's the case, I'll sail the *Hampton* to England."

"But you need men."

"Then I'll hire them."

Neal understood why Wolf had been elected captain. "I'll help all I can. Until you make your arrangements, let me offer you my stables. I have excellent horses and you may choose any one you wish to ride. Go anywhere on the island. There are no boundaries. In fact, there is a waterfall at the end of the Slipper that you'll find extraordinary."

Bender injected, "I know for a fact that Wolf is well-acquainted with horses. You'll have no worry about his riding. On the other hand, as for me, it's been ages. I'll look for a meek, mild-mannered old-timer." They laughed.

Jefferson quietly appeared. "Beg pardon, Mr. Neal, I have the rooms ready for the gentlemen as you ordered. And have taken the two to the cottage as told."

"I'm sure our guests would like to retire; they've had a long day. See to their need and anything they require."

"Yes, Mr. Neal, Sir."

Neal Durand stood and Wolf and Bender did also. Neal had to look up to Wolf, being a short man, "We'll talk tomorrow." He held out his hand to both men. "Have a good night."

"Thank you again and again. It has been a long time since I've enjoyed delicious food. What can we do for you, Neal?"

Bender nodded and said, "That goes for me too."

"Gentlemen, your appreciation is enough, for I believe you'd do the same for lost persons too."

They said good evening again and followed Jefferson.

On the way up the long stairway, Bender asked, "Are you going to check on Gully?"

"I don't think it's necessary. As long as he and Muggs have food and water, they'll be okay. To be honest, I'm bone tired."

Jefferson spoke, "I hear you and your friend be looked after good. I checked the cottage and it's clean. The little one was smiling."

"Thank you, Jefferson. Thank you for telling me." Wolf smiled at the old man.

Jefferson smiled. *These be strange men. They treat that big blackie like a friend and not a slave. I wonder how he do that.* He stopped before one door and pointed across the hall to another. "This be your rooms. I got some clothes for you, I hope they be all right. Goodnight, Sirs."

Wolf and Bender thanked Jefferson and bid him a good night. "See you in the morning, Wolf. Don't go to town without me." Wolf grinned and closed his door.

Chapter Twenty-Three

Port Charles was thriving at mid-morning with locals, sailors, and slaves intent on carrying on, some laughing, some busy, and others going about their business while in port.

Neal left Wolf, Bender, and Barslow at the bank planning to meet them later for lunch. With their letter of credit and money in their pockets, the three men headed to the island's only tailor.

Coming out of the tailor's carrying their bundles of canvas pants and shirts from stacks of ready-mades.

Barslow, no longer surprised at the two aristocrats, said, "You'll blend in for sure."

"That's the idea," Bender offered.

"Are you certain about sailing the *Hampton* to England?"

Bender shifted his bundle to his other arm, "If Wolf says we're going to do it, I'm going to be on board."

"Whoa, I only said if it became necessary, I'd do it."

"Oh you will, Wolf," Bender grinned, "and I'll be right there with you."

Barslow slowed his steps. "We're supposed to meet Neal... I can't remember where."

Taunting his solicitor, Wolf said, "Can you imagine, Bender, turning my affairs over to a man who is lost?"

"It's that cafe across the road with the palm tree covering the window and three kids playing in the flower box."

Wolf cautioned, "Remember, Barslow, we met on the ship; don't be overly friendly."

"*Derrick?* Derrick Staunton… is it really you?"

Wolf froze. He raised his head to look down the wooden walkway. He said to Bender and Barslow, "Go meet with Neal. I'll catch up with you."

Stunned, saying nothing. Bender reached and took Wolf's bundle before hurrying off. The man approaching Wolf strode forward, disbelief plainly written across his face.

His white naval uniform cut a distinctive path as the locals stared. His hand reached out to Wolf, "This is an unbelievable surprise. It is *you,* brown as a bear, but I'd know you anywhere." Before Wolf said a word, the admiral continued, while pumping Wolf's hand. "What in the world are you doing here? Everyone thinks you're dead." His features dimmed. "Sorry about the duke, he was not only a fine man, but a great friend."

Wolf clasped the man's hand. "Admiral Cunningham… you visited Penumbra often."

"Indeed. A real tragedy… a real tragedy. I understand there weren't any services," he rubbed his chin, "I thought it strange but then, when it was said you were missing, people understood. They were waiting for you to return. The Duke of Grenfell, no doubt about it, a great well-liked gentleman."

"Thank you, Admiral." Wolf was choking back his grief that had never left him.

Admiral Cunningham, so pleased with his discovery and being around sailors for much of his life, at the moment, didn't register at Derrick's clothing.

"Admiral," Wolf braced himself knowing the admiral will ask details, so keeping his voice low, said, "I have much to discuss and it will be for your ears only."

The admiral's jovial mien disappeared. "Of course. For absolute privacy, let us return to the frigate. Do you have time?"

"Yes."

"What about your friends?"

"They'll understand."

Seated in the admiral's cabin with their luncheon plates being removed, the two men eyed each other.

Puffing on one of the admiral's choice cigars, Wolf said, "What I tell you must remain between the two of us. Understood?"

"Of course, your grace."

Wolf put the cigar in an ashtray in the shape of a dingy. "First, Admiral Cunningham, I respectfully ask that you not refer to me as *your grace*. I am known as *Wolf*."

"Wolf? But you are now a duke."

"That's what I've learned. I'll explain my reasons. Later," Wolf grinned, "I'd be honored to be recognized as the Duke of Grenfell."

The admiral's jaw clenched. "Tell me what you will. It will go no further."

"Thank you." And Wolf proceeded to tell how he and his father were heading for France, being stopped and robbed, his father murdered and he was shanghaied and literally sold to the *Shark Tooth's* Captain Zuber.

The admiral's mouth dropped open. "Excuse me, that ship… *Shark Tooth,* we battled with it not four days ago. It opened fire on us, we sunk it. Years ago, Zuber made off with *Silver Sails*—changed its name to *Shark Tooth* and became a threat to any ship he met on the high seas. A very sharp seaman—he knew how to captain."

Now it was Wolf's turn to gape at the admiral.

Cunningham went on, "Zuber lost his certificate for drunkenness and thievery. He turned pirate. Always a threat, no loss. You mean you were part of his crew?"

"Not by choice. He was brutal and had a crew that was just like him." Wolf wouldn't tell of the whipping.

"Didn't you tell him who you were? Not that he would have let you go; quite the opposite—he'd probably have killed you as he always ranted about the aristocracy."

"I told no one who I am." Wolf's mood veered sharply to anger. "All I thought about was surviving and getting off that filthy tub."

"Do you have any idea who killed the duke and kidnapped you?"

"No, I woke lying in dirty water with rats." He told about Muggs, Gully helping him.

"So how did you get *here?* How did you get away from Zuber?"

"Zuber came across the *Hampton.* Its captain died, the crew abandoned ship leaving a half dozen passengers with two women on board. You know what that means. I took the opportunity to take Zuber as my hostage and the rest is history."

"You let him go?"

"I despise the man and all he stands for, but I am not a murderer." *Not yet, but I soon will be.* "I sent him back to his ship," Wolf laughed, "and sailed away."

The admiral let out a long audible breath. "Now it makes sense. We picked up one of his crew when we blasted *Shark Tooth* to smithereens. The seaman was hanging on a hatch. He claimed his captain had gone crazy being shamed in front of his crew. The first mate took over but nothing went right. No one knew what to do." The admiral shook his head, "He died, weak and dehydrated."

"I'm glad to know this. Captain Zuber and his crew's deaths are no loss, payback for the scourge they were." Wolf stretched his long legs out and picked up his cigar—relit it. "Tell me what you've heard about Penumbra. I've been worried."

"The duke's death shocked everyone. Your twin held up well. He married... I think someone mentioned a neighbor, I'm not sure. I rarely visited the country except to see the duke. Mostly, we met in London."

Wolf concealed his anger. "I'm sure my brother is holding up well. He'll be surprised to learn I'm alive."

"Last I heard he hasn't been recognized as Duke of Grenfell... good thing too with you alive." The admiral thought he was parting with good news.

"That's the issue I want to talk with you about." Wolf's tone changed, it was hard and flat, "I'm asking that you not tell anyone that you've seen me. More importantly that I'm alive. I need time to handle affairs that require my immediate personal attention and I will not explain my absence with anyone. Presently, I will keep the name *Wolf*."

The admiral couldn't believe his ears, but he also heard Wolf's command. He had no right to question a duke, who was now one of the most powerful men in London.

"You have my word… Wolf."

"I appreciate your help. *Hampton* is anchored on the other side of the island. It must be returned to Southampton and that means a crew. I will be taking a black man, his name is Gully, and a young boy, his name is Muggs-with me back to England. Also a friend, his name is Bender. Naturally, I can't return the ship to England without help."

"Your grace… pardon, I mean Wolf, if you can hold over for two weeks, I have two frigates that will be returning to Southampton. It would aid me greatly if you could see yourself to it. We anchor here only to replenish our water supply. I will see that you have a crew."

"Admiral Cunningham, I am in your debt. Waiting two weeks will not be a problem. Thank you, Sir."

Wolf rose and offered his hand. The admiral felt the calloused hand and its strength. He knew the new Duke of Grenfell had survived more than just being a deckhand.

Wolf, moving to depart, stopped, "Oh yes," his voice authoritative, "Gully, a black man, and little Muggs are my friends. Advise your crew that they are to be respected."

"Consider it done, Wolf."

Wolf nodded and about to leave when the admiral spoke, "I just thought of something. I have old newspapers I can't seem to discard; perhaps you'd like to take them with you. It may give you some idea what's been happening in London."

"I'm grateful. Thank you."

"I'll have you taken to shore."

"I'm staying with Neal Durand at Lady Slipper Plantation."

"I'll not let you down."

"I'm counting on it, Admiral."

Admiral Cunningham saw a tall, hardened man with a back of iron and the tone of a nobleman. *He is one powerful man. Derrick Staunton, the new Duke of Grenfell is going to make a gigantic splash when he returns and I can't say a word to anyone. Damn.*

Wolf hopped onto the dock from the small boat. Its rocking motion seemed not to matter, his step up was light and easy, his dark beard and his raven hair making him look menacing. He was thinking about his conversation with the admiral making his features stern. Several people stepped out of his way not wanting to tangle with this sailor. Wolf's long stride took him to his waiting friends.

"Neal," Barslow explained, "will be delayed and suggested we go on without him."

Bender eyed Wolf with newspapers. "I haven't seen one of those in ages." He reached for them, giving one a cursory glance. "Do you mind?"

He handed them to Bender. He said to the two men, "I've worked out everything. There'll be no problems. I'll tell you as we ride back to the plantation." Then to Barslow, he asked, "What have you found out about taking Lady Thomas on to the colony?"

"I spoke with her this morning and she's decided to return to London, posthaste. Lucky for us, Neal found a private yacht leaving in two days and the owner has agreed to take the three of us providing we don't reveal his name." Barslow smiled. "You would know of him. That's all I will say."

"You'll get to London before me, I'll tell you what I want you to do."

"Yes, your... Wolf."

"Let's get our horses." Wolf looked at Barslow's sun-red face, "You better get a hat on or you'll be fried by sundown."

Barslow used his hankie to dab at his forehead. "I know. I misplaced it."

Bender laughed. "You'll see a skinny lad wearing it if you come back tomorrow."

Barslow's mouth dropped open. "You saw him take it?" Grinning, Bender nodded. "Why didn't you stop him?"

Bender shrugged and didn't reply. He remembered Muggs on board *Shark Tooth* where given any kind of article bought a wide smile and happiness.

Wolf, impatient to be underway, said, "Never mind. Let's go." They flipped two youngsters' coins for watching their horses and headed for Lady Slipper. Reaching Slipper's stable, Barslow left to inform Lady Thomas of their pending departure and Wolf and Bender walked toward the schoolhouse.

"I want Gully and Muggs to hear this too." Wolf's mood was positive. "It looks like we'll all be going *home,* Bender."

Muggs saw them coming and came running.

Bender ruffled his cut hair. "I say, Mate, if you don't stop eating, you're going to get as fat as Captain Zuber."

"Aw, Sir, I ain't so fat." He grinned. "But the cookin' is good. I never had so much in all my life."

"Well then," Wolf said, squeezing the little bony shoulder, "we'll see that you *always* have as much as you want."

"For Gully, too?"

"Especially for Gully and especially for you." Wolf's expressive face changed to almost somber, but then he grinned, "I've good news for all of us—come on, let's find Gully."

Muggs lost his smile. He pointed, then almost whispered, "Gully's in the schoolhouse."

Wolf looked at Muggs, "What's going on?"

"Gully's got trouble," Muggs looked at Bender, he was about to cry, but didn't.

They were about to step up on the schoolhouse porch when Gully walked out, his tall broad frame was dirty. He was shaking. "I got trouble, big, big trouble, Wolf. I'm sorry."

Wolf was beside Gully in seconds. "Sit down... tell me what I can do."

"I'm sorry I'm going to get you in a heap of trouble."

Wolf quirked his eyebrow, his gut feeling that what Gully was about to tell was trouble as Gully never said what wasn't true. "Listen, we came to tell you we're all going home in a couple of weeks."

Bender shoved at Wolf's shoulder. "And you didn't tell me all this time?"

"I can't go." They all gawked at Gully as if he were mad. "I mean I don't know what to do."

Wolf's tone sharpened. "Enough of this, Gully. Suppose you tell us what this is about and we'll make it right. Now *what* is going on?"

Muggs burst out, "Gully's got a girl in the schoolhouse." Wolf and Bender were stunned.

Gully spoke in his usual calm way. "I heard some crying back there in the woods. So I went to investigate. I thought it was a hurt animal." His mouth tightened. "It was an animal alright, a human animal. She's black and from Starwell Plantation. She was covered with blood. I couldn't leave her... she'd lost her baby. She'd been beaten with bruises covering her body and face. I had no choice."

Wolf and Bender knew that this was trouble... big trouble as Gully uttered. Slaves were property. "How is she?"

"It'll take time, if we have it." Gully's voice was just above a whisper. "Losing her baby, she also lost a lot of blood. She's weak."

Wolf moved to go inside. Gully grabbed his arm to stop him. "She's going to be scared because you're a white man. I tried to tell her you were different but she doesn't think any white man is good. She's been raped by them often."

Wolf backed off and went to stand with Bender. Gully told Muggs to go and stay with Sheena while he talked with his two friends. "I'm real sorry, but to leave her isn't the right thing to do. She's been beaten so much that even her scars have scars."

Bender's expression was grim while Wolf's was tight from strain. "Gully," Wolf warned, "we're safe here because of Neal Durand's generosity. What we have here is property that doesn't belong to any of us." He raised his hand to stay off Gully's indignant opposition. "*Don't, don't,* tell me how wrong it is to own people. I agree, but this is the law on this island. You know they are going to come looking for her."

Gully sneered. "Oh yeah, they're going to get their dogs out. I'm surprised we haven't heard them yowling already. Sheena said they probably don't know she's gone."

Wolf took a deep breath. "Do you have any idea how we can avoid Neal getting into any of this?"

"Not rightly. But I've been doing nothing but thinking about it."

"We've got to get her out of the schoolhouse. She can't stay here. I won't put Neal in the middle of this." Wolf began to pace.

Bender leaned on the porch post. "Wolf, you've got to be careful. This is dynamite and you can be shot... accidentally, of course. They won't tolerate abetting a slave escaping. We're strangers, that makes us doubly vulnerable."

It was as if Wolf wasn't listening to Bender. He stopped, his strained countenance created a stony mask. "Can Sheena walk at all?"

"Not without help."

"Look, Gully, she's got to walk. She must get herself down to the water. She's got to enter the water as though she wants to drown."

One corner of Bender's mouth twisted upward. "Right... clever, Wolf, but then what?"

"We've got to get her on board the *Hampton*."

Gully broke out with the biggest grin they could ever remember seeing.

"At the stable this morning, the groom asked if I liked to fish and said there's a boat down on the beach—pulled up and anchored to some bushes. I'll find it. We'll borrow it and take Sheena to the ship. But we've got to do it tonight. Like you said, those dogs are going to be on us and they'll come right here."

"I already scrubbed down the porch and everything she touched. Those dogs will lead her to those bushes, but I carried her out of them."

"You know better than to think they won't come this way," Wolf admonished.

Gully nodded.

Bender said, "Look, I'll go up to the house and pretend you're still visiting with Gully and Muggs. If we're all here too long, someone might become suspicious. Especially Tishee, she seems to be peeking around a lot."

"I noticed that too."

Picking up the newspapers, Bender headed for the mansion.

Wolf looked at Gully. "As soon as it's dark enough, you must get that girl walking and to the beach. It's quite a way—have Muggs go along and sweep your footprints away. When you get to the beach, I'll be there. I'll find that boat and between the two of us, we'll have to row out to the ship. We won't have all that much time but my being with you won't cause too much interest. Be sure you take the quilt and anything that was touched by the girl. Those dogs will sniff her scent; you can say you and Muggs were off somewhere in case they track her to the schoolhouse. Keep this in mind, we must keep Neal Durand out of this and there must not be one iota of proof that we are involved."

"I promise, Wolf."

Wolf was worried. "Definitely she will be traced and followed right to the beach. Cross your fingers and hope they believe she drowned on purpose."

Gully, agonizing over the trouble he had brought to his true friend, said, "I know I'm putting you in this difficult spot, Wolf, but when I saw her bloody body, I remembered the life I lived. I *couldn't* leave her, I just couldn't."

Wolf clasped Gully's arm, his bronzed hand against the black arm making a striking contrast. "I know, Gully. Your heart is giant in size. We'll make this happen—just be extra cautious."

"I will."

"I won't go in to see her. She doesn't need any more upset if she'd going to have to walk. There will be a quarter moon so it will help us negotiate your trek to the beach. Wait for me there. Be sure to tell her she's going to have to walk into the water and the salt will eat at her skin, but it's the only way. Her trail must end at the beach."

"I'll be with her, Captain." He looked at Wolf, the water in his eyes hung on his lids. "Thanks."

Wolf nodded, turned, and left. He heard Gully call out to Muggs.

Chapter Twenty-Four

Gully was holding Sheena as far from him as possible so Muggs could sweep his prints away with a palm frond. Muggs was walking backward and doing away with his also. It was a slow process, but they kept on. Then they heard the howls, the whining, and the crashing through the bushes. The dogs were on their way.

"Gully!" Muggs cried as quietly as he could.

Gully lifted Sheena in his arms and began to run. "Come on, Muggs, we haven't got time. They're at the schoolhouse now."

Sheena began to whimper. "Shh, girl, hang on to me best you can. We'll make it, don't give up now."

Muggs passed Gully showing him the way. The dogs' barking got louder. "It's right up here, Gully. Not much further."

They reached the beach but didn't see Wolf. "Get yourself lost, Muggs. I'll do what I can. Don't get caught."

"I don't want to leave you, Gully."

"You do what I say. They're just about on us. Go!"

Muggs ran down the beach and hid in the palmetto bushes. He was shaking. He wanted to stay with Gully and help him, but Gully ordered him to go and he had to obey. He tried to see his friend, but a cloud moved over the moon. He was breathing hard and quivering.

Gully was holding Sheena and taking her into the water. "Listen to me, Girl, like I said the salt is going to burn and hurt. But you've got to keep still. I will not let you go. Trust me." She nodded.

Gully being tall, it took a while for him to reach the deep water to submerge him and Sheena. "Ohh," she softly cried, "it hurts."

"I told you it will, but it will also cleanse your bruises. Now hang on to me. That's right put your arms around my neck as we're going to go under the water. I'll not let you go. Take a deep breath when I take us under. As soon as I can, I'll help you float. I'll stay with you."

The dogs hit the sandy beach and ran straight to the water lapping at the shoreline. Two dogs ran in splashing while the others continued to howl on shore.

Gully dove deep, barely moving his legs so as not to be discovered. Holding his breath, he could have stayed down longer but Sheena began to struggle so he rose as gently as he could and hoped the cloud stayed. Slowly, oh so slowly, Gully moved further out to sea. He needed to get as far from shore as possible. He didn't know how long he could keep going but his priority was to save this girl.

The dogs hung about the water's edge. He could hear men yelling but couldn't make out what they were saying and didn't particularly care at the moment. He was gasping for air and holding Sheena up was taxing his energy. He kept moving out to sea. If he ended up drowning, at least it was for a good reason.

Sheena began to whimper. "Hush… sounds carry," he panted, "those dogs have ears that will pick up our sounds." Trying to fill his lungs with air while his arms and legs felt like lead, Gully continued pushing into the cool water. The noise from the beach no longer in his hearing, either because he was tired and his ears were filled with seawater or the searchers had given up. Yet Gully continued to move forward. He didn't think he could go further. The cloud no longer followed them and the slight moonbeam glistened on the water. *Not a bad way to die,* he thought. He drew Sheena to him as best he could. She was squeezing him around his neck and he smiled to himself—it being the first time in years that he held a female in his arms. He was getting ready to apologize for not saving her when his knees found sand.

He kicked his legs and found himself lying on a sandbar. He wanted to roar, to shout their good luck but he only stopped moving and let the water cover him as it lapped over his long body. Bringing air into his lungs, he held Sheena's head up as he relaxed and let his body go limp. *A sandbar.* He couldn't believe his luck. Soon judging that there was about two or three feet of water, he whispered, "Stay absolutely quiet. Those dogs are out there, make no mistake. Do you understand?"

She nodded. Gully couldn't see her but because he was holding her head above water, he felt her movement.

"We're going to stay right here. If I know the captain, he'll find us."

Stocker, the overseer from Big Star Plantation, was yelling at the dogs to quiet down.

One ran to the palmetto bushes and howled. Smiling, Stocker hurried over and yelled, "Come out of there, you slut. Thought you could get away, did you? You'll feel my whip for sure. Maybe then you'll learn not to make me have to hunt you up again."

Muggs began to cry. "I didn't do nothing." He crawled out, the dogs growling. "Whaaat? Who are you? What are you doing here? Where's my slut? You better tell me or I'll whip your hide."

A voice of iron came out of the darkness. Its tone had depth and authority. "I don't think you'll do any such thing." Wolf walked toward the overseer. Three slaves that had accompanied Stocker moved away to stand behind him. Even the dogs stopped their howling and softened their whine—settling in the sand.

Stocker wasn't intimidated; after all, he had Mr. Medwill Starwell to back him and no one dared challenge the owner of Big Star. "Who the devil are you?"

"That is none of your business. I'm here to teach this lad to swim. Do you have a problem with that?"

Stocker's voice was heavy with sarcasm. "Swimming, huh? I just bet." What Stocker thought was that this man was having a rendezvous with the boy. He sneered. "I don't care what you call it but my dogs followed my runaway slave here."

"Well, look all you want, but I doubt that this boy has *him.*"

"It's not a *him,* she's a slut and Mr. Starwell wants her back."

"Then I suggest you continue your search. It isn't my business."

Stocker stood back and tried to see Wolf. The moon didn't offer much light and the lanterns his slaves carried burned all the fuel. "Who are you? What are you doing on this beach? It's private property."

Wolf responded matter-of-factly, he didn't want to raise this man's ire, he had to find Gully. "Yes, it belongs to Neal. I'm aware it belongs to Lady Slipper Plantation, that's why I thought it would give me a chance to teach my little friend how to swim without anyone seeing him learn. He's shy."

"You know Mr. Durand?"

"Yes, of course. I'm visiting with him."

Stocker backed off immediately. "I didn't know. Sorry." He turned on the slaves. "Get the dogs, you lazy buzzards, let's go." Grumbling, he added, "Mr. Medwill ain't going to be happy with tonight's work."

Muggs, sitting in the sand, jumped up as soon as Stocker was out of sight. He hugged Wolf around his waist. Wolf was surprised at the intense pleasure he got from Muggs' response. He lightly punched Muggs' arm, saying softly, "You did well." Bending his head for Muggs' ears only, "What about Gully?"

"The dogs were coming and Gully carried the girl out into the water. He ordered me to hide and wait for you."

"That's what a good sailor does, he obeys orders." Wolf began walking. "There's a boat over there. Let's get it in the water and see if we have luck finding him."

"I'm scared."

"So am I, Muggs. We'll do the best we can—come show me where Gully entered the water and if we don't get twisted too much, we might be able to find him. We've got to hurry."

They lugged the small boat into the water. "What's in that canvas bag?"

"Provisions. Let's hope we need them. Come on."

They began to row, remaining silent hoping to pick up some sound from their friend. All they heard was the swish of the oars as the boat rode over small waves. Wolf pulled on the oars; it felt good to use his muscles again.

"Want me to help you row?"

"Not yet, Muggs. See if you can make out anything on the water."

Wolf rowed and then let the boat drift. He called out as loud as he thought wise. "Gully… Gully." Nothing. He rowed some more, his heart in his mouth and his stomach coiled in a knot. "Gully… Gully?"

"Could he swim out this far, Wolf?" The worry in Muggs' voice was evident.

"I don't know. I'd like to tell you everything will be all right, but I don't want to lie to you, Muggs. We've got to keep trying."

"Gully's smart. He said he had to save that girl. He's always saving someone."

Wolf took a deep breath as his shoulders moved in unison with his strong arms pulling the oars. "Gully saved you and then he saved me. Now it's our turn to save him."

"I'm glad you talk like that, Wolf. No one liked Gully 'cause he was black, but that didn't matter to me. He's always been nice to me. Should I call out?"

"Okay, but keep your voice low. Wait, I'll stop rowing, we'll float quietly."

Muggs cupped his hands around his mouth, calling out, "Gully… Gully, please answer. Where are you?" His little shoulders slumped and he began to cry.

"Easy… hold on, Muggs. Don't give up." He put the oars to work and moved further out to sea, when he suddenly lifted the oars. "Listen… listen." They heard nothing. "Call again, Muggs."

"Gully… Gully… it's me and Mr. Wolf."

"Over here, about eleven o'clock. Then straight ahead," he called out, just loud enough to be heard.

With new energy, Wolf yanked on the oars.

They came upon the sandbar, but far from Gully; it mattered not. "Stay quiet," Wolf ordered, "we must not be discovered."

Jubilant, Muggs whispered, "Right you are, Captain."

They pulled the boat onto the sandbar. They could hear the swish-swashing water's movement as Gully made his way to them.

There wasn't time for greetings, but there were smiles, though barely visible. Gully spoke, "Sheena needs shelter." He was carrying her and moved to get in the boat.

The quilt he had her wrapped in was dripping, still he held her wrapped in it. "Muggs, will you sit and hold Sheena's head. It wouldn't be good to let her bounce over the waves."

"Sure, Gully," the youngster was happy. "I sure am glad we found you. You're so smart to find this sandbar."

Whispering back, he said, "It was luck, pure luck."

They were in the boat and beginning to row. "I'll row first and then if you feel okay, you can do a few pulls. Okay?"

"I can do it now, Wolf. In fact, let's do it together and make a giant wake. How far away is the *Hampton*?"

"I can't say, but it's this way." They both worked the oars. "We've got to get back before dawn."

Wolf spoke quietly to Gully who was sitting beside him. "Are you sure she can handle being alone on the ship? We can't stay with her."

"She knows that I'll keep her safe. And I was thinking maybe you could say Muggs and me are going to stay on board and sort of look after it."

"Good idea. I think Neal Durand might like that. You know he's been kind about your staying at the schoolhouse and now with the missing slave…"

"Say no more. I understand. But I also know it was you that got us a nice place to stay. It'll be better if we're gone."

"We've got to be careful. If we get caught, it's not only our necks, but Neal Durand's too. I've got news… we'll all be sailing to England in a couple of weeks. I met with a Navy man I know and he's going to see that we have a crew."

"You sure you want me along?"

"How can you ask? You've got to know I wouldn't think of leaving you or Muggs. You have a home with me for as long as you like. You have my word."

Gully looked sideways at Wolf, his voice thick and unsteady. "Thank you."

The night air was warm, stars filled sky, quiet as two muscled men made their way, cutting smoothly through the light chop of the Caribbean Sea.

Chapter Twenty-Five

Wolf slept longer than usual. The exercise from rowing had felt good but by the time he got to bed, he was exhausted even having regained most of his stamina.

When he got to the stable to ride the black horse, *Night,* he'd admired, it was gone.

Thinking Neal had taken the horse, Wolf chose a golden-brown gelding. "It's a good ride you'll get from *Striker,* Mr. Wolf," the black groom said. Wolf smiled, thanked him, and was off in seconds heading Striker toward the beach.

The sea's teal colored water was the most beautiful water Wolf had ever seen. Galloping along its shore and splashing in the surf with the breeze blowing his hair in all directions, gave Wolf a sense of freedom—riding again, almost like at Penumbra. He raced a long distance and saw another horse way ahead and raced toward it.

Nearing the horse that was trotting, Wolf couldn't believe his eyes—it was the blonde; her long hair flying in the air. She sat on a *black... black... that's Night! What the devil is she doing riding Neal's thoroughbred?* He kneed his horse to catch her but when she turned at the sound of pounding hoofs, her eyes about popped out of her head.

Marvalea gulped. "I'm in for it now, but not if I can get away." Talking to her horse, "Come on, Sweetheart, let's go." Rather than race on down the beach, she turned around and headed toward the pirate. After all, she knew this beach better than he.

Her charging forward stunned Wolf, pulling Striker to a halt. But she didn't stop as he thought she would. Instead, she made a wide arc and sailed on down the beach. When he realized she had no intention to stop, he watched, totally amazed at her flawless riding. He laughed, she was riding astride. She wore those white shorts with her blouse knotted at her waist. She was a vision of wild loveliness.

Wolf nudged *Striker* to follow. He saw *Night* make a left tum and disappear. Wolf couldn't figure how that could be as that wasn't the way back to the stable.

Galloping on, he knew he had somehow missed the turn. But how? He put the horse at a slow trot and turned back, this time conscious of the hoof prints left in the sand. Sure enough, there was a small opening that looked as if was just a notch in the dune. It was where the hoof prints led and he carefully set *Striker* onto the path. It wound through the palmettos, their sharp edges sticking out here and there scraping the horse's legs as well as Wolf's, but he kept going. He was going to trail the blonde servant and find out how she was able to filch one of Neal's finest horses to ride, especially if she should be working. He'd threaten to tell on her, but he knew he wouldn't.

Slowly, making his way down a narrow path, the breeze stopped causing perspiration to build and his shirt to stick to his body. Birds flew among the overhanging branches but didn't chirp. Bugs were abundant buzzing around evidently not liking being disturbed.

Wolf pushed his hair back off his face feeling its wetness, still determined to find her.

Moving forward he heard the waterfall; the closer he got the louder, it sang. *This must be the one Neal mentioned.* The noise from the fall concealed his approach and just before coming to the full opening, he halted *Striker* and stared. He couldn't believe his eyes. Suddenly, he was in paradise. Wolf swallowed his breath not wanting to make a sound as he watched the beautiful servant girl floating on her back wearing absolutely nothing. Her golden body in crystal clear water was bronzed to perfection. Her long blond hair floated above her head. Her eyes were closed and every so often, she'd wiggle her feet and hands slightly to move through the water. Her voluptuous breasts would most certainly fit into the palms of his hands. His eyes traveled down to her womanhood and he could feel himself harden. Wolf leaned forward with his elbow on his thigh, not wanting to disturb the beauty one moment. But the hushed scene didn't remain for his horse snickered, wanting to have a drink of cool water.

Marvalea leapt forward, her beautiful body sinking into the clear water, creating rings around her. Certain that her pounding pulse made ripples in the water—she glared at Wolf as she spat out contemptuously, "What are you doing here, Pirate? Get out!" Continuing to tread water moving further from him to the other side of the pond where her clothes lay on a rock.

Aware of what she was about, he had no intention of allowing her to escape him. He was out of the saddle in seconds, kicking off his canvas shoes and diving into the water to catch her. His long arms swiftly made the distance closer to her but to his amazement, she had powerful strokes and was about to leap onto the small ledge to reach her clothes. He laughed as he caught her ankle. Now he was standing in the water waist high when he pulled her back into his arms, her wet luscious body sliding down against his.

She struggled as he pressed her wet body to keep her close to him. His strong arms meant to keep her there.

"Let go of me, you filthy cur." She felt his hard body, trying to hide her panic.

But he squeezed her to him, causing her to gasp. She tried to kick him but he held her so close it was impossible. She tried to beat him on his face and ears, but he moved so quickly grasping her wrists and holding them with his one hand over her head. Marvalea was literally floating in the water as her feet couldn't find the bottom.

A sense of urgency drove Wolf to lower his head and kiss her. His voice turning husky, almost laughing with joy when his mouth met her tightly sealed lips. "My god, you're beautiful... wild to perfection." He moved his mouth toward her again, touching her lips with his tongue, feeling the coldness from the waterfall. He wanted to devour her. When she didn't respond, he picked up his head eying her, "Surely, you sassy little wench, you've been kissed before." Sarcasm took over as he scowled, "What's wrong, I assure you this man will please you."

He lowered his head to kiss her again, but she spat at him, trying to kick him, "You're disgusting!"

In a flash, he dropped her; she splashed into the water trying to get her balance. His features were a glowering mask of rage. He didn't move a muscle as she moved to put distance between them.

"Worry not, you nasty piece of baggage. I've never forced a female. Take yourself away from me before I turn you over and paddle your derriere. That might encourage you to learn some manners. A lady you are not," his tone colder than the waterfall, "and I doubt that you even care. Perhaps…" he took a breath, "never mind. Go!"

Marvalea having reached her clothes pulled on her shorts and misbuttoned her blouse, but she didn't care. Now that she had herself covered, she could brazen it out with the pirate. Seething with anger and humiliation, she said, "Manners? You, sir, have none! How dare you think you can manhandle me? Did I give you any reason to think I'm in need of your service? Have I given you reason to think I'd permit you to touch me? You, Pirate, are an overbearing lout and why Neal Durand invited you to stay on his plantation is beyond me. I might even tell him how you invaded *my* territory."

Wolf roared, "Your territory? Perhaps because you are his servant, but believe me, this is not your territory." Even though Wolf was angry at her despicable behavior when all he wanted was to make love with her, he was fired up over her willingness to argue and the rosy color that infused her golden cheeks. Remembering her blonde hair floating like a mermaid, her beauty, her golden skin. He wondered how she came to work on this island… and why?

Marvalea knew she should leave, but looking at the pirate standing waist deep in her pond did something funny to her stomach. He looked dark and mysterious, but she realized he wasn't vicious as when she spat at him to get him to release her, he dropped her when he could have slapped her or really turned violent. She thought she would play with him. "Oh please, I'm sorry. You won't report me to Mr. Durand, will you?"

Wolf cocked his head to one side eying her, "I think you're a shade sorry, so no I won't say a word to Mr. Durand." He looked beyond her to the black horse munching stray grasses. "Tell me how you're able to take that horse to ride? Who taught you to ride so well?"

Pleased with his praise as riding being her one passion, she glanced toward *her* horse, and then turned and smiled at Wolf. It was a warm smile that lighted her eyes. "I'm allowed to ride when I have the time… as long as I'm careful."

Wolf surmised for her to ride the beautiful stallion as well as she does, she had to ride often. Well, he wasn't going to mention it to Neal, it wasn't his place to do so and in all fairness he didn't want to cause this sassy angel trouble. But he couldn't let her know. "I suggest," his voice belligerent, "you get yourself and *Night* back to the stable. Unless…" he flashed an intense eye piercing look, "you're hanging around here for me to fulfill my desire for you."

Marvalea backed away toward her horse and then suddenly stopped. Shock and anger lit her eyes, contempt filled her. "You are worse than a cur. It's too bad I don't know something worse to call you." With that, she was up on Night's back and trotted off. She didn't look back.

Wolf wanted to laugh, but he didn't for he knew he hadn't behaved as a gentleman. Regardless of someone's status, he always respected them if it was their due and surely, she didn't deserve his brazenness. If the opportunity presented itself, he'd apologize.

Removing his saturated clothes and tossing them on the rock, Wolf dove into the deep cold clear water with his thoughts on the blonde beauty floating in this same water. *She calls me Pirate.* He burst out laughing because he liked it… he liked her.

Chapter Twenty-Six

It was mid-morning as he led Striker from the waterfall back to the beach. Leaning forward Wolf gently patted the stallion's neck. He had no idea the picture he and the horse created—both sturdy and handsome looking. The horse's tail swished as it stood like a statue. Both so quiet the lapping water surrounding them seemed settling and calm.

Wolf stared out at the horizon, taken in by its arc, his thoughts traveling to Penumbra. His heart had never ceased its aching over his father's death. His hand tightened on the reins until it indented his palm, gradually he loosened his grip and taking a deep breath turned to head for the schoolhouse and check on his friends. They had a busy night.

Sitting on the schoolhouse porch, Gully and Muggs appeared to be waiting for him. Gully whittled on a piece of wood leaving a pile of shavings at his feet. Muggs sat with his back supported by the building, his head cradled in his hand, talking. When Muggs saw Wolf approach, he was about to run to him, but Gully held out his hand, stopping him. Gully looked at Wolf, said nothing at first, his eyes moving around in his head.

Wolf barely nodded his head, he understood.

"Oh Captain," Muggs called out, "we be so glad to see you."

Wolf laughed. "I'm glad to see you, too. Do you think you'll be able to keep your head above water now? It was a pretty good swimming lesson."

Muggs grinning, said, "I'll be the best swimmer yet. Guess what? I had fresh strawberries, all I could eat. They're so sweet. I never had them before."

Gully kept whittling, his voice low as Muggs kept talking, "We're being watched."

"Well, Muggs, I think you better pack your things as I'm taking you and Gully back to England with me. Then you can have all the strawberries you want."

"Really? You mean it?"

"Yes. We're going to sail the *Hampton* across the Atlantic. Think you can manage it?"

"Gully and me?"

"Of course, and Bender too."

Wolf rose and stepped off the porch. "I've got to be going… give me a hand, will you, Gully? I think my horse has a spur lodged in its hoof."

Gully walked with Wolf and then lifted *Striker's* front leg. Both men bent down.

Gully's voice low, "We been watched when I woke this morning. Told Muggs to stay put and not say anything. Can you get us on the boat without trouble?"

"I'm sure. I'll talk with Neal this evening. Get what you want to take ready. If I can't come, I'll send Bender. Don't tell him about the girl. Get on board and wait."

"I think I got it, Captain," Gully said quite loud, he patted the horse. "Bet that feels better now."

"Thanks, Gully."

Muggs yelled out, "Bye Captain, don't forget to take us with you."

Laughing, Wolf called back, "We'll be moving in a day or so. I'm going to clear it with Mr. Durand." He trotted away, his stomach coiled, he hated leaving his friends, but he had no choice. The sooner he got them on the ship, the better-off everyone would be.

Wolf turned over wanting to go back to sleep, the swim at the waterfall and after last night's stint he had little sleep.

There was a tap on the door and Bender walked in, grinning. "I've never known you to be in bed in the middle of the afternoon. Time to get your butt out of that bed and dressed." He whistled softly, "You must have had some morning. Care to tell me about it?"

Wolf stretched. The sheet barely covering his midsection with his tanned hairy legs protruding out across the mattress as he yawned and said, "The blonde servant…"

"Ah, now I see. But one thing I can't put together is that all the slaves here have black hair and hers…" he grinned.

"I know, I've thought about it, but who knows. Her skin tone is light but darkened from the sun to golden—she's a golden angel."

"So?"

"She must have some kind of arrangement with who knows, but she rides that black stallion like she's glued to it and mind you, rides astride and bareback." Wolf was silent as he thought of her galloping toward him and then past him and finally finding her floating in water.

"Well, come on, are you going to dream about it and not share?"

Wolf chuckled. He'd already decided he wouldn't reveal that she was swimming without a stitch on. "I caught up with her at a small pond and dove in with my clothes on to catch her when she spied me. Naturally, I did what a very normal man would do, I kissed her and she resisted me. Can you believe that?" They both laughed. "She called me a cur, a lout, and a pirate. I let her slip away." They were grinning, "She took off on that beautiful black stallion astride with no saddle. That's it. I stripped off my wet clothes and swam. There's a waterfall and its ice-cold water disposed of my romantic ideas. The iciest water around this warm place made my skin tingle and it's the best feeling I've enjoyed in ages."

Bender's eyes twinkled, "Better than sex?"

"How the devil would I know… it seems like eons since I've been there. I thought for a moment this morning was going to be my lucky day, but I've never forced my intentions and that little spitfire wanted nothing to do with me."

"Be that as it may, you'd better get yourself up and dressed. Neal invited some friends of his over for a casual supper. He said not to worry about our clothes."

"That's a blessing."

"The owners from Big Star Plantation will be here. From what I gather, their son is in love with Neal's daughter."

"Neal has a *daughter*?"

"Remember someone said she's been incapacitated. Lady Thomas and Miss Regina visited with her. Oh yes, they'll be leaving in the morning. Barslow is anxious to get to London. It's working well for them."

"The ladies recovered well, I heard."

"Mrs. Durand took personal care—they blossomed almost at once. I'll tell you that as nice as it is here, I'm looking forward to seeing England again and be part of its lifestyle."

Wolf threw back the sheet and stood naked, his eyes hooded like a hawk. "It can't be soon enough."

"I'll go on down and make your excuses. I won't tell them you were lolling around on their soft bed wishing you had an angel for company."

Wolf pitched his pillow at him, but the door had already closed but he heard Bender's laughter.

Tishee, helping Marvalea dress, shook her head, "What are you going to say? Val, if that man tells your daddy that you were swimming naked and the pirate saw you and even touched you, I'm telling you, Val... there's going to be trouble."

"Do shush, Tish, before someone hears you." She sighed in exasperation. "He won't say a word. I did nothing wrong, *he* did." She laughed. "I'd like to listen to him explain how he tried to molest me." Marvalea was enjoying the coming introduction of meeting the pirate— right there in front of everyone. She couldn't wait to put him in his place and being silent was just how she'd do it... pretend.

"What dress have you decided to wear?" Tishee tried to hide her envy.

"The green silk… it hugs my body and he told me my body was perfect, it'll just remind him of his words."

"Oh Val, you're looking for trouble."

"I know… isn't it exciting?"

"What about Medwill Jr.? He's here with his parents and you know he's planning on marrying you."

She ground her teeth, "He can plan all he wants, I'll never marry the likes of him. He's like his father—selfish and mean."

"You got that right and you can add stupid. They scare me. I stay as far away from them as I can. You know, Junior always asks Mr. Neal to sell me to him. I think I'd kill myself if that happened."

Marvalea hugged Tishee. "Daddy would never do that."

"Thank goodness."

Marvalea went to sit before her dressing table. "Help me brush my hair and put it up your special way. It makes me look older."

Wolf entered the large summer room wearing his white pants and shirt, its sleeves folded halfway up his arms. It was necessary as the sleeves were too short and he had to make the best of it. His raven hair against his sun-bronzed skin made quite a contrast, though it was the man whose grace overshadowed his looks.

Neal smiled warmly. "Wolf, I'm glad to see you. I hear you had a long day riding. Good for you."

Jefferson carried a tray to Wolf. The tall glass filled with cloudy liquid with a green sliver of lime on its rim told Wolf it was lemonade. What he needed was a good stiff drink. Much to his surprise, his drink had a tangy soured mix. "This is delicious."

"Wolf, I'd like you to meet our neighbors. Medwill Starwell, his wife, Jean, and over here is Medwill Jr."

Medwill Sr. held out his hand. "Glad to meet you. I heard about you running into trouble in a storm-lucky you landed on our island. I own Big Star Plantation."

Wolf shook Medwill's hand and then turned to his wife. Wolf nodded and smiled, "Mrs. Starwell, it's a pleasure to meet you."

Junior came over. "Oh don't bother with my mother, she doesn't know much. We're just talking about losing a slave. The little sl—"

"Junior," cautioned Senior, "these are Neal's guests." He looked toward Lady Thomas and Miss Regina as well and Marcella.

"Oh yeah," mumbled Junior.

Wolf and Bender eyed one another. They didn't have to say a word, they knew a good for nothing jackass when they heard one.

Ignoring Junior's remark, Wolf asked Mrs. Starwell if he could get her something to drink.

She smiled. "No thank you. I'm fine."

Wolf greeted Marcella, Mrs. Thomas, and Lady Regina.

Junior's boisterous voice carried across the room, "Jefferson, how about finding what's keeping my girl?"

Jefferson looked over at Mrs. Durand. She just barely moved her head *no* and he walked from the room.

Wolf moved back to Bender saying without moving his lips, "She's got to have rocks for a brain if she's attached to *that*. Have you met the daughter?"

Before Bender could answer, with Wolf's back toward the doorway, Marvalea walked in, stood for a moment, looking around.

Bender's mouth dropped open. "Ahh, wait…"

Junior jumped up. "There you are. You know I don't like to be kept waiting."

She ignored him. Neal smiled. "Here's my daughter, Wolf. She's been unwell but is fine now. I'd like you to meet her."

Bender reached for his arm, but too late.

Forming a smile, Wolf turned and then froze. Fighting to control rage, anger and fury auguring inside his head… *she knew and all this time she played me a fool.* His pride aided in concealing his inner turmoil. *Neal's daughter…* he bit the inside of his cheek.

Neal brought her to Wolf's side. Proudly smiling, he said, "Wolf, this is my daughter, Marvalea." Looking at her, he said, "This is our guest, Wolf," and then he nodded to Bender, "and this other gentleman is Bender. I'm sure your mother told you about our house guests."

Marvalea swallowed hard, lifted her chin, and boldly met Wolf's accusing eyes and without flinching, said, "So nice to meet you… what did you say his name is, Daddy?"

"He prefers *Wolf*, Sweetheart." He looked at Wolf, who hadn't said a word yet. "You know we don't stand on protocol. Please feel free to use my daughter's name, Marvalea."

She waited, challenging him as she held out her hand.

He took it. Rage ready to burst within him like hot cannon ball. Make a fool of him, would she. He squeezed her fingers but she didn't utter a sound, only glared at him in defiance. "Hello, Marvalea." He dropped her hand without saying another word.

Neal didn't understand, but took his daughter's arm and introduced her to Bender and Barslow.

Jefferson came with another tray. Wolf reached for one glass and then set it back. Softly he said, "I'd appreciate a double of something in one of those glasses, please."

Jefferson blinked, "Yes, Sir… I can do that."

The evening continued pleasantly with the exception of Junior trailing Marvalea while she obviously tried to shun him. She'd look at Wolf and he'd tilt his glass to her, grin, and then ignore her.

Junior went to stand with Wolf and Barslow. "Wolf… now that's a funny name. How come you got a name like that?"

Wolf replied with heavy irony, "Because I like it."

Evidently, it went over the jackass's head because he persisted, "I think I would have chosen *Tiger,* which would make you fierce."

"Then why don't you?"

Junior laughed. "Hey Marvay, do you want me to go by the name of *Tiger?* Wolf here thinks it would be a great idea."

Wolf frowned in exasperation. Barslow stepped away. Bender, grinning, looked over at Wolf who shrugged his shoulders and turned in annoyance.

Marvalea's embarrassment turned to aggravation. "Mr. Starwell, will you please ask your son not to shout?"

Starwell Sr. laughed. "You know, Missy, that he's crazy about you, as we all are. He likes teasing you."

Neal came to his daughter's side, lowering his voice, "Easy, now is not the time to explode."

Unshed tears hung on her long lashes. "Daddy, will you make my excuses? I am sorry, I don't feel well."

"Go then. It'll be all right." He held her arm. "But I'll see you in the morn, you can't stay in your room any longer."

"I won't." She kissed his cheek and quietly left.

Wolf saw her depart. He knew she was humiliated over the jackass's attempt to impress her, in fact he even felt sorry for her. Yet, he was angry for being played a fool. It bothered him more than he cared to admit because he liked her. Her sassy wildness was appealing. Nothing like the mamas' daughters he'd had thrust at him because of being the Duke of Grenfell's heir.

Supper seemed long and drawn out. The breeze barely reached the room and small children moved feathered fans back and forth by pulling on a line. Wolf couldn't enjoy the scrumptious meal as the little ones tried not to watch as they moved the feather lines.

Not believing in slavery and even though Neal treated his slaves well, he still *owned* them. Finally, the last course was served and the women left while the men went out on the patio to smoke.

Medwill Sr. grumbled about losing a female slave. "The dogs tracked her to your beach, Neal. I know she can't swim so she either had help or she drowned."

Neal became indignant. "Surely you don't think Lady Slipper aided in her escape?"

"No, no," Medwill hurriedly replied, "I just can't understand it. I've never lost one in all my years."

Wolf took a draw on his cigar and released it slowly. "I met your overseer last night."

"He told me."

"I didn't see anyone other than my little friend. He's only nine years old. I assure you he didn't come in contact with your lost slave."

"I understand that you were there to teach him to swim."

"That's right. You see, he's been living as a cabin boy on a ship since he was six and afraid of drowning, but didn't want anyone to know. I promised to teach him before I take him home with me." Wolf took another draw on his cigar. "The water here is more conducive to relax. Its warmth takes away fear."

Medwill conceded, but you could tell he didn't like it.

Junior grumbled. "I don't see why you allowed Marvay to leave. She's feeling okay, she sure gets some quirky ideas." He laughed with a sneer, "But I can change that."

Neal's words ripped out, "Don't count on my daughter accepting your marriage proposal. She's told me she's a long way off from getting married, and I agree."

Medwill Sr. tried to temper the situation. "You know how these young bucks are, Neal. Only time will tell."

By now, they were ready to join the ladies.

Wolf and Bender decided to call it a night; they made the expected pleasantries and escaped.

Chapter Twenty-Seven

Wolf lay in bed unable to sleep. The sheet twisted around his naked body as he tossed and turned. He knew having been played a fool by that sassy blonde was infuriating, yet more than that, he had molested Neal's daughter. It was a cross between guilt and rage at the angel floating in the pond. Oh how he had wanted her. He hardened just thinking of her; this had to stop. *Thank goodness I'm leaving and hopefully, Neal will not learn of my having already met his beautiful daughter… unclothed.* If Wolf told, it would not only anger Neal, and rightly so, but perhaps he'd no longer trust strangers in need.

Wolf unwound the sheet and stood. He needed fresh air. He'd go swimming in the salty sea knowing he'd never find the pond in the dark. He pulled on his canvas pants, yanked a towel from the rack, slipped into his canvas shoes, and quietly stepped through the slider-doors leading out on Slipper's vast lawn and gardens. His pace quickened as he headed for the beach.

The night air fanned his warm body, immediately improving his frame of mind. He'd talk with Neal in the morning and tell that they were all going to stay on board the ship to get it ready to sail. He wouldn't see the angel, but would ask Neal to extend his goodbyes to his family for him. Wolf wouldn't mention that after he straightened matters at Penumbra, he'd do something nice for the Durand family in some way to thank them.

Wolf reached the hedgerow of palmettos and stumbled on a root. Carefully taking his next step, he heard the water kissing the shore. The beach just on the other side of the dune, he picked up his pace.

The moon's quarter offered enough light to shimmer on the water. The gentle sound of the sea helped calm Wolf's guilt. He kicked off his shoes, pushed down his pants and stood naked letting the salty sea air soothe his rock-hard torso and his iron muscled thighs. A breeze stirred the hair on his chest and legs as he stretched his arms wide a few times—unaware of his glorious image.

Walking into the sea waist deep, he leaned forward and swishing the cool water over his form and pushed off to swim. His strokes were smooth, barely making a ripple. He turned his body to swim horizontally with the beach planning that when he tired, he would go ashore and saunter unhurriedly back to his clothes.

Slowing his breast strokes, the tension easing, his mind traveled to Penumbra.

Though these thoughts tightened his stomach muscles, he kept his strokes even. He knew he had to get home. *I promised I wouldn't let you down, Father, or our Staunton heritage* and he relaxed, soon he'd be on his way to England. Wolf's calloused hands plowed more strongly cutting deep. Tiring, having swam a good distance he headed for shore.

Marvalea couldn't sleep and stood at her opened slider-doors looking out into the night. She saw a movement out across the lawn and recognized the tall form. "It's the pirate," she murmured. She hurried to step into her slippers, rushing out, not bothering with a robe. The night air penetrated her short nightie but with her intent to spy, the cool air went unnoticed. The dew soaking her satin slippers, she picked up her pace, "He's going to my pond," she muttered.

As Marvalea cut thought the same palmettos, she was startled at the form standing at the water's edge. She smothered a gasp and stayed still, sucking in her breath sure that he could hear her. She saw only his back, the little bit of moon outlined his long legs. She could imagine what was beyond his narrow waist. It stirred a sudden unknown kind of pressure within her. *I must be having a heart attack.* She sank to the sand and continued to watch the man walk into the sea. She never lost sight of him for she couldn't have closed her eyes if she wanted to and she certainly did not want to. His magnificent body took her breath away. She'd seen her brother naked a time or two by accident, but it never affected *her... Marshall doesn't come close to Pirate's build.* She smiled.

Marvalea sat watching the man take long strokes and move through the water. She knew immediately that he was a strong swimmer as he moved barely kicking up any water. Soon he was further down the beach from her and she sat for a moment, excited. She stood and tried to catch sight of him but it was impossible.

Without thought she walked toward the water. She knew she'd have time to disappear before he returned. It was then she stepped on the pirate's pants, shoes and towel. Picking them up, a huge grin blossomed. Quickly, she rolled them under her arm and went back to the palmettos, sitting off to the side so she could watch the pirate's reaction. *Oh what fun.* She sat waiting, watching the water; he'd be coming soon for his clothes. She laughed thinking of him stunned, surprised. It'd be like this evening when she walked into the room and was introduced, she could tell he was furious, she enjoyed the moment. Now she was going to payback for invading her waterfall. *I kept our secret, Mr. Pirate, now you'll have to keep this one too. We're even!*

Wolf knew his stamina still wasn't as it should be, so he took one last dip and waded to shore. Shaking the water from his hair to keep it from dripping in his eyes, he pushed it off his face. His felt rejuvenated; he looked forward to a good night's sleep.

He sloshed through the water making what seemed like a racket, but it mattered not as he was alone. He thought of the sassy angel and decided to skip any apology and just get to the *Hampton* after speaking with Neal. He'd never see her again; he'd best leave things as they are. His mind made up, Wolf walked up the sandy beach, swinging his arms before starting to jog. He felt so much better.

He kept running and running, trying to locate his clothes. He was sure they were right about here or there. He surmised he must have gone too far and turned around. He was at the spot where the path opened through the palmettos, kicking his feet in a wide arch hoping to feel them He began to get frustrated. Concluding that if he didn't find them soon, he definitely couldn't return to the house naked, he'd have to wake Gully. He grinned thinking what Gully would say when he stood at his door naked. So they'd have a good laugh; he turned to go toward the schoolhouse.

Wolf stopped! *She* was standing near the path seeming to come out of nowhere. A vision so small he might have missed it if the minuscule moon didn't attach its beam to her white nightie.

She was laughing and holding up his pants. "Hey, Pirate, is this what you're looking for?" Her silky voice floated through the air bringing shivers to his body along with another reaction he had to hide. Yet he stood there, astonished.

"Cat got your tongue, Pirate?" She waved his pants at him.

"You're mighty brave standing so far away," he taunted. "Why don't you bring them to me?"

Marvalea was enchanted. He was so tall and admittedly handsome. Her voice purred, "Oh no, Pirate, I don't trust you."

"I promise you can trust me, Angel. Come on… afraid?" He knew that would get her.

Excited, yet provoked, she responded, "Afraid? *Of you?* I think not. But I owe you for entering my domain… that pond is mine and you weren't invited."

Wolf whispered just loud enough for her to hear. "You're right, but I didn't know. You have to admit that."

"True, but you certainly didn't act like a gentleman."

"Now there you've got me. But I am a pirate, am I not? And pirates always go after gold." He waited to hear her retort but none came. "What's wrong, Angel, cat got *your* tongue?"

Marvalea was stirred with his gentle teasing. She was beginning to like him. *I must be crazy.* Still she answered, "No, no cat… just me."

Now Wolf came to his senses, standing nude and teasing Neal's daughter. He had nothing to shield himself and his body reacting to this seemingly childish play with this woman he wanted more than he could remember. "I'll tell you what, I'll go back into the water and you can bring me my clothes and return to your hideaway. How's that sound to you?"

She goaded him. "Don't tell me you're afraid I might see your body? Are you deformed?"

Wolf thought of his scarred back, but he laughed and said, "Not so you'd notice."

"You're not like my brother." Goodness, Marvalea wondered whatever made her admit that.

"Oh?" Wolf snickered. "How so?"

"Just… never mind."

Wolf backed into the water. He felt the sea at his ankles and then his knees and finally covering his erection. Now waist high, he called to her. "What are you doing out? Won't your mother and father worry?"

"They don't know. I often go out at night when it gets over-warm. The night air is refreshing." She was walking closer carrying his things—dropping them at the water's edge and stood there.

Wolf felt that if he made the slightest move to retrieve his pants, the water would soak them… well he'd just have to wear them wet. "Okay, Angel, how about you turn around and allow me to get my pants. Surely you don't want me to be embarrassed?"

She began to laugh. It was a sweet melodious sound. "You embarrassed? I don't think so." She bent down, picked up his pants. "You want these? Here!" She tossed them into the water.

"Why, you little devil." Wolf went for them. "And all the time I thought you were an angel." He got his pants and struggling, got them on. All the while she didn't move, but stood and watched.

Wolf began to walk out of the water but Marvalea didn't move. She couldn't. There was something about this man that made her realize she was no longer a girl but a woman.

She wanted him to kiss her again so she could kiss him back. His smile wide, he tweaked her under her chin, "Thanks."

182

Her voice barely a whisper, "Don't mention it." She peered up to him in the semi-darkness. She came to his shoulder. She waited.

Something transpired between them. A vibration causing both to take a swallow of air. Wolf fisted his hands to keep from taking her in his arms, the magnetic pull strong.

The moon didn't have to be full to show off her golden hair... her stance daring him. He said, "This will not do, Val. You shouldn't be here, especially with me clad in a pair of wet pants, and you," her sleepwear hiding nothing, "scantily dressed. What are you thinking coming to play games... again?" He took a step closer, "That is a gorgeous night shirt, if I weren't going to act a gentleman, you'd be in danger."

Blatantly, Marvalea reached for Wolf's arm and felt his corded muscle react to her touch. "Don't be a gentleman," her silky voice challenged.

Wolf's manhood responded, but his brain was also in working order; without saying a word, he picked her up in his arms and walked back into the sea.

"What are you doing? Put me down!"

He was laughing. She felt so good in his arms he didn't want to let her go. "Since you asked..." He swung her around, dropping her in the water and causing a splash that brought her up coughing.

She scrambled to get her footing. Her hair unraveling and dripping. Wiping the water from her face with her hand and pushing back her hair off her face, her voice bitter, "I knew I couldn't trust you."

She slapped at him but missed as her fingers slid down the hair on his chest.

To Wolf it was like lighting a match and setting him on fire. He couldn't have stopped himself, "You little spitfire, you're here looking for trouble and you've found it."

Instead of being frightened, she began to giggle. Unexpectedly, she stepped away and began to run toward shore, but she wasn't fast enough, the water slowing her. Wolf dove and grabbed her ankle.

She splashed down and tried kicking with her other foot but Wolf's strength held her in place.

"You little wildcat."

The voice she heard was insistent and oddly gentle, she shivered.

Wolf held her, wading into shallow water. He had no intention of letting her go. He couldn't. He wanted to keep holding her and his need to feel her lips became an obsession. Hitting ankle deep water, he sat her down giving her no chance to escape as he fell down beside her and continued holding her at her waist.

The dark night, water slicing over them and around them increasing sensual feelings neither could deny. Marvalea didn't struggle; she held her head up so gentle waves wouldn't wash over her. Looking up at him but unable to see him, she raised her arms and put them around Wolf's neck.

"Oh Angel, you don't know what you're doing," he spoke against her forehead.

She felt his warm breath creating a tremor run through her. His mellow voice caressing her generating new feelings—she didn't want to move out of his arms.

"I must be out of my mind," Wolf's sudden tone turned harsh. He took her hands from around his neck and scrambled to shore, leaving her to get herself up.

Only this time, he wasn't the aggressor. Marvalea spun around and just before he reached the water's edge, she tackled him. Laughing, she fell on top of him, Wolf lying on his stomach. She stretched her full body on top of him. She was panting from exertion but she managed to challenge him. "Don't tell me, Pirate, you're afraid of me?"

As quick as a wink Marvalea found herself on her back and Wolf's face inches from hers. There it was again, this incredible magnetism expanding and taking hold. She knew of intimacy between a man and woman. She felt his hardness against her belly. It did funny things to her belly and on down to her private area she had never felt before.

Wolf's strained voice reached into her, "I'm going to kiss you, Angel, and this time you better respond or I'm going to drown you."

She felt his smile as he touched her lips, brushing over hers so gentle it raised goose bumps. She liked it. Then she felt his tongue trace the outline of her mouth. She liked that too. Then Wolf tenderly took her bottom lip between his teeth and nipped. Oh, she liked that even more. When he released her lip, he matched his mouth to hers only this time his tongue wanted entrance to hers and without thinking she opened for him as he delved into the recess looking to mate his tongue with hers.

Marvalea felt her body warm as she joined the dance with Wolf's music. Their tongues met and moved and he sucked hers and she liked that too. He pulled his head up, breathing hard. "Don't stop," she pleaded while reaching to bring him back to her.

He couldn't hold back a chuckle. "Oh baby, you fire me up as no one ever has." He rubbed his body over hers and she moved with him. He lifted her wet nightie and kissed each of her perfectly formed breasts. His tongue traveled over and around them and Marvalea held his head in place, not wanting him to stop. Wolf put his fingers onto the tops of her panties, about to lower them-Marvalea raised her hips to help, crying out for him to, "*Hurry.* I'm so glad, Pirate, that you'll be the one to show me what I've been missing."

Her words slammed into his senses. *What have I almost done?* He was off her in a flash, lying on his stomach in the water, trying to catch his breath and disgusted with what he had been about to do and that he had allowed his sexual desires to precede common decency. *She's not only a virgin, but Neal's daughter.* If he could have felt the whip, he'd have deserved it.

"What's wrong? Why did you stop?" She was over him and began to rub his back, she needed to touch him. Then she gasped, feeling not a smooth muscled back but one scarred with welts.

Wolf's heart continuing to hammer, he growled, not wanting to explain, "Stop that!" He flipped her over and was up and on shore before she could jump up on her own.

Marvalea froze, shocked at his sudden rage. She reached the beach and sat down, waiting for him to join her.

Wolf's ardor slowly cooled while he castigated himself for his behavior. He walked to where Marvalea sat and kneeled beside her, but not touching. "I apologize, Angel. I acted as a complete clod. I ask your forgiveness."

Taken by surprise, she blurted, "You mean you stopped for that reason?"

His angel never ceased to amaze him. He grinned. "First, a gentleman doesn't attack a woman. Secondly, you are the daughter of the man that has treated me and my friends with kindness and respect. He deserves the same from me. And thirdly, my sassy angel, you have never been *touched*. *That* is your gift to your husband. He'll treasure you for it."

"I know, but I've heard Marshall and his friends talking and there are girls that haven't waited to marry." She touched Wolf's arm and it was as if she branded him. He pulled away. But she seemed not to notice, continuing, "Maybe you should marry me, Pirate. Then it would be okay."

Wolf laughed and laughed. She had no idea who he was and in the back of his mind he treasured that this sassy wild angel was willing to marry *him* and not his title. He turned serious. "Marvalea... Val, your innocence means a lot to me, but I'm not the marrying kind and even if I were, your mother and father would be abhorred at such a suggestion. No, my sweet, you'll fall in love and then you'll live happily ever after, as the saying goes."

"But..." she wasn't giving up, "maybe I'm in love with you. And maybe you'd come to love me... for real."

"Oh angel, you couldn't be in love with me... it's passion talking. This is new to you, so it feels right."

"Perhaps. I don't know. But will you do me one favor and I'll release you from any commitment I'm trying to force upon you?"

He stood and pulled her up to stand near him. "We've got to get back to the house. Soon it'll be time to rise."

"You haven't answered me. Don't change the subject."

"You're a persistent little nag. What favor?"

Moving toward him with barely enough moonlight but each aware of their nearness. "Will you kiss me one last time, Mr. Pirate? A kiss like you really mean it?"

"Ohhh, Angel, that would be so dangerous."

"No, I promise, if you give me one kiss, we'll turn and walk back immediately."

Wolf wanted to kiss her now and forever. The glow she brought to him turned him into jelly and he relished that feeling. He reached for her and with both hands on the side of each cheek, his voice husky, "Promise?"

Her pulse skittering, her mind reliving his warm velvety touch of his mouth on hers, she needed *her* pirate's kisses to sustain her, she whispered, "I promise."

Wolf took her in his arms. First he brushed his lips on each of her cheeks. Then he moved his lips over her forehead and then kissed each of her closed eyes, her lashes tickling his lips. He nibbled her earlobes. Marvalea felt a heady sensation travel through her to the tips of her toes. Wolf wasn't done; he seared a path down her neck and let his tongue linger at the cleft at the top of her breasts, but made a point not to go further, this was a promised kiss, nothing else, he told himself and knew he was lying. *My angel is magic.*

The caress of his mouth touching her skin set her aflame. She gripped his pants at his waist and tried pulling herself against him. "Slow down, love, this will have to last us a lifetime." Wolf moved his mouth over hers devouring its softness and then plunged into her sweet nectar, pressing her to him, his kiss turning into intense savagery and fusing their mouths together. And then slowly, with masterful strokes, he eased taking possession of her totally, knowing he had to let her go but loathed the idea that he had no choice.

Lifting his head, he showered her with kisses along her jaw and tenderly planted a peck on her nose. Taking her arms from around his neck, his voice hoarse, knowing it was over, he put his arm around her waist and began to move. Neither saying a word.

They reached the dune and Marvalea broke the silence. "You know, Pirate, I would have floated up and away if you weren't holding me. I'll take an encore anytime you say, just give me a nod or a look." She smiled at him, though he couldn't see, but he knew.

That pleased Wolf but he wouldn't tell her. In fact, when he thought of someone else kissing her and then making love to her, he mentally recoiled.

Marvalea reached taking his hand. "Okay, a promise is a promise. If you aren't going to talk, then we'd best get going."

They moved forward in their wet clothes. "This has been quite a night. I hope you won't live to regret it, Angel. I wouldn't hurt you if my life depended on it. Please remember that. Know that you are precious to me."

Elated at his words—they were approaching the house, she squeezed his fingers. "Of course, I'll never forget this night. And you didn't hurt me, Mr. Pirate. Don't forget; I encouraged you a tad."

He stopped short but kept her at arm's length. "Angel, you must not willingly be asking for kisses. There is danger when a man gets in a... let's say a romantic stage and sometimes a man won't let a lady say *no*. Please be careful."

She tried to see him in the dark. "Do you think I'd let just any man kiss me? Now that I've had a taste of you? I'll wait until you decide to change your mind and marry me. You know, I can be a nice person if I put my mind to it."

Wolf laughed. He pulled her alongside of him and they walked together with their arm around each other's waist. "Well, let me put it this way—if you find someone you love, you go ahead and marry. I'll understand."

She tried to retaliate by pinching his flesh at his waist but all she got was muscle. "I'm not going to let you go, Pirate. You belong to me. I don't care that you've probably done a lot of bad things, but you can change."

Hearing her serious tone, Wolf knew it was time to put an end to her fantasy. "I shouldn't have kissed you, but then it's been a long time since I've kissed anyone and after all, you are available. You're not bad for a youngster, but I prefer my women older and much more knowledgeable."

"How could you?" He heard her voice crack as she dropped her arm from his waist.

He stopped to let her go, but before she ran off, she slapped his face.

It hurt, not the slap but the words he had to inflict to make her realize he would never consider marriage, especially at this time. Slowly, he headed toward his room, unaware that Neal was standing on the darkened patio.

Chapter Twenty-Eight

Wolf woke early. He didn't sleep well knowing his abominable behavior—using Neal's daughter even though he had left her untouched, his conduct unforgiveable.

Entering the morning room, he was alone. The windows open with fresh air surrounding him still didn't alleviate his guilt.

Jefferson entered bringing a plate of scrambled eggs, bacon, the island's favorite grits, and buttered biscuits. He set a glass of orange juice next to Wolf's freshly poured coffee. "Is there anything else I can get for you, Mr. Wolf?"

"No thank you, Jefferson."

"Excuse me, Mr. Wolf. Mr. Neal say when you finish, I'm to show you to his office."

A momentary twinge of discomfort shot through Wolf. *Could Val have said something to her father? No, I don't think so. Though I feel summoned.* He took a sip of hot coffee, not touching his inviting breakfast. He rose and nodded to Jefferson.

Jefferson took Wolf out a side entrance and across a stone walkway to a whitewashed building surrounded by fragrant bougainvillea. But Wolf didn't see any of their beauty as he reached the small unadorned porch. Jefferson called, "Mr. Neal... I bring Mr. Wolf, sir." Then he turned and left.

Neal came to the screened door pushing it open. His expression grim. Wolf knew immediately this was not a social visit. "Come in. My office is the only place I have total privacy. I need it with you." His tone not the least welcoming.

Wolf nodded. He felt like a school boy coming into the director's office—guilt not a stranger at this moment.

"Sit down, if you will." Neal walked around the crowded space and sat behind his desk. He made no overtures of friendliness. Glaring, infuriated, he said, "I saw you and my daughter coming in very late last night, or rather this morning. I gather from the beach." His tone harsh. "How dare you?"

Wolf's hand swept through his hair. "Nothing happened."

Neal pounded his fist upon his desk. The papers laying there fluttered and a pencil rolled. "How dare you take *my daughter* and plan a rendezvous with her? I trusted you. I thought you a gentleman." Neal pursed his mouth so tightly that his lips disappeared.

Wolf leaned forward. "Neal, I'm telling you nothing happened. I went for a swim because I couldn't sleep. When I came out of the water, your daughter was standing on the beach. That is the truth. We planned no rendezvous." Angry with himself and insulted that Neal would even think he'd take full advantage of Marvalea—Wolf's fingers curled on the chair's wooden arms. He stood and, eying Neal, said, "I rose early to tell you that I was with Marvalea during the night. I didn't invite her or tell her that I would be swimming." He shook his head. "I didn't even know I would go swimming. I couldn't sleep and that is all there is to it."

Not to be deterred, Neal's voice edged with control. "I saw you both walking arm in arm. If nothing happened, that would not have occurred. Do you think I'm dim-witted?"

"Of course not." Entering Wolf's mind at being chastised and he a Staunton, his name noble, his back stiffened, his eyes narrowed; he no longer felt the school boy. "Neal, Sir... I owe you an apology for accepting your generous hospitality and then acting a cad. When I say nothing happened, I'd like to correct that."

Neal's mouth dropped open, before saying, "You didn't?"

"Don't go there." Wolf's iron voice warned. "I kissed your daughter. *That is all!*" He wouldn't tell of the Angel looking for trouble and his willingness to fulfill it. "Marvalea is a beautiful young lady. She teases without knowing the consequences. When I kissed her, I explained the danger there is when a man kisses a lady. *It went no further*."

"Why were you walking arm in arm?"

Wolf let out a swoosh of breath. "Your silly daughter thinks we should marry."

"What?" Neal shouted.

"Look, I'm truly sorry. I'll tell you what Marvalea said." He couldn't hold back a slight smile. "She is innocent and I know that. When she suggested that she could marry a pirate, I wanted to laugh, but she was serious in her own innocence." Wolf paced in the small space. "I knew I had to discourage her ridiculous thinking so I told her that she was great and having been away from a woman for so long, kissing her was a delight, that I always looked forward to kissing the ladies. I had to make her believe that is what I do." Wolf rubbed his cheek. "You know what she did? She slapped my face and I don't mean with a light tap. She truly let me have it. And I couldn't blame her as I had insulted her—as was my intention. I did so because she put too much meaning into our kiss."

Neal wasn't born yesterday. When Wolf said *our* kiss, there was more to it. "I've never asked anyone to leave Lady Slipper, but I'm asking you now. In fact, I'm telling you. I want you away from here within the hour. Please take your two friends at the schoolhouse with you. Bender is welcome to stay if he chooses, but I doubt he will. I will say nothing to him; you best explain your behavior. I find it appalling." Neal stood and walked to the screened door, holding it open, waiting for Wolf to leave.

"You may not believe this but leaving is exactly what I was going to tell you this morn. There's no way I want to embarrass your family." Wolf held out his hand, but Neal refused to take it.

"Goodbye, Neal. Again, I apologize." Wolf walked away, not looking back for if he did, he would have seen the sorrow on Neal Durand's face.

Chapter Twenty-Nine

Wolf, Bender, Gully, and Muggs were living on board *Hampton.* They worked to get what they could in order, awaiting Admiral Cunningham's crew. They were looking forward to setting sail.

Gully took care of Sheena, bringing her up on deck for fresh air, but only on very dark nights. No one suspected that she was on board.

One night when Muggs slept, Gully decided it was time to confront Wolf. He found him on deck stretched out using a coil of line for a pillow. The moon cast its beam on the water, the boat rocked—offering ease in this silent night.

Gully squatted down near Wolf. Gully wasn't his usual smiling self. His somber tone alerted Wolf to peer up at his friend.

"Okay, Wolf," his voice low, "has my helping Sheena caused you trouble that you're not telling?"

"What do you mean, Gully?"

"Well, you haven't left this ship in three days. It appears as if *you* are exiled from the plantation. I'm sorry I got you in this mess."

"Get Bender, Gully, if you will, and I'll explain."

"I'm right over here." Bender moved from the other side of the deck. "I'm enjoying the cool night and couldn't help hearing Gully."

"Bender, you and I are here because Neal asked… no, he insisted *I* leave his property."

"You're kidding? Why? Me too?"

"No, you were welcome to remain." Wolf ran his fingers through his hair. "The night we had dinner and discovered Val was Marvalea, Neal's daughter, it was later, after turning in I couldn't sleep. So I threw on my pants and headed for the beach to swim." He laughed. "Marvalea saw me leaving and followed. I didn't know. When I stripped and took off swimming, she stole my clothes."

Gully's smile brightened in conflict with the moon. "Ahhh," was all Bender said.

Wolf continued, "When I went to find my clothes, I stood there in the nude and after looking and kicking sand as it was dark, I heard this giggle and then she asked if I was looking for my clothes—she had them. To make a long story short, I went back into the water and she tossed them to me, yes, they were sopping wet and you know putting on wet pants is an ordeal, but I did and all the time she stood on shore and watched."

Bender whistled and Gully kept grinning.

"When I finally made it to shore, she taunted me about losing my clothes. I told her she should be careful that she was in dangerous territory. We were headed back to the house when she asked me to kiss her. 'Really kiss me,' she said. Well now, I've been dying to do just that, so even knowing I should not, I did."

Bender whistled again and Gully was still grinning.

"Neal's daughter is pure innocence, but still how could I refuse?" He couldn't hide his smile. "And kiss her I did. After, as we're heading across the lawn, she said that even my being a pirate that she'd be willing to overlook all the bad things I've done and would be willing to marry me."

Now Bender was grinning and Gully lost his smile—his big brown eyes got bigger. "I knew this was trouble so to discourage her thinking, I implied that I always went around kissing ladies and she was just another one. Callously, I added that she'd do in a pinch. I believed it was the only way to stop her. I don't like myself for saying that to her—I still don' t. But I admire her for what she did next; it was the right thing to do... she slapped my face and I don't mean a tap. I had it coming."

"You didn't have any choice," Bender agreed. "So how did Neal find out? She didn't tell, did she?"

"No. In fact, I had every intention of telling him without mentioning my being without clothes. Neal spied the two of us coming across the lawn, I guess around two in the morning, and suspected the worse. Early the next morning, he asked me into his office, told of seeing me with his daughter, and asked me to leave within the hour."

Gully spoke, "Didn't you tell him it was only a kiss?"

"I tried and I think he believed me, but Marvalea is his precious daughter and he did what any father would do—protect her. So here I am. Of course, Gully and I were planning on staying here, Neal made the decision easier."

"Well, thanks for telling me," Bender accused. "Were the two of you going to include me?"

Gully laughed. "You were the one that was supposed to get Muggs and me on board. Then you and Wolf would follow as soon as you could."

Smiling, Bender said, "That's better."

"This is all my doing. It isn't Neal's daughter's fault. I know better but she is a tease and I thought kissing her like I meant it would scare her off and it did just the opposite. She's an angel in disguise."

"Too bad you won't see her again."

"I think it's the only way, Gully. I'll admit I like her."

"I'm glad Muggs and I didn't cause you to lose Mr. Durand's friendship." Gully stretched. "I'm going to go down and talk with Sheena and catch a few hours' sleep." His voice was somber. "This sure isn't like Shark Tooth and Zuber got his just reward... he... became fish food."

Bender smoked the last half of his cigar.

Wolf stretched out again. "You know, Bender, that blonde spitfire proposed to me. She thinks I'm a pirate. It's the first time in my life that someone looked at me as a person and not as a future *duke*. I can imagine what I'll run into when I get back home. I dread thinking of the marriage market."

"I know how that works. Me? I'm going to stay away from Almack's. There you know the mamas are going be overbearing to latch a title for their daughter."

"Sad, isn't it?"

"It is, but it's the way, necessary to make a great match—noble blood and all that."

Wolf's voice echoed his own longings. "Tell me, have you ever met anyone that you cared enough to marry?"

"If you're talking about *love,* no not really. But I'd like to think that I might find that someone special to spend the rest of my life with. I want to be a true father to my children. You're lucky—the Duke of Grenfell is tops... oh, I'm sorry."

"That's all right. I've yet to come to grips with his death. It'll hit me more when I'm home at Penumbra."

Both men sat in silence—each with their own thoughts.

"Daddy," Marvalea cried, "what do you mean? How could the pirate and his friends just up and leave?"

Marcella eyed her husband and then busied herself with her embroidery.

"Marvalea, it's as I said. Wolf and his friends are anxious to return to their home in England and decided to get busy and settle their arrangements. You know the black man is traveling with them and they treat him as an equal. That is not recognized here. The opportunity came for them and they took it. That's all there is to it."

Tears filled her eyes and slowly rolled down. "I wish I could have said goodbye."

Neal studied his daughter. "Is there any particular reason?"

She hesitated and then said, "He turned out to be a very nice person."

Marcella looked up. "You mean Mr. Bender?" Neal watched his daughter.

"Yes. And also the pirate, Wolf."

Marcella turned the needle so that it came through the silk material tightened by the hoop. "Why do you insist on calling him a *pirate?* I'm sure he's not."

Their daughter laughed. "I know. It's sort of a joke between us."

Marcella put down her embroidery and glared at her young daughter. "Just what do you mean *between* you? Has he misbehaved? Are you telling me that you have been in his company *alone?"*

Marvalea knew she was getting into deep water. She'd better leave well enough alone.

The pirate and his crew were gone and she'd never see him again, but she also knew she'd never forget him. She also admitted to herself that she wanted him to ravish her and he wouldn't. "It's really nothing, Mother. They're all gone and it has been an interesting visit. We've never had guests like them on Slipper."

"We certainly haven't. I can't say I'm sorry to have them gone." She looked at her husband and the meaning was clear. "But I will say that Lady Thomas sung his praises. She claimed he saved their lives." She picked up her embroidery and began to stitch.

"I think I'll find Tishee and go for a swim."

"Be careful, dear."

"I will, Mama."

Admiral Cunningham returned four days earlier than expected and was pleased to find Wolf and his friends ready to depart. He ordered men from each frigate to sail *Hampton.*

"We'll get provisions on board and set sail." The admiral was in a congenial frame of mind. "If the winds are good to us, we'll see England in three weeks."

Wolf was pleased. He not only needed to get home to Penumbra, but he had to put distance between him and his sassy angel.

Hampton set sail with two English frigates two days later.

Wolf stood on deck looking out at Port Charles as it slowly receded from view.

Goodbye, my angel, I'll never forget you.

Chapter Thirty

Meanwhile, back at Penumbra

Vicky, the young maid, shook entering the Duchess of Grenfell's bedroom. "Your Grace," the maid's voice carefully above a whisper, "His Grace insists on your company within the hour in the east room." The Penumbra household often felt the sting of the duchess's wrath and the maid knew waking Her Grace would surely have repercussions.

Eudora rolled over in her heavily quilted bed, "You dare wake me?" Yet Eudora heard it was Delbert's command, she scowled, "What time is it?" Her hair, once the highlight of her beauty, needed attention. Curls hung limp matching her red blotchy eyes.

"It is two hours past noon, Your Grace."

A spasm of irritation crossed her face. "Bring warm water at once and make sure it's warm. I don't want it hot or cold. Do you hear me? Or you will pay."

Vicky's knees wanted to give way as she bowed her head while backing out of the duchess's boudoir. "Yes, yes, Your Grace."

Eudora stood before her mirror, letting her nightgown slide down her body to the floor. She smiled wickedly until eyeing the red marks on her shoulder and legs. Her mouth contorted while turning to view her backside. The black and blue spots would soon turn yellow and green. *Someday, Delbert, I'll get even with you. I'll make you sorry.*

Vicky came in with an ewer of water. She walked slowly not wanting to spill any. It was hot when she left the kitchen and hoped it would be the right temperature now. She filled the rose ceramic bowl. "It is ready,

Your Grace." Sneaking a finger in the water, Vicky silently breathed a sigh of relief.

Eudora was naked. "What are you staring at?" She moved to the water bowl and put her finger in it. "You stupid slut, it is cold."

Nervous, the maid blurted, "But, Your Grace, it isn't."

"How dare you contradict me?" She moved like lightning and slapped the young maid's face. "Get out my lavender afternoon dress and help me into it."

Shaking, feeling the slap's sting and hiding her tears, Vicky went to the armoire for the dress.

Eudora grabbed it and began to step into it. She was having trouble pulling it over her rippling hips. "Help me," she yelled. Together they got the dress on but when it came to buttoning the back, Vicky had a problem. It was tight and the buttons were pulling against their holes. She didn't know if she should say anything but when she felt the heat on her cheek from the duchess's slap, she decided not to. Finished with the buttons, Vicky picked out the matching slippers. She kneeled to help put them on Eudora's feet and having accomplished that feat, she was about to rise when Eudora's evil smile simmering, she gave Vicky a sharp kick. The young maid fell over. "You are so clumsy." Placing a couple of silver combs in her hair to keep it in place, she snapped, "Now get up and get my flowered shawl that I wear with this dress."

Vicky obeyed, helping Eudora lay it around her shoulders.

Eudora walked toward the door. "See that this room is in order when I return. And get rid of that *cold* water."

Vicky began to cry. She hated the duchess as much as she hated the duke. Both were cruel. The duke carried his whip with him and used it to taunt and spread fear. The duchess not only yelled, but would strike out for no reason other than to be mean. Vicky thought they made a great pair and told Cook. But Cook told her to button her lip.

Today, with tears falling, Vicky decided she wouldn't take any more abuse. She received her month's wages in two days and then she was quitting. Her contribution to her family's income wasn't that much. She just wouldn't eat that much. "I'll find somewhere to work, I'm not lazy," she cried into the empty room.

Chapter Thirty-One

Delbert's eyes narrowed with contempt while slapping his whip on the top of a chair's back; said, "Well, I'm glad to see that my duchess is obeying my command. I'd hate to have to punish her."

Eudora pursed her lips with suppressed fury. She sat at the table and tinkled a crystal bell. It was answered immediately. "I want a cup of tea and three croissants along with my usual dish of peach and strawberry jams."

"You keep eating like that, my darling, and you'll turn into a sow. Right now, you're a little piglet."

Eudora had heard it all before and it hurt but she'd not let him know. She didn't reply as the butler entered with her food.

The duke snarled, "Close the door when you leave and all of you go to the kitchen until you're wanted."

Eudora delved into spreading peach jam on a croissant, ignoring Delbert.

Delbert didn't appreciate her silence. He slapped his whip upon the table. "I'm talking to you."

"When you can say something less despicable, I'll be willing to converse with you."

"Don't get uppity with me."

"Your Grace, did it ever occur to you to treat me with respect? Get this, Delbert, I just don't care anymore. I'm resigned to the fact that for you to be a man," smiling maliciously, "to be able to perform as a man, you must beat me. It gives you sordid pleasure. So be it. I'll have to tolerate it but some day," she fixed him with a level stare, "I'll turn the

202

tables on you. After all," she taunted, "you really aren't the Duke of Grenfell, are you?"

Delbert's face turning red, then almost purple, shouted, "Enough!"

Eudora popped another piece of croissant into her mouth. "Whatever you say, Your Grace."

Delbert began to whine. Eudora knew it was a sign that he was going to capitulate. He was perverted, but still they were part of noble society. The *ton* couldn't discount them. They owned Penumbra, the envy of many.

Taking a sip of tea and then spreading strawberry jam on the other croissant, she sat back. "So dear husband, what is so urgent that you had to have me taken from my bed?"

Delbert pulled out a chair and sat. He laid his whip on top of the polished cherry wood table. "I've been in touch with Medford..."

"Oh please, Del, that old skinflint is half dead."

"Will you listen?" He reached for his whip and instead danced his fingers on top of the table. "He's interested in buying some of Penumbra. He'll pay top dollar."

"You can't! Are you mad?"

"Then I suggest you tell me where we are going to get the blunt to hold the ball you want so badly? I can't get extra funds until I'm recognized by the crown as Duke of Grenfell."

"I know that. But it's sure to happen this season. We're going to London in three weeks. Surely when the parliament meets, you'll have a voice."

"That's why I need Medford Tayford. He will speak on my behalf."

"You don't need him," Eudora admonished. "You can't sell any part of Penumbra. Your father will turn over in his grave."

Delbert laughed, "Not likely."

"Listen, you shouldn't have gotten rid of Barslow. He could have helped you through all this. He knows what can and cannot be done." She pleaded, "Before you agree to anything, why not get in touch with Barslow when we're in London?"

Delbert hesitated. He hated when his wife was right.

Eudora went on, "We've got to get Penumbra back in pristine condition. Barslow can help you. You can't ask the tenants to pay more rent. They're barely making it themselves." Eudora reached across the table to touch Delbert's arm. "Please, let's work together on this."

"I suppose I can hold off Medford. But Eudora, I need to be recognized as Grenfell's duke. It's nearing two years. When I spoke with the crown's consort, I was asked about my crest. I was dumfounded. I had no idea what he was talking about." He rubbed his jaw. "I told you about that and even you have never heard of such a thing. This is hanging over my head. Maybe Barslow knows."

"We'll get in touch with him. In fact, why not write to him asking for an appointment? I'm sure he'll be relieved to have Grenfell business again. You've hired Payne but he's worthless."

"I agree. But I had to get rid of Barslow at the time as he was insistent on waiting for Derrick to return." They both stared at one another but said nothing.

"I wish we could have found the Grenfell jewels. I wonder where they're hidden."

"They've been sold. I know you won't accept that, but how could my father have maintained Penumbra without money? He was a sly old fox and never told how he managed."

"I'd give up just about anything to wear them. Everyone would envy me." She got a glassy look and moved her fingers up to her neck.

"I admit they'd mean a lot; it'd prove I'm really the Duke."

Neither of the culprits realized it but this happened to be the first time they actually had a conversation without sniping at each other.

"Eudora," Delbert's voice as low as he could make it, "what do you think happened to Derrick?"

Her eyes opened wide as she whispered back, "What brought that up?" Leaning forward for his ears only, she said, "We saw his dead body. Does it really matter?"

"I guess not. But I have this strange feeling... I can't explain."

"It's probably because the time has come for you to be named the true Duke of Grenfell." She spread her hands flat on the table. "He's *dead* and good riddance."

A hot clammy feeling passed through Delbert; he said nothing.

Eudora pushed back her chair and stood. "You get busy and write to Barslow and I'll start making arrangements for our London sojourn. We'll straighten this mess once and for all. Then you'll see the *ton* clamoring for our attention."

Chapter Thirty-Two

From Penumbra to London, three weeks later

The Staunton mansion was impressive. Its mansard roof with dormer windows incorporated classical Renaissance elements. Heavy white monumental columns appeared to stand sentry at the main entrance while holding up the Greek portico for cover from inclement weather. The exterior of gray stone mixed with tinted colors emitting and inviting radiance. When the afternoon sun aimed its rays upon the stone, it reflected a myriad of soft colors creating a warm glow. White trim adorned the long leaded windows. Its huge black front door displayed a brass knocker with the Staunton crest.

Upon stepping into the entry, one couldn't help but pause and gape. Its walls painted green to bring some of the country of Penumbra to town. All else was white; from the newel posts and railing that took the curved marble stairway up to the mezzanine. A golden chandelier's hand painted flowers on white globes with matching sconces lighted the area. A mirrored wall doubled the view enlarging the already huge entry. The only furniture-a cushioned brass bench on one side and a marble table holding fresh flowers, and a sterling salver. Tucked away in one corner stood a tall ceramic urn, its colorful flowers and ferns designs, holding several umbrellas. Rare paintings drew the eye, their colors dominating-welcoming invited guests.

Unseen were six salons, an immense dining room, but most imposing and envied is the Staunton mirrored ballroom. There were many rich and beautiful mansions but none had one like the Staunton ballroom. Intricately carved cherubs attached to wide cornices surrounded the vaulted ceiling where an artist's clouds hovered above with their silver linings increasing their radiance from eight enormous crystal chandeliers. The inlaid dance floor reflected the chandeliers lighted candles along with colors from the ladies' gowns. It appeared magical. The added high ceiling kept the temperature comfortable.

The orchestra played from a wide arched niche built especially for musicians so their music carried evenly throughout the ballroom-at the opposite end a raised mezzanine section with soft cushioned chairs and benches for those not wishing to dance but to sit and view the dancing. Also it was where the mama's literally put their daughters on display hoping to interest a titled nobleman. One side of the ballroom opened onto a veranda lighted with lanterns. Carefully tended pots of greenery enhanced the area and many of the dancers could dance out on the veranda as it enjoined the ballroom.

The card room, two doors down from the dancers, offered respite for those choosing to gamble, smoke, and talk—mostly a man's haven. If gambling, markers were exchanged, but never money. Should one not follow the wishes of the Host, they were no longer welcome.

Off limits in the mansion was the Staunton library. It became known that anyone entering this private domain without a personal invitation from the duke would be banished with no explanation.

George Richard Staunton, Duke of Grenfell, had been the most respected man in London—known that if he gave his word, writing in contract form was unnecessary. His integrity, fairness, and welcoming character were constant. An invitation to the Staunton ball always coveted, now the aristocrats were waiting.

Since the accidental deaths of the well liked Stauntons, the mansion had been closed. It was thought that the second son waited for his twin to return, thus making no effort to attend a season.

When word came that the Staunton mansion was being prepared for the next Duke of Grenfell's arrival, curiosity reigned. Many in the ton aware that the second son had yet to be recognized as the next duke—their tongues began to wag. Bets were placed at White's as to when it would happen. Also, attending a Staunton soiree had been a much enviable invitation and now the *ton* questioned if the second son would have any of his father's extraordinary uniqueness. They remembered little about him, it was the duke and his heir that had captured their admiration.

Eudora clenched her mouth tighter, dropping her pelisse on the floor. "What do you mean not all the servants have been hired? I left specific orders what I expected."

The older woman wasn't the least intimidated. She had raised Eudora since she was ten years old and because the Earl of Sherbrooke found it difficult to manage his motherless daughter, had given Nora a freer hand. Eudora used to complain to her father but he didn't back down. So Nora stayed with the spoiled chit and they learned to live with one another.

Eudora would never admit that she relied on Nora, though she tried to treat her as a lowly servant. It didn't work.

"Listen, Duchess, unless you're willing to pay extra, you're not going to find top-of-the-line help. Everyone knows of your cruelty. Look what you did back at Penumbra," Nora boldly reprimanded, "callously treating that young maid, Vicky, even when her family needed her wages, they'd not tolerate her being abused. You have a horrible reputation."

Without shame, Eudora dropped onto her bed, ignoring Nora's scolding. "I'm tired. His grace is a wretch," she laid an arm over her eyes, "I wish—"

"There's no sense going there," the older woman interrupted as she bent, picking up the pelisse. "You know the saying; *you made your bed and now you—*"

"Oh stop."

"So make the best of it."

"I'm trying."

Nora moved to stand next to the bed. "If you really mean to *try,* I suggest you stop gobbling all those sweets and make yourself act and look like a duchess. It's what you've targeted all these years."

"Sometimes, Nora, you overstep your bounds."

Nora chuckled, ignoring her outburst. "Get some rest and I'll help things get settled. The duke has gone out."

Eudora sat up in a lurch. "Gone out? Where?"

"He didn't report to me."

"With all there is to do and he just ups and leaves everything for me to do."

"Enough, Eudora." Nora's annoyed tone went on, "Get yourself together and start acting like a Grenfell duchess. Show your husband how competent you can be."

Conflicting emotions crossed Eudora's face. "Tell me what I should do." Arrogance being her forte, she mocked, "I want to show the *ton* that the Stauntons are back in town and things will be better than ever. They will crave an invitation from the Duchess of Grenfell." She rose walking toward the cheval mirror, touching her neck. "If only I could find the Grenfell jewels, then I'd be praised and envied."

Nora, shaking her head, left her mistress.

Chapter Thirty-Three

Escorted by two frigates, the *Hampton* docked at Southampton
Wolf and Bender reported to the naval authorities telling only what was pertinent to their taking over *Hampton's* command. Admiral Cunningham would fill in further information.

They were down on the wharf with people moving quickly about. Other sailors were laughing and looking for a night on the town. Wolf and Bender, dressed in their sailors' clothes, collected Gully, Muggs, and Sheena needing to locate a place to stay. As they began walking, Gully brought a lot of stares.

"You know, Wolf, we're going to have a problem finding a place, especially with so many ships in port. Rooms are going to be hard to come by."

"I know, Bender, and I've been thinking. How about we hire a carriage to take us closer to London? I'll find a place for Gully and Muggs, and then we can plan on what we're going to do."

"Good thinking." He grinned. "Are you going to continue being a sailor? I mean, this charade will have to end."

"I don't want anyone to know I've returned until I find what is happening at Penumbra. I understand you're anxious to get to Tayford, I don't want to hold you up."

They were walking away from the port. "I've been away this long; a couple more days shouldn't matter. I'm sure my father is still the miserly old man that I left behind."

Wolf's fist touched Bender's upper arm. "We do have our crosses to bear, don't we?" He looked at Gully. "How do you like England?" The air was damp and cool and filled with unwelcome odd smells. "Just like Port Charles, isn't it?"

Gully's wide smile warmed Wolf's heart. "It'll be all right as long as we're together."

"Yeah," grinned Muggs, "but I never seen such brown water. It doesn't smell like the sea. And it sure ain't pretty to look at."

Wolf and Bender smiled at the youngster's discovery and definition. Gully, taking Sheena's hand to bring her along, shortening his stride.

They found a carriage for hire and Wolf decided to go to Horsham, not far from London. "I know the place, governor, if you've got the blunt—I'll take your crew anywhere."

They arrived in Horsham late, the tired travelers waited while Wolf and Bender went into the inn; returning with a heaping tray of rolls, bangers, and three kidney pies and a pitcher of ale and two mugs of milk. Gully, Muggs, and Sheena sat behind the inn devouring their bounty. The food tasted strange but being so hungry they sat back and ate it all, smiling.

Wolf and Bender sat inside the inn. "I've got to see if I can find something to let." Wolf took a drink of ale. The inn-owner's wife came to refill his mug, Wolf smiled. "Pardon, Ma'am, would you know of a furnished cottage I could let for about three months or so?" He put two sovereigns on the planked table as he picked up his mug. "There'd be no trouble; we just need a quiet place to rest before traveling further."

The greed showed on the woman's face and wasn't missed by either man. "I suppose you plan to take those," she moved her head in the direction of the kitchen, "with you? You'll all be need in the same place?"

Wolf knew he could catch more with honey, so he'd not let his tone sting. "Why yes, Ma'am, they're my responsibility. I must take them with me." Wolf made it look like he accidentally put his mug down on the sovereigns and nonchalantly pushed them aside.

Bender could hardly keep from laughing.

The woman's eyes bugged. "My sister's got a place about three miles from here. It's by itself without neighbors. Her husband died and she's living here with me." Turning toward the kitchen, she yelled, "Hilly, come out here."

Wolf rented a cart from the stable. Filled with everything they could think they needed, they set out for Hilly's cottage. Arriving, they found to their surprise that it was well tended and surrounded by woods.

Muggs was delighted. "I never lived in a place like this… sure is something." Wolf thought of Penumbra and how he'd be able to give them all a home.

"Gully, will you come outside with Bender and me? We've got some things to talk over. Muggs can stay with Sheena." He smiled at the strange black girl who hung back when either he or Bender were near.

Standing on the broken-brick walk, Wolf looked up at Gully. Before he could say anything, Gully spoke. "You're leaving us, Captain? But don't worry, we'll be just fine."

Wolf swallowed, knowing this man was his good friend. "Gully, I have to get to London and it'll be easier for me to travel alone. Bender is going to go on to his home. Believe me, I'm not abandoning you. It's just that I don't want to draw attention to myself. When I get matters straightened, I'll come back and we'll go to my home where we'll live together. I told you and Muggs, and now I'll include Sheena, that you have a home with me for as long as you want it."

"You worry too much, Captain. I know your word is good." Gully looked at Bender. "And that goes for Mr. Bender, too."

Bender held out his hand. "I'm proud to shake your hand, Gully. Anytime you need my help, you have only to get word to me at Tayford Manor."

They shook hands. There were tears behind their lids, but none fell.

Wolf gave Gully a swift squeeze on his arms. "Muggs," he called, "bring Sheena out here."

Muggs came running. Sheena, walking slowly, not knowing what to expect in this strange place, stopped near Gully. Muggs' spirited voice asked, "What is it, Captain?"

"Bender and I need you to look after Gully while we're gone. We've got to go on ahead. Do you think you can handle things here until I return?"

Muggs, grinning and nodding his head, grasped Gully's hand.

Wolf put a leather pouch in Gully's hand. "This will hold you over. Get what you need and tell them you've been ordered to act on my behalf. That way no one should cause you any problems. Especially when they see the coins you offer."

"I've got it, Captain."

"Bender and I will return the cart." He ruffled Muggs' shaggy hair, "I'll be back as soon as I can, just know that I will come back for you all." Wolf turned, waved, and he and Bender left their good friends— their good and loyal friends.

"Good sailing, Mr. Wolfman," Gully called out. And then he turned to start this new temporary adventure. "Let's get ourselves settled." *Mr. Wolfman, you aren't no murderer, so whoever you're after, I lay my bet that you won't kill anyone.*

Muggs held the door open for Gully, wearing a happy smile.

Chapter Thirty-Four

Wolf and Bender returned the cart and purchased two horses to take them to London. Their mounts had seen better days and both men decided after getting to their destination they'd retire the two nags, letting them live out their last days in leisure.

"I look forward to arriving at Penumbra and seeing to my stables. I have great thoroughbreds." Wolf's upbeat tone made Bender smile, it being the first time Bender heard Wolf regard Penumbra in an upbeat frame of mind.

They clopped along as fast as they dared to push. Wolf was silent for a long while. He broke out with a wide grin. "I was just thinking of what that sassy angel would say if she saw us plodding along on these racehorses. Probably laugh at us two pirates."

Bender returned a chuckle. "*Your* angel can ride. I've never seen a lady ride astride and control a stallion as she does."

Eying Bender, Wolf said, "There were a few moments when I wished that she was *my* angel. She set me on fire."

"That's why Neal asked you to leave, isn't it?"

Bender's question stabbed at Wolf's heart, but he never lied, just avoided the truth if necessary. But now he wanted to tell his friend. "Yes. I couldn't sleep so as I said I went swimming and she was there before I knew it." Remembering, he laughed. "Angel? Ha! You know what she did... she took my pants and left me bare. I didn't know she had them, it was dark and I thought I just couldn't find them. I planned to high-tail to the schoolhouse as I couldn't return to the house bare-butt. She showed herself, taunting me. I did dive into the water," he laughed, "had to."

"Ah ha. I know what you mean."

"Finally, she tossed my pants into the water and I got them on and then she decided to run but I tackled her." Wolf stopped talking, his face taking on a faraway look. Bender wasn't fooled. Suddenly, Wolf added, "I kissed her, nothing more, a kiss that lit my fire; still I did not take advantage though she was willing. I reminded myself that she is Neal's daughter, our gracious host. And common sense prevailed. We were walking back, to the house and she put her arm around my waist and I couldn't help myself, I pulled her to my side. Our hips met and our steps were in unison on the dewy grass." Wolf hesitated, savoring the memory. "Now you'll never believe this."

Bender grinned, "She propositioned you."

"Worse than that, she said we should marry. She hadn't planned on marrying a pirate, but for me she'd make the exception."

"That must have been some kiss."

"Truthfully, I think I would like being married to her. Life certainly wouldn't be dull. But I knew I had to discourage her nonsensical idea, and as said, I insulted her, received a slap on my face, well deserved, and that's the last I saw or spoke with her."

"So how did Neal find out?"

"He was awake and saw us. He thought the worst. I can't blame him as she was in her nightie and me wearing wet pants."

Bender whistled.

"And the rest you know. He summoned me to his office and didn't ask me to leave, he ordered me to go within the hour. He was furious. I tried to impress on him that nothing happened other than a kiss, but his rage wasn't listening."

"She got to you, though, didn't she?"

"Yes. And you know what meant more to me is that she thought I was a pirate and even if in her innocence claimed to like me enough to marry me, it was *me* and not the title. Of course, it was passion speaking, but she didn't understand. Still, life with her would have been something special."

"That something is what many of us noblemen wish for and very few find." Bender bridled, "You know, once it's known we are back, invitations will run amuck to attend balls, musicals, and especially Almack's." Bender shook his head in disgust. "Mamas will be parading their daughters in front of us." Suddenly, Bender chuckled, "The shackles will tighten on you before me. The parson's trap will be ready and waiting as you're already a duke and will be the most sought after. Me? I've got time."

"Don't remind me. I know my duty as you know yours."

Frowning, they set their horse clopping toward their next stop, the *Silver Bell.*

Wolf called to the young lad, his clothes clean yet tattered. "Will you keep an eye on our horses?"

In hopes of making a coin, the lad grinned, "Aye, Sir," and wrinkled his nose, giving the horses a quick onceover. He recognized the value of a good horse and these didn't meet his idea of quality, but the man did ask and not order, so any amount of coin will do.

"Stopping here, Bender, will prove beneficial. Household servants gather here to let off steam to each other knowing they'll get their share of sympathy."

"I know. I've never heard a ripple of complaint about your family."

Proudly, Wolf said, "That's because of my father. I intend to see that nothing changes."

Unshaven, wearing dusty pants and shirt with their arms, neck exposed, they looked as travelers stopping for a drink. Nodding as they took seats at a scarred table, ordering ale like everyone else. The silence ended after Wolf and Bender lifted their mugs and began to drink, ignoring the men standing at the hewn oak bar. The two men appeared to be passing though and it meant nothing to this working class.

Seemingly unconcerned with the strangers, *Silver Bell's* patrons began to continue talking. One taking a long swig from his mug—

outfitted in brown work clothes, grumbled, "I hope I gets my wages soon for my wife keeps telling me the cupboards are getting down."

A lanky man leaned over and looked at the guy complaining. "Hey Melvin, why don't you just come up and tell the duke you needs your blunt?"

"Sure now, you've got to be joking. Me tell his high and mighty, who isn't a duke yet, that I need me wages when the witch he's married to is running around town trying to get credit and takes all her anger out on me and the cattle. Can't do it, work is hard to come by," taking a long swallow of ale, "you know that."

Another voice agreed.

"I hear there's talk that he'll be recognized this season as the next heir."

"That's if old iron-fisted Medford makes it."

Bender looked at Wolf, bent forward at the table so as not to miss a word. His ire building.

"What's with the skinflint?"

"Haven't you heard? There's talk that he's suffering from apoplexy, but more likely he had to spend some of his blunt." There were laughs as they raised their mugs in full agreement.

Wolf went to the bar tossing a sovereign on it. They all stared at him, looking at the gold piece, and waited.

"Gents," Wolf's voice smooth as he rubbed his beard, with his big bronzed working hand, seemingly relaxed leaning his elbow on the bar. "I'm willing to have you enjoy all the ale and food you want for some answers."

None of the six men were willing to jump at the offer, now eying him suspiciously.

Wolf continued with his nonchalance attitude. "You see, I heard you mention the new duke, it's got to be at Penumbra. I once met the Duke of Grenfell. We talked about thoroughbreds and he invited me to see his and mayhap I could get some work."

"He's right," one man said, "*that* duke loved his horses and had a son that did too."

Wolf bent his head to look at the man speaking. "What do you mean *that* duke?"

"Well now, I suppose I spoke out of turn, it's just gossip you know." But the man couldn't help wanting to contribute as he spied the gold piece. "You see, the real Duke of Grenfell died some time back and the son that like horses, they say he died too. The son that's left to inherit doesn't care much for cattle. They say he's a mean one."

Wolf choked back anger, narrowing his eyes, controlling his temper. "I hoped to go to Penumbra and visit the Duke. I'm sorry to hear he's dead."

The man that had complained about not getting his wages spoke, "You're not as sorry as the rest of us. I was so proud to get a job at Penumbra—everyone wanted to work for the duke, but not anymore. The new duke and his duchess aren't liked. I'm sorry I gave up my job working for the Earl of Tunbridge."

The youngest man there piped up, "My sister had to quit 'cause the duchess hit her so often for nothing and my ma said we'd have to make it without extra wages; she didn't care if she is a duchess, no one hits what's hers."

Another younger man said, "My Becky says the duchess is planning a ball and she's having trouble getting credit. I guess they' re waiting to see if the other twin gets named duke. My Becky hopes so, she needs her wages."

"What's the hold-up?" the innkeeper asked.

"Don't know, but every time he's supposed to take title, it doesn't come about." Wolf pushed the sovereign toward the innkeeper and shrugged toward Bender. "You're leaving already? Mind telling where you're headed, Mister?"

"I'm thinking of taking a look at Penumbra. I remember it a long time ago when I was there. It's a beautiful place."

Bender, standing next to Wolf, said, "What about Medford? Is he really a skinflint?"

There was laughter all around. One man said through his chuckles, "You've heard the saying, you can't get blood out of stone; believe me, old Medford's tried."

"Is he really sick?"

"That's the word passed around, but nobody knows. He's supposed to be coming to town but they say he's still in the country. Why?"

"I heard he's rich so I thought I might ask him for a bit of financial investing." Now they all roared, a couple of them choked on their ale.

Wolf and Bender grinned, saluted the men, and hurried out. Bender gave the lad a handful of coins and they rode down the road out of sight.

"I've got to get to Medford, Wolf. If my father is ill, he'll need me."

"Go. I'm going to straighten out some things in London and then I'm heading for Penumbra."

They shook hands and then looking at each other, they clasped each other in a big hug. Neither wanting the other to discover the water building under their eyelids. "Take care, Bender. Let me know if I can help. Let's keep in touch."

"Will do." Bender cleared his throat. "You're a good friend, Wolf. I wish you luck." Wolf nodded.

The men got on their horses and each went in a different direction.

Chapter Thirty-Five

Wolf's first stop just off Fleet Street was to talk with his solicitor. Barslow was away and he encountered Spangler, Barslow's trusted man, and got right to the point.

Spangler didn't blink or show any sign of surprise when Wolf entered telling, "I'm Derrick Staunton of Penumbra." He held out his hand to shake the old man's—careful not to apply pressure to the bony fingers. "My identity is to remain secret. I want you to furtively spread the word that any and all Staunton debts will be honored. Bills are to be delivered to this office for payment." Wolf, incensed that his family name was being besmirched in any form, said, "The Staunton name will not be tarnished. Do you understand, Mr. Spangler?"

"I do, Your Grace."

"You have a quiet way about you, Mr. Spangler, that I admire. No doubt my solicitor has advised how I want to remain unnamed."

The old man shuffled, yet his movements were quick and level. His nearly bald head with wisps of white hair matched his colorless skin. It appeared Mr. Spangler spent his days indoors. He knew of many nobles, but none treated him with respect as did the previous Duke of Grenfell and now his son is following in his footsteps. "Is there anything more I can do, Your Grace?"

Wolf had been sitting in Barlow's big chair, yet the chair didn't look that big with the new duke's frame. Spangler stared, waiting.

Combing his fingers through his hair, he said, "Yes. I'm going to Tattersalls and look over the cattle being put up for bid; I'll check the horse I want and I'd like you to handle the transaction."

220

"I can do that. They'll naturally ask and I'll say I'm buying it for my employer's client, which will be true."

"Of course. Use Barslow's name on the papers. Have the horse delivered to his stable. I'll pick it up in a couple of hours."

"Will there be anything more?"

"No. I'm going to Penumbra. However, I understand my brother and his wife are giving a ball. See that their needs are filled. Let no tradesman *ever* believe that a Staunton does not honor their debts or that they linger unpaid." Wolf again held out his bronzed hand. His calluses had thinned, yet strength permeated his grasp. Mr. Spangler's hand was lost in Wolf's but not before gripping it as best he could.

"I'll see to everything, Your Grace. And I'd like to say that I'm pleased that you are well. My condolence for the Duke of Grenfell's passing. He was a fine, fine man."

"Thank you, Mr. Spangler." And Wolf departed.

Next, Wolf required clothing. He walked into the tailor shop that had outfitted his father for years. Wolf didn't see Mr. Pearson and walked past his assistant, not wanting to explain. He pushed to open Pearson's door.

"Now see here," the assistant said right behind him.

Wolf turned, eyed him with one brow raised, no smile, but the stare was enough to stop the man.

Pearson, not wanting to provoke a patron, said, "I'll handle this." The assistant backed away. Wolf stepped into the sparse office and closed the door.

Pearson stood, curious while thinking this tall man was a force, but with noticeable restrained character.

Wolf held out his hand. Pearson noticed it was a working hand, yet maybe from holding reins for a long period of time, though he doubted it. He accepted the offered hand.

"Forgive my intrusion, Mr. Pearson, but my time is limited. I trust that what I say will remain in this room."

"I see no reason to disagree."

Wolf nodded. "I'm Derrick Staunton. My father purchased his clothing from you."

Pearson fell back into his chair, staring. "The Duke of Grenfell... you're his son... you're alive?"

Wolf smiled. "I believe I am."

"What I mean," he gasped for breath, "everyone thinks you perished."

"So I've heard." Wolf leaned on the tailor's desk. "I haven't time, I must be on my way; what I need is a pair of britches, clean shirt, coat, and a cape. I want them all in black with the exception of the shirt. You have two hours. Will you comply?"

"I'll try." He looked into the gray eyes and responded, "Yes, two hours. I'll have to take your measurements."

"Of course. In fact, take all that you need. Send a wardrobe to me at Penumbra. Send all that's required. However, I want my clothes made in black, grays, buff, and also some navy. I want no fancy colors with lace even if they are the rage. Plain, Mr. Pearson, simply cut and plain."

Mr. Pearson couldn't hold back his smile. "I believe anything you don will look right. Even those canvas pants do not look out of place."

Wolf laughed. "By the way, have you heard if Hendrix is now my brother's valet?"

The tailor shook his head and wrung his hands. "I knew Hendrix well, being he cared for all the duke's clothes. I'm sorry to say that your brother dismissed him. I don't know what happened to him."

Wolf's forehead furrowed, this tone low, speaking to himself, *is there nothing Del hasn't massacred?*

"I beg your pardon?"

Wolf shrugged. "Sorry, it's nothing. I rely on your discretion."

"You have it, Your Grace."

Wolf's next stop was the back entrance to Staunton Manor's stable. Knowing that servants gossip, he began his clandestine investigation.

"Hey you there, you ain't supposed to be on this property. You better go before the duke finds you, he's a mean one, he is."

Wolfs straight posture and aloof manner caused the young groom to back off and then wait. Wolfs tone sounded aristocratic but still polite, "And who might you be?" Surprised, though the man wasn't dressed like a dandy, the groom relaxed, "Me name's Jolly. I'm in charge of the stable and the duke's cattle."

Wolf moved toward the horses' rumps and running his hand over one of them. "It doesn't appear you're all the good. These are scars along with new welts."

Jolly was glad he finally had someone to tell. "Don't I know it. The duke isn't kind and uses a whip."

Wolfs reply shocked Jolly. "I agree. Tell the duke you have orders from the grave and that his brother was here and told you to give particular care to all the cattle."

Jolly's mouth gapped. "You? His twin? Oh my god, they say you're dead." Gawking at Wolf, "Are you really the lost brother? Really?"

Wolfs smile reached his eyes, "Yes, but you mustn't say a word except to my brother. He'll want to know. I expect you to say absolutely nothing about my being here to anyone else." Wolfs voice deepened, "Do you understand?" He squeezed the young man's shoulder. "I'm going, just remember to give my brother my message."

Jolly excited over knowing such a great secret, "Not a word. Yes, Sir, I won't forget."

Wolf squeezed the young man's shoulder. "I've got to go. I want you to keep treating those welts. You have enough feed for them?"

"That's one thing I won't short them on."

"Very good. And remember to give my brother my message." Jolly, excited over knowing a secret, could only nod.

Wolf left without looking back.

Chapter Thirty-Six

Anxious to arrive at his beautiful Penumbra, Wolf rode long hours, stopping only to rest his new horse. He paused at a rill letting the stallion drink and munch on grass. The oats he'd carried was long gone. "This will have to do, my friend. But when you get to your new home, Rutley will bed you in a stall all your own."

Smiling, Wolf leaned against a tree, his black cape thrown back over his shoulders and took a bite of the polished apple he'd rubbed on his sleeve. His horse came over and nudged his shoulder. "You're a greedy one." Wolf took one more bite and gave the rest of the apple to his horse.

The rushing water from the rill blocked all sounds. Before Wolf could move, a large man stood off to his side. His red beard matched his long hair. His eyes were warm against his sun-reddened skin.

Wolf put his hand on his sword that was protected in its scabbard.

"No need for that, Sir," the deep voice said. "I'm wondering if you have another one of those reds."

"No, this greedy horse took the last." Wolf's congenial tone put the man at ease. "I do have a half loaf and a slab of cheese you're welcome to."

"Right you are, Sir." Wolf gave the man the last of his food. The redhead bent over it pulling a hunk of bread and with a knife taken from his boot sliced off a chunk of cheese. He smelled the cheese and grinned. "This will be tasty." He returned the remaining bread and cheese to Wolf.

"Going far?" Wolf discovered he missed the camaraderie he had had with Bender, Gully, and Muggs. "I'm resting my mount." He handed the food back to the man. "Take it. I don't have far to travel."

"I have no special destination. I'm in search of work. I'm having no luck. Would you know of any?"

"Where do you hail from?"

"Up near Edinburgh. Lung fever wiped out my family and I had to get away."

Wolf held out his hand. "Sorry."

"Thanks." Both men's grip was strong. "My name's Quinn." He was about to walk away, but turned. "Thanks for the bite. It was good of you to share."

Wolf's natural empathy immediately came into play. "If you have no special destination, why not ride with me?"

Quinn turned, somewhat suspicious of the invite. After all, this was a well-speaking gent, why ask a stranger for company? "Would you know of work around these parts?"

Wolf's smile was genuine. "Do you like horses?"

"I do. I have a fine chestnut in the woods back there. His welfare comes first before mine." He laughed. "Where he goes, I go with him."

"Then I know of a stablemaster that would more than likely be happy to have you work for him."

Quinn's grin brightened his already red face. His clean crooked teeth enhanced his ruddy complexion, making his hair seem twice as red. "Then I'll get Scully, that's his name."

The two men rode in silence for a short while. Quinn peered over at Wolf. "You've got the bronze that one can only get from being at sea. Are you a ship's captain home for a spell?"

Wolf liked the direct inquiry from the big Scotsman. "Yes and no," and then he laughed. "I've been at sea nearly two years and now I'm home to stay."

"I tried the sea, but as soon as the boat rocked, I turned green and wished for death." He shook his head. "Misery, the worst case I ever had. I think that's God's way of telling me to stay on dry land." Quinn looked over at Wolf in awe, "You never got those ailments?"

Wolf shook his head. "It is the one thing where I lucked out."

"Did I guess right? Were you a captain?"

This time Wolf didn't smile, animation left his features taut. "You could say I captained a ship." He said no more.

Quinn was wise enough not to probe. "Would it be all right then if I call you *Captain*?"

Wolf shrugged, "Why not?"

"I'm Quinn Weems. How far do we have to travel to reach this fine stable you know of?" Quinn assumed this man had well-off friends.

"We'll be there by nightfall."

Chapter Thirty-Seven

Back in London

Eudora, glowing and in high spirits, perused the acceptances to *her* ball. A contemptuous laugh escaped—*this is going to make the ton envy me, definitely signifying that I am the Duchess of Grenfell*. Tapping the Earl of Tunbridge's note against her fingers, she was positive the earl had written it. It was written on his personal stationery inquiring if he may include his visiting sister and niece into his invitation—trusting it would not be an inconvenience. Eudora's stomach did somersaults; after all, it was well known the Earl of Tunbridge rarely acknowledged invitations. Even so, no one would dare slight him by not sending him one. Never for a second did Eudora think the earl would deem to attend, yet now that she thought about it decided it was because *she* being the new duchess, he would not slight her.

Eudora recalled when at one time she had thought to set her sights on the earl for herself when his wife died. He retired to the country and ignored the *ton*, seldom coming to town. But the title of duchess had more status and she certainly didn't want to be confined on his country estate so she dismissed setting her cap for the very wealthy earl.

Eudora wanted to sing. Euphoric as some of the *ton* had yet to accept her as the Duchess of Grenfell; the earl's attendance answered her longing for recognition. There wasn't a doubt in her mind that her husband was a-second class duke. She bit the inside of her jaw thinking of his twin and what a masterful duke he would have been. But then, she'd never be the Duchess of Grenfell and being its duchess had always been her aim—its money, power, and the Grenfell jewels. And bearing the Staunton name was the highest honor bestowed; the tradesmen came to their senses after hesitating to fulfill her demands. It was humiliating and when this ball was over, she would be sure to put them in their place.

Eudora, still holding the Earl of Tunbridge's note, watched Delbert slowly enter her ornate boudoir without so much as a scratch at her door. His legs weren't going to hold him much longer. He rushed to grip the back of the chair near the fireplace, and began to shake while trying to take air into his lungs.

Not giving him one iota of attention, her voice melodious, "Your Grace, you'll never guess who is accepting my invitation… I'll be the envy of everyone." When Delbert made no sound, she looked up and gasped. "What is it? You look like death. Don't tell me you're sick with the ball in just a few days." Her features contorted into ugly lines. "If you spoil *my* ball, I will not only maim you, Delbert, I might even kill you."

Exasperated, Eudora went to him. "I mean it, if you're even thinking of getting sick," taking a good look at his pallor, groused, "what in the world is wrong with you?"

Gripping the arms on the chair, his knuckles white and then blue as he tightened his hold, stopping the flow of blood to his fingers. His eyes swelling in their sockets with fear, trembling; unable to speak, he stared at his wife.

Eudora huffed. "You're frightening me. What is wrong with you?"

"He's… he's *alive*." His words were so low Eudora had to strain to hear.

"Delbert," she stood with her hands on her hips. "You're spoiling my surprise. Who's alive? What has this to do with *my* ball? Stop this nonsense… I mean it."

Taking a deep breath and easing his grip, he began to laugh and laugh and laugh. The more he laughed the eerier the sound. It frightened his duchess.

"Have you gone mad?"

Delbert slowly collected himself. "No, my darling duchess, I have not gone mad, but beware, soon both of us will wish we had that for an excuse."

"Stop it! You are mad... I won't have it!"

"*It,* my dear, is the title of duchess and you are so right," he began to shake again, "you won't have it... you see, Derrick is alive."

Eudora began to laugh. "You are out of your mind. Derrick *alive?* We know better."

"I'm telling you, he's alive and well. He visited the stable and ordered special care given to the cattle." Delbert stared into the burning embers as though mesmerized. "Who do you know worries about animals as much as Derrick? I used to laugh at his and Rutley's obsession."

"You're an idiot, Delbert. Because some fool comes into our stable and says something to the numbskull you've allowed to be groomsman, you believe him." Eudora walked away in a huff. "And I thought this to be the most wonderful day since coming to London. Why, the Earl of Tunbridge is attending *my* ball."

Recovering from the jolt of receiving Derrick's message and knowing in his gut that it was from his twin, Delbert continued staring at the embers and said, "We're in trouble, Eudora."

Seeing the need to placate her idiot husband, she went to stand beside him. Reaching for his arm, his waistcoat, tailored with the finest material, its softness tickled her fingers, she said with underlying calmness, "Let's say what you think is true. It matters not; of course, that you'd not be the next duke." She hid her despairing emotion. "We have nothing to worry about. You remember the blood; we saw them both."

Delbert choked, his head bent. "How can I forget?"

"Then don't you see, if Derrick survived, he was unconscious. We were masked. He didn't see us and those thugs have no way of knowing who we are. There isn't any way Derrick would think to connect us to what happened."

His shoulders slumped; he kept staring at the dying embers. "I hope you're right, Eudora. If you're wrong—do you know what that means?"

"Don't you think if Derrick were alive, he would come to see you and announce to one and all that he's back? This is ridiculous. Where could he have been that no one ever knew of him? Why wouldn't he have returned to his beautiful Penumbra? You know he treasured that place. No, I think you're hatching up a nest of vipers for no reason. Derrick is as dead as—"

"Don't say it, Eudora." His voice turned to iron, rusty iron. "He was my father and it eats on me; eroding any self-respect I might possibly have."

She brushed away his misgivings. "We have it all and you wanted it too. Remember that!"

Delbert looked at his wife, his bottom lip curling. "We're truly a matched pair. We went after what was not ours and pretend to be the Duke and Duchess of Grenfell. You know something, dear wife, even if I am recognized as the next duke, we will *never* be the Stauntons connected to the title. We are fakes."

Eudora's voice carried to the door, cold as death. "I've always hated you, Delbert. Derrick is the twin I wanted. He was a *man,* something you never were and will never be. You have no backbone unless you're carrying a whip." Her laugh was insulting.

Delbert stopped. Listening to his wife, he wondered who hated whom the most. Not bothering to look back, he left.

Eudora rang for her maid.

Chapter Thirty-Eight

Wolf and Quinn rode hard, reaching Penumbra as the sun began to set.

"You have some very fancy friends. Are you sure they won't mind me tagging along?"

"You'll see. You'll be welcome at Penumbra."

Wolf stopped and stared. His heart pounding as he took it all in. He was finally home. He gripped the reins to keep his emotions in check.

"Are you all right, Captain?"

Wolf's smile was broad, his teeth whiter against his bronzed skin, his eyes shining so they looked silver. "As right as I'll ever be, Quinn." He gently kneed his horse and Quinn followed.

Wolf pulled his horse to a stop. Not wanting to believe what was there before him—fallow fields, grasses uncut, and reeds growing high around the lake. *So my twin and his duchess aren't caring for Penumbra.* Rage tightened his gut, but he kept it smothered. Riding further to the stable, he saw a faint light in a single window. "Rutley is here. You'll like him, Quinn. There's no better man that knows good horseflesh."

"You sound very sure that he'll take me on." He gawked over at his new friend. "I suspect there is more to you than you let on. You're more than a captain, aren't you? You can't be a noble, they usually aren't congenial with us lower folks."

Looking over his shoulder, Wolf grinned.

"Whoa… you are a noble, right?"

Calling back as he raced toward the stable, "Come on; let's take Rutley away from his supper."

Arriving at the stable, he found not one horse whinnying, no sound of hoofs stepping in their stalls, no swishing of tails, in fact there wasn't a heavy smell of horses at all. The place was deserted. "What the...?"

A small man, the setting sun turning his wrinkled skin to an orange tint, came forward.

"Sorry, but this stable is closed. We can't accommodate you. But there is water... take all you like."

"Rutley? Rutley... it's me," he paused, *"Derrick."*

Derrick was off his horse in a flash as he needed to catch the old man before he hit the ground.

Quinn was there beside him. "Did he have a heart attack?"

"I just did something foolish." Wolf picked up the thin body and carried him to his room. He knew where to go as they used to sit for hours and talk horses.

When Wolf entered, it was exactly as he remembered—clean, yet the warmth was missing. He laid the old man gently on his bed. Quinn was already there with a mug of water. Lifting the old gent's head, Wolf helped him sip some of the tepid water.

Rutley opened his eyes and stared. "It's really you, Mr. Derrick? I couldn't believe my ears. But that beard, you look different. I'm sorry I didn't recognize you."

"Stop, Rutley. We're friends. I'll always be Derrick to you. Remember what the duke said..." They both stopped, remembering, and silence vibrated. Derrick cleared his throat. "Anyway, he said you were to treat me as one of your workers." He laughed, "And you did." He looked over at an astounded Quinn. "I shoveled more horse dung thinking I'd never finish and when I did, there was always more."

Rutley gripped Wolf's arm as his face got back some color. "I knew you weren't dead. I just knew it." Suddenly, his face twisted in pain. "I'm sorry. There was no finer man than the Duke of Grenfell. I loved him, you know?"

Wolf said nothing, he couldn't; he just nodded, not wanting to blot his eyes. Quinn stood back, waiting. He cleared his throat.

Wolf said to Rutley, "I've brought you some help. Quinn is looking for work and I told him I knew just the man. What do you say, Rutley? You know hiring for Penumbra's stable has always been your decision."

Rutley moved to sit up. Wolf moved too, to give him room. "If you say he's a good man, that's good enough for me. But I've got nothing for him to do."

Knots formed in Wolf's stomach. "Tell me."

"Well, first, will you share some rabbit stew and bread? I also have some tea and an old bottle of brandy that I've been saving for a special day. This is it."

The three men sat in the small room. Their meal over, Rutley poured a splash of brandy in three old mugs, saying, "My best crystal... this will do."

Quinn knew they were going to have a private conversation and took his mug and went outside.

"Tell me, Rutley, what's been going on. Where are Penumbra's thoroughbreds? Arcadia King and Monticon? The others? Where's Valiant?"

Rutley held up his hand. "Stop, my boy. I'll tell you what I can." He took a sip of brandy; the mug nearly empty so he tilted it back and then set the mug on the table. Deep furrows cut across his forehead, he said, "There was nothing I could do. After the duke was buried, your brother ordered that all cattle be sold, except for the grays he uses for his curricle and any required to pull the coach."

He shook his head, "I've got to say it, even though it's not my place, but Mr. Derrick, he raped Penumbra's stable. He came here one afternoon and said to saddle Valiant, even knowing his fear of riding. He tried to ride your beautiful stallion, but Valiant wasn't of mind to let him; Valiant was uncontrollable. Your twin had his whip and he kept hitting the poor horse. Valiant bucked and threw your brother to the ground. I was ordered not to sell him with the others, but to destroy him at once. Your brother left without another word."

Wolf's voice was wooden, distant. "You didn't?"

Rutley grinned. "I could no more kill your beautiful stallion than I could cut off my arm." He leaned forward. "Do you remember that old gamekeeper's cottage in the woods where you boys used to play?" Without waiting for Wolf's reply, he went on, "I took Valiant there and he's been living in splendor. Now that I have nothing much to do, I go there and tend to him. Why, that old fraud lets me ride him. He's in good shape."

Wolf reached for Rutley's hand, gripping it. "Thank you."

The old man nodded. "You haven't changed; you're still a nice boy." Leaning back and studying Wolf, he rubbed his whiskered chin. "Where have you been that you couldn't come back sooner? You know, your twin is supposed to be made duke. I hear he's having a bit of trouble but I don't know about any of it. I don't know if it's true."

"Is the staff still at the manor? I'm going to go there and I don't want to frighten them. I'm sorry I took you by surprise."

"Oh but what a fine surprise." Then a despairing look crossed Rutley's face. "The duchess let go of most of Penumbra's staff. I know because they came to find a ride to the village. It's a mess. Beg pardon, I'm speaking out of turn."

"No, tell me. I need to know."

"Your brother came out here, he didn't send his secretary but came and told me to vacate the premises at once." Rutley's tone hardened. "I told him that the Duke of Grenfell had told me that Penumbra was my home for as long as I wanted it to be and that I wasn't going." The old gent, grinning, went on, "He stuttered, hit his leg with his whip a few times, I think he'd like to have used it on me, and he turned and left and I haven't seen him since. When he wants anything from the stable, he has hired a new man, Jolly. I think a good man. I've watched him with the horses."

"What about our tenants? Do you know?"

"I heard that their rents were raised and they're struggling. They claim the old duke provided all the seed and took a fair percentage of the crop. But your brother cut their share and refuses to buy the seed. Like I said, it's a mess."

Wolf stood. "You've given me enough to think about." He held out his hand again, "My thanks. Do you think you can find a suitable place for Quinn? I'd like to put him on if I have your approval."

"You've got it." They were out in the stable. "I need to ask you something important." Wolf, eying Rutley, waited. "What do I call you? I mean *Your Grace?* Quinn called you Captain and then the name *Wolf* comes up."

Wolf put his strong arm about the man's bony shoulder. "I *am* the Duke of Grenfell and I will be addressed as *Your Grace.* But when we are alone, just the two of us, I'd like you to call me by my given name as you used to... Derrick. And you may also use *Sir.*"

"I'm so honored to do so, Your Grace." Rutley saw Quinn standing nearby and was certain Quinn overheard some of their discussion. "One more thing, am I to mention this to our new friend?"

"You have my permission, but say nothing about any of Penumbra's news—good or bad. Only my name and what you'll expect of him. We're going to have to begin filling our stable again."

"Captain?" Quinn moved toward them. "Since I figured it out that you're not visiting but you live here, am I going to be working for you?"

Wolf held out his hand. "Welcome to Penumbra, Quinn. You'll be working for Rutley and me. We're glad to have you with us."

Quinn's smile lighted the evening dusk.

Rutley took over. "Best you be calling this man *Your Grace,* or *Sir* will also work, but I don't know about *Captain.*"

Quinn Weems grinning said, "This is my lucky day."

Wolf left the two men, taking long strides, anxious to be inside his home again. Wolf knew his name *Wolf* was no more. He was his father's son, Derrick George Staunton. He'd never forget why he became *Wolf* and still had that score to settle, but as of this moment, he is Derrick, the Duke of Grenfell.

Reaching the huge oak door, he didn't use the brass knocker but pounded on the oak to get immediate attention.

The door finally opened by a slovenly clothed butler, scowling. "Here now," taking in Derrick's untailored appearance along with his black beard and long hair curling on his collar, ordered, "get away. We need nothing and you should have gone to the back entrance." He was about to push the door shut, but Derrick's shoulder leaned into it and not only pushed the door wide but took the burly man by surprise.

Derrick's tone, controlled as being the Duke of Grenfell, he'd conduct himself in that manner. Giving the man a cursory examination, said, "When you answer any summons here at Penumbra, I expect courtesy and exceptionally good manners. Do not forget what I've said."

Taken aback and ready to hiss, yet the stranger's tone came across as powerful. He made no reply.

"I want *all* the staff to present themselves here in five minutes. Make no mistake that when I say *all* that is exactly what I mean. Now go!"

The servant gaped and suddenly moved to do as ordered thinking that with them all together, they could take care of this outsider.

Assembled before Derrick were five men and six women. He recognized none of the faces. *Delbert, what have you done with our faithful people?*

Derrick stood ramrod straight, looking at Penumbra's service people. Having to hurry, some of their clothing was askew, but they had obeyed his command. He looked intently at each of them while remaining silent.

"Sir?" The burly man stepped forward. "We are here and we'd like to know what right you have to come into the duke's house and think to take over? The duke and duchess are in London, but that doesn't mean that we can allow this."

A spasm of irritation darkened Derrick's eyes; still he maintained the reserve as Duke of Grenfell. "I am Derrick Staunton, the missing son of the late Duke of Grenfell. My twin brother is in London and will be returning shortly. But know that I *do not* require his permission to be in my home. As of this minute, those of you who no longer wish to serve step away and be gone in the next thirty minutes. If you wish to continue to be part of Penumbra's staff, you will obey my orders from this second on." No one moved. "Very well. My first order is that you comport yourselves as people connected with Penumbra. You will dress accordingly. Next, remove the belongings of my twin brother and his wife's from where they are now and put them in the blue room at the end of the hall. Have the duke's apartment tidied and restored to faultless condition. Have I made myself clear?"

A young maid stepped forward, quaking. "Sir?"

"I will be addressed as *Your Grace.*"

She wobbled more. Derrick wanted to reach for her to quiet her nerves, but knew to have their respect, he couldn't back down. "What is your name?"

"I'm called Ag… Agnes, Your Grace."

Derrick nodded. "What is it you have to say?"

"Your Grace, the duchess doesn't like that room. She had it decorated and still doesn't like the color."

Derrick held back his smile. "And what color is that?"

"Red, Your Grace."

Derrick put his palm along his jaw as though giving Agnes's dilemma serious thought. "That being the case, Agnes, you're to put her things in that room and if she questions it, you may refer her to me. Do you understand?"

"Yes, Your Grace." She curtsied.

Derrick turned to the woman with a big apron wrapped around her generous middle. "I presume you are Cook… please bring a plate to me in the duke's study. Do you know where that is?"

"I-I think it's on the upper floor. I've never been there, Your Grace."

Derrick looked at the burly man. "What is your name?"

His face tight and pinched, he said, "Nigel, Your Grace."

Looking at cook, he said, "Nigel will bring me the tray." They all stood, not moving, not knowing what to do.

"You are dismissed to follow my orders. Tomorrow, I'll see that matters here at Penumbra are as I wish them to be." Tired, but not permitting his body to show it, Derrick climbed the wide staircase and went directly to the right—to his father's study.

There wasn't any doubt in the staff's mind that this man knew the location of that room. Stabs of anxiety forced them to obey this stranger's orders. He did sound like a nobleman. But they all knew that the first-born heir was long dead.

Nigel whispered to one of the servants, "Get on your horse and get to London. Tell the duke and duchess what is going on."

Chapter Thirty-Nine

London

Delbert wearing his favorite color—chartreuse satin—with its lacy collar and cuffs, white stockings hugging his muscled legs with silver buckles on his black soft leather shoes, stood at the opened door. Eudora, invigorated, glided across the ballroom. "Oh, Your Grace, everything is perfect. This ballroom, not the least bit ostentatious glows in its richness. Our flowers are in ultimate blooms. The chandeliers are magnificent with sparkle and the best of all—I've engaged the orchestra that *Prinny* considers the finest."

Eudora's momentum for their big evening didn't carry to Delbert, but she didn't care. "Also, Cook has given particular concentration for the suppers. I will be the envy of all."

Delbert's voice was edged with tension, "Gloat, dear wife, for this will be your first and last moment to shine."

Eudora stopped so sharply her bright red gown swished around her ankles, her eyes blinked with incredulity, her features pinched while pursing her lips, retorted, "Don't be ridiculous."

Delbert clamped his eyes shut, his face ashen as he then opened them, his tone racked in agony. "I'm not being ridiculous, dear duchess, Derrick is alive."

She pounced on him, her tone low while controlling it not to become hysterical. "Leave it to you to spoil my first Staunton ball. Sometimes, husband, I wish…" Eudora clenched her mouth closed.

"Pray, dear wife, don't stop now. You wish what?" His eyes narrowed with contempt.

Desperate, she needed to tamp down her temper. "I wish… I wish you'd be more understanding. *My* guests will be arriving in less than an hour. Can't you forget this balderdash about Derrick?"

"It's not balderdash, Eudora. Nigel has sent word that Derrick is at Penumbra."

Eudora's eyes widened. "He can't be." She looked about as the servants were moving here and there making their last-minute checks. She pulled at Delbert's hand and then quickly dropped it. Under her breath, she uttered, "Come with me." Her gown rustled, her diamond earrings were swinging to and fro, she hurried down the hall entering the library. She almost slammed the library door, but caught herself, not wanting to draw attention with the servants. "Are you telling me that *he* is at Penumbra?" She paced and turned to attack, "The man must be an imposter." The corners of her mouth turned, forcing a smile. "Of course, that's it. Some fool is trying to steal from Penumbra knowing that we are in London."

"If only that were true." Delbert's heart hammered so that he was sure he'd pop a button on his silver quilted waistcoat. "Nigel said a person claiming to be my brother is making himself at home and giving orders like he belonged. Nigel said that they would all obey the man until we get back to throw the scoundrel out."

Eudora began to pace, twisting her fingers. "If, now I'm saying *if* it should be true and this person is Derrick, it only means that he's back and will inherit Penumbra. He doesn't know what we've done. He doesn't know that we are involved at all. Remember, Delbert, we were masked and both the Duke and Derrick were bloodied." She shook her head, loosening a curl. "No wonder his body wasn't recovered. I wonder how—"

"Eudora," Delbert shrieked, "how can you be so nonchalant and speak as if all we did was kill a rabbit? It was a duke… *my* father and my brother. We are not home free from any of this." He wanted to cry. "And in all this time, it hasn't bothered you?"

"Keep your voice down! And just remember you were right there with me and it was you that changed their carriage and it was you that provided payment." Assuming a posture of superiority, she lowered her voice, "You listen to me—we are having this ball. *My* ball! No one knows about Derrick. We are the Duke and Duchess of Grenfell and will accept all accolades due us as Stauntons." Looking at her husband whose complexion lost all color, his shoulders slumped, she snapped, "Try to act like a duke and not a dolt."

Icily, Delbert replied, "I accept that you are truly a cold-blooded horrid lady," he sneered, "correct that, for you aren't a lady. You never were and never will be. I've overlooked your meanness and petty actions all these years; in many cases, I thought them endearing which proves what an absolute imbecile I am." He cried out in raw terror, "Now *we are* going to pay. I can feel Derrick knows what we did, and if you're not afraid, you're more an imbecile than me." Regaining a quieter demeanor, Delbert moved toward the door. "I suggest, Duchess, that you repair your hair, *your* guests will be arriving soon." He left, saying not another word and not looking back at his frightened wife.

But Eudora had to have the last word. "I'll get even with you. Just you wait and see."

If Eudora had any problems clouding her thoughts, her guests would have never guessed. She blossomed as hostess. Her gracious smile reached her eyes. Sparkling over having the Earl of Tunbridge in attendance was her pinnacle for the evening.

The Earl's low voice forced Eudora to lean close to hear. "Thank you, Your Grace, for permitting me to include my sister and niece to enjoy your beautiful ball."

Aglow, Eudora replied, "Not at all, my lord. Your niece is very lovely." Eudora nodded to the earl's sister. "Mrs. Durand, I hear you live on an island with wonderful weather year round."

241

Marcella Durand, her petite form in gray satin adorned with a string of pearls and matching drop earrings, sipping champagne, eyed the duchess. "Yes, Your Grace, we're from Port Charles in the Caribbean Sea. My daughter and I are enjoying a long overdue visit with my brother." She touched the earl's sleeve. "His insistence that we join him this evening is a dream come true for my daughter." She peered out over the dance floor and saw Marvalea dancing with a young man. Marcella recognized the smile that didn't reach her daughter's eyes.

"I am so pleased the Earl accepted my invitation," gushed Eudora, "and so happy that you agreed to join us."

The earl half smiled. "If you ladies will excuse me, I believe I will see what is transpiring in the card room." He nodded and departed, stopping on his way to greet some of the *ton* that were fortunate to be in his path.

"Your brother is well respected," Eudora offered.

"I don't know of anyone that thinks ill of him." Marcella took a step with Eudora hovering. The dance over Marvalea's dance partner returned her back to Marcella.

"Mama, I'd like you to meet Viscount Changly."

Viscount Changly lifted Marcella's gloved hand and bowed, "Mrs. Durand." He smiled at Marvalea. "Please remember you've promised me a waltz."

"Of course."

He moved away.

"I hope you're enjoying my ball, Miss Marvalea."

"Very much, Your Grace."

At that moment a servant, with a slight nod with his head, required Eudora's attention. "Excuse me, please."

Alone, Marcella looked at her beautiful daughter. "Blue becomes you, Val. I wish your father could see you. This is how he pictured you—only he hoped you'd be happy."

"I am happy, Mama."

"Don't try to fool me, darling." She blinked her eye ever so slightly. "You're still pining over that pirate. How I wish he'd never landed on Slipper… of all the plantations, why ours?"

Marvalea reached for her mother's gloved arm. "Really, I am having a wonderful time. Though I worry about Papa. Do you think the uprising from the other plantations will reach Slipper?"

"We can only hope that the slaves on our land stick with us. We've always treated them right. But please do not worry, not this night. James wanted it to be special for I know that he never accepts invitations, he likes living privately in the country. He's attending tonight for me and for you."

"I'm enjoying the music, Mama… and though I wish my pirate didn't leave without saying goodbye, rest easy," she smiled to ease her mother's worry, "as our paths will never cross. Still, I think of him and wonder where he's sailing."

A young man stepped forward and said to Marvalea, "I believe this is our dance."

Marcella watched her beautiful daughter lightly touch his arm and smile. But she knew that the pirate had marked Val's heart and she didn't like it at all.

Chapter Forty

Derrick ordered a hearty breakfast to be packed and ready for him in thirty minutes. He had already bathed and shaved. Looking in the mirror, he laughed at his bronzed skin and long hair—he did look like a pirate. *Oh Angel, if you only knew.*

Walking into the stable, the sun having risen an hour ago, he spied Rutley and Quinn. Hauling the basket on his shoulder, he didn't look like a duke. "Sleep well?" he inquired.

They said they did and began to devour the food. Derrick joined in. "Rutley, I'd like Quinn to come with me, if you don't mind."

"Not much to do around here. No problem."

"Good." Derrick eyed Quinn. "I must have your word that what I do now or at any time, it remains between you and me and no one else. Can you give me your word?"

"Captain… sorry, I mean, Your Grace, my word is my life and I'll not give either up. You can trust me no matter what occurs."

Derrick nodded and held out his hand. Both their grips were strong. Then Derrick heard a whinny and rushed to a stall further down, grinning, he called out, "Valiant, you handsome devil." He opened the gate and actually hugged the black stallion. "You haven't forgotten me." He yelled to Rutley, "Thanks, Rutley, I'll never forget this." He moved to saddle Valiant. "I'm going to take him for a gallop. When I come back, Quinn, be saddled and if you have a weapon, bring it. If not, Rutley will give you one."

Rutley, looking up at the man sitting straight on the stallion, said, "I don't suppose you have use for an old man?"

"Not for this, Rutley. I want you here so I know what's going on. I'm going to be bringing two friends with me, plus a girl they rescued. Gully is a black man and Muggs is a youngster that's never been on a horse. I promised him a chance to learn." Speaking to both Rutley and Quinn, "All I'll say about them is that they saved my life. I owe them, but most important, they're my friends."

"You can count on me, Your Grace," smiled Rutley.

"And me," said Quinn.

Derrick barely kneed Valiant as he gave his horse free rein.

Rutley watched his protege disappear over a knoll—horse and rider were one. "I've loved that boy when he was young and I love him still. A fine man, duke or not."

"As I told you, it was my lucky day when we met."

Chapter Forty-One

Derrick tossed his rein to a raggedy lad. "Watch our horses and you will be well paid."

Then he pushed open the door entering Pigwhistle.

Quinn, not knowing what to expect, walked behind and then stopped, keeping a few steps away from the duke. Whatever was about to happen, Quinn was sure that being in this run-down sty was serious.

"Where's the owner of this place?" Derrick's tone wasn't friendly.

Big Mike, older but still monstrous in size, walked behind his bar and said, "I am."

Derrick leaned on the makeshift bar. "I'll have a whiskey, your very best."

"Yes sir, yes sir." Big Mike brought out a bottle pushing it toward Derrick. With his other hand, he placed a glass upside down—it was the signal to his men to be ready, this man had a heavy purse.

Derrick's sword swept across the bar, knocking the upside-down glass to the floor. "Hey," yelled Mike, "what do you think you be doing?"

Quinn, alert, keeping his hand on the dagger strapped at his waist, waited.

Derrick's eyes narrowed, his jaw tightened, and his voice threatening, said, "Move to get your weapon and you're a dead man, Big Mike."

At that moment, Quinn's knife whizzed across the room pinning a man's hat to the wall with the man still wearing it. Then Quinn reached into his boot and produced another dagger he held for all to see. No one moved.

Derrick didn't turn. He watched Big Mike. "Over two years ago, you killed my father and sold me to Captain Zuber." Watching Big Mike's eyes fly open, he continued, "I see that you recall. You see I've never forgotten… that's why I'm here. And I see that you still have your followers with you. Good!"

There was a gasp from someone in the room. He remembered too.

Big Mike not wanting to give up, thinking he could make a deal of some sort, tried to smile, "Ya know how it is, business is business."

Knowing Quinn was keeping an eye on the rest of the cowards, Derrick pointed to a young boy among the men. "How old are you?"

"Ten and two, I think," he answered.

Derrick knew he was too young to have been there that horrendous day. He ordered him to free all the animals, but to keep a horse and wagon and to take it across the road and wait. The boy didn't think twice not to obey.

Big Mike groused, "Why?"

Ignoring him, but keeping his sword at the big man's middle, ordered two of the men to carry all the edible or worthy food out to the side of the road. "And hurry back or I'll personally come after each of you."

They followed his instructions. Now they were all standing and waiting—some twisting their hands and another mopping his brow with his dirty sleeve. Their fear evident by their silence.

That night long ago, there were four men plus Big Mike. Derrick counted five in the group. He only wanted the thugs that took part in his father's murder as well as those that killed the innocent men that worked for Penumbra. "Which one of you was not there?"

One man stepped out. Rafferty was not about to let anyone go if he couldn't and yelled, "We was all in on it. We all shared the blunt. Johnny was off as our lookout."

"Shut up, you lying sneak."

"You were too."

"Quinn," Derrick said, "that rope hanging on the hook, get it and tie all of them together in chain fashion. Tie them well and then gag them."

Quinn pulled his knife out of the wall, loosening the man named Rafferty's hat. Not saying a word, he did as directed. "What about the big one?" Quinn meant Big Mike.

Laying his sword on the bar, Derrick said, "I'll tie this one." Mike began to move, but Derrick having learned from *Shark Tooth* chopped his neck and Mike went down. As he was about to tie Mike, he saw a dagger sticking from his dirty boot. Pulling it out, he said, "What went wrong... no one dared buy this from you?" Derrick recognized the pride of Tunbridge, the gem-encrusted gold dagger had the earl's family crest embedded in it. It was stolen and their steward was killed. Now more determined, Derrick tied Mike's hands behind his back and then pulled it up around Mike's neck and then back down, trussing his legs bent behind him, continuing until ending with the rope around Mike's ankles. If Mike pulled at his ankles, he also tightened the rope around his neck—just enough to keep the man hurting. Derrick knew he'd not kill any of them but he still wanted vengeance. He was going to see that each man paid every minute, hour, and day, the rest of their lives remembering... until death claimed them.

"Your friend Captain Zuber is no longer living or I'd be sure to introduce you to him so you all could be part of his crew. Instead, you'll be transported to Botany Bay and serve your life sentences prescribed personally by me. Those salt mines you'll be working in... you will know who put you in them—this is payback."

He ordered the roped men to haul Mike's carcass out to the wagon. They struggled but they completed the job. With all of them gagged and watching, he returned to Pigwhistle and knocked over the lanterns, setting fire to it. First there was smoke and slowly fire and then ablaze. The dry wood denied water popped and crackled and collapsed.

The men in the wagon struggled against one another but to no end. Big Mike's eyes bulged. He moved and the rope cut into his throat; he stopped.

Assured that no one was in danger, Derrick said to the two young raggedy boys. "Are any of these men related to you?" They looked questioning. "I mean are they part of your family?"

Answering, they each shook their head, one saying, "We're brothers."

"What were you doing in there?"

"I help in the kitchen and get food. I take it to my ma."

Derrick gave each several coins. Nodding to the piled foodstuffs, said, "Take what you want and share it with others. If anyone asks where the men have gone, tell them they left for London and won't be coming back." Derrick turned to Quinn. "I'm going to tie Valiant to the wagon. I'll drive. Come with me."

Quinn nodded, got his horse, and began to follow the wagon.

It was slow and tedious but worth it as far as Derrick was concerned. He headed for the Thames where ships heading for Australia were docked. Finding one with a captain that asked no questions when a handful of sovereigns hit the captain's palm, all necessary fake papers for six men, loaded below deck, would quickly appear. The ship would sail on the next high tide at dawn.

Derrick felt a giant boulder lifted off his back, but not from his heart. He knew his father would not have wanted him to become a murderer. As much as he hated, he could not kill, not even for revenge. His next plan was to return to Penumbra and take care of the two people he despised.

"Quinn, we'll get something to eat and continue on. I've got two people I must pick up and take to Penumbra. I'll need the wagon. They can't ride."

"Whatever you say, Captain." Then he smiled, "I mean…"

Derrick nodded. "Later."

Chapter Forty-Two

Muggs ran out laughing and grabbed Derrick's hand. "We knew you'd come back. Gully said so. Are you stayin' or are we going with you?"

Gully came forward. "Hold on, Muggs. We've got to let Wolf catch his breath."

Derrick gripped Gully's hand. "It's good to see you. Any problems?"

"None that I couldn't handle," he replied, smiling. He looked over at the big red-headed man, noticing he stood quiet, listening. "Gully, this is Quinn. He works for me."

Gully didn't hesitate to hold out his hand and Quinn clasped it, smiling. Then Gully said, "Muggs, come and say hello to Mr. Quinn, Wolf's friend."

"Whoa, hold on... the name's Quinn, no Mister."

Greetings over, they all went into the house. It was clean and shiny, better than when they first arrived.

Gully said, "I've got some good food cooking, real coffee, and spring water."

They sat in comfort with Derrick explaining that his real name was Staunton and that he no longer used the name *Wolf.* Looking at Muggs, he told him he had to remember that.

"What do we call you then?" Muggs was confused.

"Because we have rules, you must follow them. You must call me *Your Grace* as I am the Duke of Grenfell. However, if you slip and call me *Sir,* that will work." Derrick realized that Muggs wouldn't be in contact with any nobles, so not wanting to confuse him further, he said he could also call him *Captain,* until he got used to his new name.

Gully said to Muggs, "Say it."

All smiles, Muggs said, "Thank you, Your Grace."

"Well done." Derrick patted Muggs' shoulder and felt more flesh.

Derrick stood. "Gully, I'll have duties that need my attention and I won't see you as often as I'd like, but please let us remain good friends that we are. No protocol, just shipmates. I'll never forget your saving my life more than once."

"Captain, you can never imagine what my life has been, so we're even."

Quinn, taking in their conversation, added, "You know, Gully, His Grace is a good man and I know between the two of us, we'll never let him down."

"You got that right," said Gully.

The next morning, they packed their meager belongings. Gully went over everything in the cottage, securing the windows and sure that it was left in fine condition. Derrick said he'd drop off the key at the inn and they'd be on their way to Penumbra. It would be a long drive, but he assured them it would be worth it.

Sheena hung back, trying to be inconspicuous, trusting only Gully and Muggs. Derrick and Quinn let her be. In time, she would heal and perhaps smile.

Muggs asked if he could ride on the horse, fearful of the black stallion, but not with Wolf in charge. Giving the youngster a nod, Derrick lifted Muggs up, with Muggs leaning back against Derrick's chest and gripping his pant leg. They left with Gully driving the cart and Sheena quietly sitting beside him.

Quinn held back his grin, knowing their entourage would have people taking a second look. A tall tanned man, his black hair long and tied with a leather strip, wearing plain black pants and white shirt, sitting straight in the saddle, all elegance regardless of his clothes, with a small happy youngster, badly in need of a hair trim wearing clothes too small, holding on for dear life. The black stallion moving sideways now and then, obviously wanting to gallop, but controlled by the powerful man.

Then, following him a wagon with a giant black man and a black girl with big eyes full of fear riding beside him, gripping her shawl. And coming up last, a big Scotsman with shaggy red hair that when the sun shone, looked afire. Quinn's thoughts whirled about in his mind, taking to his new life. His grin broke through, he leaned forward patting Scully's neck, he had found a home with an aristocrat that he not only fully respected, but liked. *The Duke of Grenfell is a man with heart and courage like no man I've ever known.* Quinn nudged his horse and rode to ride beside Gully. He smiled.

Chapter Forty-Three

London

Her heart aflutter, her eyes bright, as excitement flowed from Eudora. Her ball was a success. She just knew it. After all, the Earl of Tunbridge had attended and that he'd traveled from his country estate was proof.

"I told you, Delbert, we are part of the elite *ton,* the Duke and Duchess of Grenfell have arrived and everyone knows they'd better give us our due or else…"

Having over imbibed, his shoulders slumped, his eyes bloodshot, his hair askew with his neckpiece undone and hanging lopsided, Delbert chided, "You're a fool, dear wife, you aren't a duchess and when it's known, you'll be the laughing stock of the *ton.* "

"I hate you, I hate you… I *loathe* you! I wish I'd never gotten tangled with you."

"Too late, my dear depraved wife, we are a pair. You arranged the assassinations and I willingly paid for them. Now my twin has returned from god knows where, but believe this, Eudora, we are going to pay dearly." Delbert wiped the sweat from his brow. "Derrick will have his revenge for he knows it was us there that night."

"You dolt, if that really is him taking over Penumbra, he knows nothing. He can only be guessing. When we meet, you'd better put on a big smile and welcome him home. Derrick's a Staunton through and through and he'll protect that name, mark my words."

"How sinister you are, still weaving a web of deceit. Have you no fear? If you do not, you are the dolt. I'm telling you Derrick is like our father," Delbert choked as he drank from his glass, "a man who believed in justice no matter what heads fell." He gulped the rest of his whiskey and began to whine, "I'm no good and I should be punished… we both should."

Eudora's lips pursed, furious, she said, "You listen to me. Stop your whining and keep your head. We can handle this if you don't show your cowardice." She was scared but she'd not let her spineless husband know. "Get a grip, we'll take it a step at a time, with Derrick taking the first step." Her expression grew hard and resentful. "You've spoiled this greatest evening in my life and I'll never forgive you." She spun and left the room.

Chapter Forty-Four

Rutley, shaking his head, said, "Your Grace, what do you expect me to do with the three of them?" Gully, Muggs, and Sheena were over at the paddock staring out at the green knolls, the breeze moving the grass like waves.

"Rutley, Gully saved my life. Because of him, I'm alive. He's my loyal friend. The youngster is also a friend. Someday I might explain, but now I need your help. I want them to have a cottage, do what you must to see that it will be in excellent living condition. I'll leave word at the house to give you anything you ask for to fill it with whatever is needed. Give Gully anything he asks for, do not question it." Derrick grinned. "And I'm asking you to help Muggs learn to ride. He can be your right hand, give him work as you did me. I want him to earn his way, but I also want to give him freedom to be a boy."

Rutley swiped at a tear. "I'm so happy you're here and well. I'll get the gamekeeper's cottage set for them. It's got all the makings of a good place and they'll have privacy. Quinn can give me a hand." He walked over to Gully, shook his hand again, and said, "The duke thinks you'll like living on Penumbra, welcome. I'll show you what I have in mind for your quarters and if you like it, we'll get it fixed up. Okay?"

Towering over the little man, Gully smiled. "Thank you. Whatever you say is fine with us. Tell me what to do and I'll see to it." He pulled Muggs to him. "This is my good friend. He'll be staying with me and Sheena. Sheena has been hurt… you'll have to give her time to learn to live our way."

"We won't have any problems. If I'm not around, tell Quinn what you need." Derrick walked over and took Gully's hand to shake. "I have a lot of things to see to, Gully. I won't be around for a while, but Rutley knows to help you in any way he can."

"I need something to do, Your Grace. You know I'm an active person."

Rutley spoke, "We'll work at getting your cottage in order and adding a couple of rooms will take some doing. After that, we can sit with the duke and figure out what's good for us all."

"I like that. Thanks."

"Then you won't mind if I put your young boy to work, if he does a good job then we're going to have to get him a horse and show him how to ride."

"Oh boy," glowed Muggs. "Can I start now?" Looking at Gully, "Is that all right?"

"Whatever Mr. Rutley says."

"It's just *Rutley*."

Gully shook his head. "If you don't mind, I'd like this boy to learn manners toward everyone. It's got to be *Mr.* Rutley."

Rutley eyed Derrick, saw him raise his eyebrow, and then said to Gully, "Then *Mr.* it is. But not for you, understood?"

"Aye, I got it, Rutley." They laughed.

Chapter Forty-Five

London

Derrick went to see James Conlow, Earl of Tunbridge. They'd been friends from school days. Today, Derrick was going to return the priceless Tunbridge dagger. Looking forward to seeing his friend, he slipped into town, keeping his existence shrouded.

The butler advised that the Earl was in his garden and would find if he was available, but Derrick, his demeanor straightforward, said he'd find Conlow on his own. Before the butler could dismiss such a notion, Derrick was on his way. The butler anxiously hurried after him, and then decided to wait for the Earl's call.

James Conlow was studying a bush and turning over its leaves. So intent that he didn't hear Derrick's approach.

"If you think you can turn that bush into silver, I want to share your knowledge."

James turned, first his mouth fell open, he blinked, his voice odd and then vibrant. *"Derrick?* Derrick… it is you! My god, we all thought you'd perished at sea." They were laughing and slapping each other's shoulders. "This is… this is fantastic." He gave Derrick a quick onceover. "You look great. Healthy is the word. What happened? Long hair and golden skin, plain white shirt and black pants—you'll be setting a new trend." Elated, he continued, "Whatever you've been doing, you look magnificent."

"James, you haven't changed. Still the nicest man with words."

"I'm so glad to see you. No one said a word."

"I've not yet announced my arrival. Trying to get settled."

"Sure. Still, I'm probing."

"Perhaps another time. The main reason I'm here is that I've come across something of yours." He held out the Tunbridge priceless dagger, the sun picking up the gems and turning them to fire. He was about to hand it to the earl when running down the walk, a woman shouted, "No, don't, don't!"

Derrick turned and saw his angel. He was flummoxed.

She grabbed Derrick's arm, pulling it away with the dagger still in his hand. Her face flushed, her eyes blazing, she was shaking. "Pirate, what do you think you're doing? Don't you dare! This is my Uncle James and although I forgive you for all your other plunder, I will never forgive you for this."

The Earl of Tunbridge stood astounded, listening to his niece. He was about to say something when he caught Derrick's eye and a slight motion of his head. He remained silent.

Derrick withheld his laughter, almost choking so that Marvalea thought he would not heed her warning.

Pulling on his arm, she demanded they step off the walkway into the secluded bushes so no one at the manor could see them. "Uncle James, you'll understand when I explain, but first I need some answers from *my* pirate."

Derrick let himself be maneuvered with James right behind. He needed answers too—James, his friend for years, *her* uncle?

Marvalea thought she was the one in control. They waited, especially James because his sister mentioned Val having feelings for an undesirable and Neal had ordered him to leave their home.

Looking up at Derrick, she scolded, "What are you doing here? Where did you come from and why aren't you at sea? Don't you know you could be caught? You're lucky I saw you from the window and I can try to convince Uncle James that you meant no harm and he'll let you go, but only if you promise to stop your disgraceful way of life."

Then she smiled, her blond hair escaping from its ribbon, her complexion so peachy with eyes that told him she was happy to see him.

Before Derrick could say a word, she turned to her uncle. "Please forgive him, Uncle James. He's very nice and I still plan on marrying him. He won't have me, but now that I've caught him committing a crime, I want you to help me blackmail him into accepting my proposal."

Speechless, James looked at his niece and then at his friend. Derrick barely moved his head and so James went along. "Marriage? I don't think so, Val. Your mother said I was to find you a suitable husband, but you called him pirate. *That* is not suitable."

"I know you can talk your sister into allowing me to choose with whom I want to spend the rest of my life. I'm sure my pirate can become respectable with your help. No one has to know about his buccaneer past. Surely you can find something for him to do."

Derrick was about to burst, mostly from knowing she wanted him with no knowledge of his title or wealth. Gruffly, he pushed her hand off his sleeve. "Listen, Spitfire, I told you I'm not a marrying man." He wanted James to know that nothing untoward occurred while he was with her, so he said, "Just because we had a kiss or two doesn't mean marriage. You let your uncle find you a good man and live happily the rest of your days."

Her jaw tightened. "Uncle, will you excuse us for just a minute or two?"

"I don't know, Val. He sounds dangerous."

"Of course he's not. I have something to say to him in private, for his ears only."

Curious as to what his niece was up to and knowing he could trust his friend, he agreed but said he'd stand a few feet away.

Marvalea didn't waste any time. "Pirate, this is our chance. Won't you reconsider about my offer?" Her voice lowered—caressing, "I think only of you. I've missed you. Please don't go away. Can't you say that you can care for me a little?"

Derrick yearned to kiss his angel, but wouldn't under the circumstances. "Angel, I don't know what to say. You are precious to me, but I remind you that your father ordered me to leave Slipper. He saw us coming back from the beach. So it would not be right to take advantage of your offer when we both know your parents will oppose it."

She boldly met his eyes, placing her hands on her hips and challenged, "Then let us run away and marry. Once the deed is done, I know Uncle James can talk Mother into accepting you because you make me happy. Then my father. I'm serious, Pirate, I will marry no other because I've already given you my heart."

She was going to argue and Derrick knew the longer he stayed, he'd take her in his arms and never let her go. So he did what he thought best for the time being, especially when he had his twin and sister-in-law to address. He took the dagger from his boot where he'd slipped it and said, "Do me a favor, Angel, and give this to your uncle. It belongs to him." With that, he kissed her forehead and bounded into the trees, disappearing before she could protest.

Disappointed, Marvalea met her uncle on the walkway and handed him the dagger. "At least, I talked him into returning this. He said it's yours."

Carefully taking the heirloom, he wrapped it in his handkerchief. "Do you know who he is, Val?"

"Yes. He may be a pirate, Uncle James, but he's also brave. He saved a lot of people from a horrible tragedy at sea. If you get to know him, you'll see has good qualities. I know that for a fact, but I won't go into it now." She used her knuckle to rub a tear from her eye. "He has attributes to make a real gentleman."

Because Derrick didn't identify himself, James would wait. Though where his friend had been was more mystery. Derrick had changed from quiet strength and now emanated power—a force to be reckoned with. He took in his niece's cheerless expression, deciding to delve further.

"Marriage is a big step, Val. How will you live? Can he support you? You know you've always lived in comfort."

A smile appeared. "I'd bet my life on him to be successful if he wants to try. You know, if we're happy, we can live anywhere as long as we're together."

"But, Val, he didn't seem to be marriage minded. And what makes you think you both would be happy... that's a big word in marriage."

She laughed. "Because he makes me want to touch him and never let him go. He's got some kind of magic. I know he feels something for me, but he won't admit it because he thinks he's not good enough for me. Don't you see, he's not looking for an easy way by marrying me-he could, but he's not that kind of man. How he became a pirate, I don't know. Do you know Lady Amelia Thomas?"

"I've heard the name."

"Well, she sang Wolf's praises."

"Wolf?"

"That's what he's called, but I didn't care for the name, so I called him *Pirate*."

The Earl became more intrigued. His friend, now Duke of Grenfell, had been living a mysterious sojourn... but why? "I don't know, Val. This is very mystifying. Why not keep this afternoon meeting between just us? I promise if I meet your pirate again and if he reconsiders your proposal, I'll speak to Marcella. That's the best I can do."

She hugged her uncle. "Fair enough. But we've got to find him yet; in the meantime, let Mom think I'm letting the two of you be matchmakers." She quickly held up her hand, adding, "But, Uncle James, I'm determined to marry my pirate." She giggled. "I'll tell you a secret—he loves horses and rides like a champion." Her eyes gleaming, she went on, "When he was on Slipper, I followed him to the beach late one night. He had no idea and then I taunted him. I begged him to kiss me and I'm glad I did. He kissed me and I felt I went to heaven. I didn't want him to stop, but he wouldn't listen to me. Now if that isn't love, I don't know what you'd call it."

"Just a couple of kisses? I think for the time being, we keep this our secret. I won't lie to Marcella, but I'll not tell her about your pirate showing up."

"Just know, Uncle James, I'm going to marry him. And if Mom and Dad refuse to accept him, we'll make it." Suddenly, her eyes opened extra wide. "You could hire him to work with your horses. I bet he'd be excellent." She was grinning. "That's it... don't let me down, we can live in one of your cottages."

"Don't make plans, Val. I don't want you disappointed. We'll have to wait and see." The Earl of Tunbridge was smothering his smile that wanted to explode and thinking, *Your angel, Derr? Welcome to the family.*

Chapter Forty-Six

Derrick entered the Staunton mansion through the rear entrance. His stature caused the servants enjoying their supper to gasp.

The butler stood immediately and explained that at the moment, the duke and duchess were not hiring. "And you should have knocked and waited for someone to attend the door."

Again, Derrick saw no one from Penumbra. Agitated, he flipped off his cape and tossed it to the butler. "Where are the duke and duchess?" He was moving toward the entry to the main hall.

"See here…"

Derrick stopped, eying the man, and said, "You will be notified if I wish to keep your service." Leaving them all flabbergasted, he took the steps two at a time up the long stairway and went directly to his father's library.

Pushing open the door, he found Delbert sitting at his father's desk. Derrick stood staring, rage filling him from head to toe. When the butler hurried in, Derrick angered over his blatant intrusion and said, "Get out and do not enter this room unless you are summoned and that goes for all of you."

The butler didn't hesitate to see if Delbert approved—he sped from the room leaving the door open.

Derrick pushed it shut, knowing he had to control his temper as the servants' gossip would fill London's drawing rooms and clubs. He would not allow the Staunton name to be tarnished.

Delbert, shaking but hoping his twin didn't see and praying that he didn't know of Eudora and his complicity, tried to be as nonchalant as possible. "Well, Brother, you've stormed in here so I gather you've decided to come home and tend to business?"

Standing with his hands fisted, seething, demanded, "Get your wife in here… no, don't pull the cord, *you* get her; you have three minutes or I will personally come after the both of you, to hell with what the servants will spread around."

Delbert was up and moving—actually glad to have his wife's support—and nearly ran from the room.

Derrick walked around the desk, picking up and scanning papers pertaining to bills owing. He dropped them when the two vipers entered.

Eudora, no longer the slim, elegant woman, smiling and pretending she was happy to see him. "Derrick, I couldn't believe my ears when Delbert said you were here. What a wonderful surprise." She took in his tall muscular build. His broad shoulders, *massive*, she corrected in her mind, caused his shirt to cling to his body. His hair long and different, but it made him all the more handsome. Eudora swallowed, wondering where he'd been as his bronze skin and dark eyes were giving her the onceover and never could she remember feeling so wretched about herself. He stood there like a towering oak—big and powerful.

"I'm going to report my returning to the crown in the morning. I want the both of you out of here at sunrise. You will go directly to Penumbra and wait for me. You will talk with no one. What excuse you give for departing suddenly is yours to make, but make it! Under no circumstances is the Staunton name to be dishonored." His tone was low and menacing. "Now get out of my sight."

Delbert began to move but Eudora wasn't going to be pushed so easily. "Really, Derrick, what's come over you?"

"You'll know soon enough. Now get out!"

Chapter Forty-Seven

Penumbra, one week later

Derrick knelt before his father and mother's graves. He allowed tears to fall as there was no one to see. *I remember your words, Father. I will keep my promise to you and to our ancestors.* He heard the carriage wheels and knew Gully would be delivering his twin and Eudora. He knuckled his eyes and moved to greet them at the gate. He met them away from the house, privacy with no ears but theirs.

Delbert sat, stoic, saying nothing. Eudora, her nose pinched and her mouth pressed tightly in anger.

Gully said nothing, keeping two bays quieted. "What is the meaning of this, Derrick?"

"It's *Your Grace,* Eudora—do not have me correct you again. Now, I want the both of you to step down. Gully, please take the horses over to let them graze. I'll let you know when to return."

"Aye, Your Grace."

When Gully was far enough not to hear, Eudora charged, "Why do you have that brute on Penumbra and I don't like him coming and giving me orders."

Smoldering, but keeping his temper, Derrick said, "First, I do not have to explain my reasons to you or anyone. Second, Gully followed my orders—you are here. And thirdly, do not call him names or anyone connected with Penumbra."

He looked at Delbert. "I imagine, dear brother, that you're frightened and well you should be. The first thing I'm going to do before I condemn the two of you is… give me that ugly whip you use as your pacifier."

Delbert, trembling, thinking Derrick was going to use it on him, meekly held it out.

Derrick took it and splintered the handle and then with the leather strip took out his dagger and cut it into several pieces. He ground out his question between his teeth, "Do you know what damage a whip does? You used it freely, not caring of the hurt you perpetrate. Because of you and your *sweet* wife, I'll show you an example." Derrick pulled up his shirt and displayed his scarred back with welts on top of welts—crisscrossed.

Eudora gasped and Delbert's already pale face turned gray.

Derrick pulled his shirt back down. "I knew I'd survive because I had to come back for the two of you vipers."

Neither of them said a word. Eudora gripped Delbert's hand, it being the first time she had ever leaned on him.

Spacing his words evenly to keep control, Derrick said, "I will not tell you what I know or how I know. But know this; the two of you will pay for the rest of your lives." His voice lowered, mockingly. "No, I'm not going to kill you, though I would be justified. That punishment would be too easy, I want you to think the rest of your days of what you did and the innocent lives of people murdered because of you."

Eudora spoke, her voice shaky, "We can go to Sherbrooke Hall."

"Oh no… that will never happen. For you and Delbert who always claimed you wanted each other… well, you shall have your wish. From this moment on, you are exiled to the dowager house here on Penumbra where I can keep an eye on you. You will have no transportation—no carriage, no horses, nothing to carry you off Penumbra's land. You will have no personal maid or valet and no servants. I will see that someone comes in once each week to replenish your food. If you require anything other than I provide, leave a note and it will be delivered to me."

"If I agree, you'll have what you ask for. If I don't agree, you will not. Delbert, I understand that you've become quite a drinker. So, to help numb your conscience, I will see that you have one bottle with each week's delivery. You will see and talk to no one and if you're foolish enough to try to leave, I'll make you more than sorry."

Derrick looked at his twin, his tone edged like iron. "Why Del? How could you? Our father, the most hospitable, fair-minded, and caring… he loved us both." Derrick choked. "I'm ashamed that we're related. You smear the Staunton name and because of you, I have to lie as I'm going to say that you and Eudora have left for the continent and who knows when or if you'll return." His voice harsh as he stared at the two of them, "You are being taken to your new home *now* and I hope to never set eyes upon either of you again." Derrick waved to Gully. "And you will treat Gully with respect. I won't hear one bad word from either of you."

"But Derrick… I mean, Your Grace," Eudora tried, "we're sorry. You can't… my father will be…"

"I can and will do as I wish, Eudora. Best you remember that or I can let it slip that you and your husband knew all along that I was alive yet you wanted to play duchess."

She shrank back.

"And as for the earl, he'll not worry about his daughter traveling knowing you're in good hands with your husband."

Gully pulled up. "Take them to where I showed you. And Gully, if you ever see them outside those premises, you're to report to me immediately."

Looking at his twin and Eudora, Derrick's last words were, "You both are despicable, yet I wish you a very long life."

Chapter Forty-Eight

Earl of Tunbridge's Home, London

Derrick entered James Conlow's library, concern obvious, his brow creased. "I came as soon as I got your message." He didn't change, still wearing black pants and white shirt opened at the neck. "It said urgent."

"Sorry, Derr, didn't mean to worry you." James held out his hand. "I have concern because of the ball this evening and you will be our esteemed guest." He pulled a cord and when the butler entered, said, "Please have Lady Durand attend me."

Derrick raised his eyebrow.

"No problem, but I did tell Marcella about you. She was surprised and shocked." James grinned. "And knowing her daughter is intent on marrying *that* pirate, after she got over the shock, she couldn't stop laughing."

Marcella entered the library.

Derrick admired her aplomb, she looked directly at him. He nodded, no smile, but his eyes held warmth as he greeted her.

James spoke, "Marcella, I believe you know this gentleman. Here in England, he's known as the Duke of Grenfell."

"Your Grace." She smiled, and then added, "I knew you were a gentleman but never did it occur to me that you would know my brother. Small world, isn't it?"

"Lady Durand, it's nice to see you again." He took her hand and bowed, "I apologize for not revealing my identity; it was important that I remain in disguise until I could return home. Also, know that never did anything untoward occur with your daughter. I'm sorry the impression I left caused you and Neal anguish. I never intended to impinge on your hospitality nor would I inflict disgrace of any kind."

"I'll speak frankly, Your Grace, you did worry my husband and me. Marvalea is precious to us and we didn't want her hurt. Her protection will always be our utmost priority. That said, you left your mark on her heart and she has confided in me that she has seen you here in London as *her* pirate and she intends to marry you. You understand that she is too young to arrive at such a serious decision."

James handed Derrick a drink. Then passed one on to his sister. "Derrick, Val is so intent on shackling you that she's begging me to hire you to train my horses. If she has any inkling who you are, I don't know what her reaction will be. She's set her sights only on this man *Wolf*."

Derrick sipped his whiskey. "Now I'll speak frankly." His voice soft but forceful, "I think your daughter is precious, too, Lady Durand. She is the first female that likes me for *me* and not my title. That is essential because it will make for a happy life for whom we are and not because of titles. I am going to marry your daughter; I hope with both Neal and your blessings; however, I will be the one proposing. It is my choice to make her my duchess. Now that you know my situation, I ask you and James to withhold telling her who I am. I will do that when the time is right, perhaps at the ball this evening. Will you do that for me?"

James went to stand next to his sister. "Marc, I believe we will do as Derrick asks. You won't be sorry," he grinned, "I want to be there when she finds out she's been proposing to a duke… the Duke of Grenfell, no less… whom London's mamas wish to snatch for their little girls."

Derrick ignored James' flaunt. "I'd like your word, if you please."

Marcella Durand knew this man, though a gentleman, had a will of his own, not to be defied. "As long as James agrees, I will also. But I do not want my daughter to be hurt."

"You have my word." Just then the door flew open and his angel entered.

"Pirate! Oh Uncle James, you found him." She went to Derrick, reaching for his hand. "Mother, you' re here. Good." She looked adoringly at Derrick. "Did my uncle tell you we can have one of his cottages and you can train his horses? I told him how good you are with them."

Derrick, grinning, said, "Slow down, Angel… nothing's been decided. I'm surprised to meet Lady Durand again. I didn't know the earl is related and it gives me much to think about."

"But what difference can it make?" She literally hung on his arm.

Marcella spoke, "Really, Val, conduct yourself as a lady. Step away from… the man."

She did, but went on to say, "I'm serious… we're going to marry. I know you think I'm too young to know what I'm doing, but I'm not! And if you give this man half a chance, you'll see he's quite a gentleman. And Mom, you've got to convince father that my pirate and I belong together."

"But dear, you don't know who he is. What's his name?"

"I'll figure all that out as soon as I convince or blackmail him into agreeing to marry me." She laughed and then winked at Derrick. "We can elope."

"Marvalea!" Her mother just about had a heart attack.

Derrick had to get out of there or else he'd sweep this spitfire into his arms right there in front of everyone and kiss her until they both couldn't breathe. "My lord, Lady Durand… I've got to be on my way." He tweaked Marvalea under her chin, smiled and without looking back, went out the window, onto a tree limb and disappeared.

Marvalea ran to watch, laughing. "Isn't he wonderful?"

"Val?" Marcella scolded. "How can you be enamored with that man? Really," her voice disproving.

"Mom, I'm more than enamored, I truly love him. And I know he cares for me more than he'll admit. But that day will come." She looked at her uncle. "You'll help me convince your sister that it's right that I marry him. He's got a good heart, truly."

James eyed his sister. "Tell you what, Val, after the ball, we'll get together and see that all our cards, so to speak, are on the table. And if your pirate truly wants to marry you and you haven't changed your mind about marrying him… then I'll work on getting your parents to accept him as your future husband."

Marvalea hugged her uncle. "I knew I could count on you." Then she kissed his cheek.

Chapter Forty-Nine

Night of Tunbridge Ball

"You look beautiful, Val." Smiling, the earl went on, "You'll be the star of the ball."

"Thank you, Uncle James."

Marcella shook her head. "I don't know why you aren't elated. James is giving this ball in your honor."

"I don't think so. I heard all the excitement from the servants that some duke came back from the dead and he will be attending." She giggled. "I guess I can put my best foot forward and perhaps the old man will ask me to dance if he remembers how. That's if the minuet won't tax his heart. Will that meet with your approval, Mama?"

"Don't be impertinent, young lady. And whatever you do this evening, do not embarrass your Uncle or me."

Marvalea's straight emerald dress over a simple chemise gathered at the waist and pulled in the back floated around her. Opera length gloves, a strand of pearls set off her curls over each temple with long curls down on her shoulders. "I promise to be on my best behavior, only…" looking at her Uncle James, "only I wish it were possible to have invited *my* pirate. You could have provided him with proper clothes, though I doubt he'd leave off wearing his boots. I think that's all he owns."

"Val, you've got to get over that man."

"Mother, surely you remember being in love with Father and giving up your life *here* and going to the islands."

"She's got you there, Marc," laughed James.

272

"I guess. I just don't want you hurt; you're our special daughter and your father would never forgive me."

"Just watch me; I'll be the epitome of propriety."

James walked toward the door. "I suggest we get ready to greet our guests. It's time."

Marvalea smothered a yawn as she greeted the earl's last arriving guests. She whispered to her mother on her left, "I guess the old dodder couldn't make it up the stairs; may I be excused?"

James leaned forward, taking his sister's arm. "I believe we can all join the rest of our guests." He didn't seem overly concerned about his duke friend not showing.

"James, what do you think happened? He's coming, isn't he?"

"Yes, I'm certain, Marc. But being a duke gives him privileges."

"Well," spoke Marvalea, "his manners need to be enhanced. It appears that everyone keeps watching and waiting for your nobleman. I hope he doesn't disappoint you, Uncle James."

Grinning, he said, "Not to worry, Niece, I look forward to his arrival, late though it may be."

"Where are you off to?" Marcella's tone held disapproval.

"I thought I'd make my way around and end on the outer porch with its lighted torches." Marvalea patted her mother's arm. "I'll be good and polite and I'll dance as soon as I see you and Uncle James opening the ball." And without waiting for a reply, she took off to mix in the ballroom.

The ballroom was warm, the doors leading out to the wide-long porch were open and the fresh night air exhilarating. Marvalea leaned on the balustrade enjoying the conversation with Viscount Joelton. He seemed interested in her life on an island, saying it was a strange way to live without strict rules.

"Oh believe me, there are rules, Viscount, but there is freedom to do what one enjoys without worrying what others might say."

"Give me an example, if you will?"

"Well, here and even at the earl's country home, ladies have to ride side-saddle. On the island, I can ride astride just as men do and no one thinks it strange."

"You mean you ride without a saddle?"

Marvalea laughed, "Yes and also with a saddle, not just the side kind."

His mouth gaped and she was going to add more to their conversation when suddenly, the ballroom quieted and murmurs carried out onto the porch.

Viscount Joelton quickly turned toward the open doors. "I bet the duke has arrived. Will you excuse me, please? I've just got to see him." He was already backing away.

"Of course, do go." In several steps, he was gone and Marvalea turned back to peer out into the garden, breathing in night air. *I'll go in and meet the missing duke, but first let everyone get their fill. I certainly won't stand in line even though it would make Mother happy.* A short while later, she pulled her gloves higher, patted the front of her dress at the waist, and decided to be a good daughter and niece and do her duty.

She entered the ballroom, music was playing but there was no one dancing. *He must really have come back from the dead.* She saw everyone surrounding her uncle and a tall dark-haired man with long hair tied with a black leather strip and gasped. He was holding court as though he belonged. *Pirate, what are you doing? No wonder everyone is looking at you! I've got to get you out of here, but then why is Uncle James smiling?*

Marvalea hung back, wanting to be inconspicuous until she could get to her pirate. She watched seeing him so handsome even being the only man there with long hair. And what she could see of his coat, it was black and he wore a frilly white shirt, *bet he's got on his riding boots*; she smiled to herself. She didn't care, he belonged to her and she'd claim him as soon as his mystique slowed.

Derrick, being gracious, kept an eye out for his angel. *Where is she?* Just as Reggie predicted, the mamas were pushing their daughters forward to meet the Duke of Grenfell—title meant everything, *but not to Angel.* And then, he spotted her standing off to one side, not blending in with the crowd. He smothered his smile and suggested to the Earl of Tunbridge that dancing should continue and would the earl be kind enough to introduce him to his niece.

James voice was low for Derrick's ears only, "Are you sure you want to do it this way?"

Grinning, all he did was nod.

After announcing that dancing should ensue, the earl and the duke slowly made their way to the beautiful green-eyed woman standing alone. It was as if the guests knew their intent and parted to give them a clear path.

As they neared Marvalea, she froze; he looked so handsome and he was smiling at her and she knew right then and there that he did love her as she loved him.

The earl reached for Val's gloved elbow and said, "I'd like you to meet my niece, Marvalea Durand, Your Grace. She is visiting from Port Charles with my sister." He said this so that all those listening would think it was their first introduction and rose to *ton* etiquette.

Before Derrick could say a word, Marvalea burst out laughing. "Don't tell me this is your missing duke? You're hamming me, Uncle."

Gasps were heard along with laughter.

Derrick took matters in hand. "My lady, it is a pleasure to meet such charm. It is true I have been missing, but no longer. You see, my plans are set and I hope to include you in them, if you will?" Derrick held her hand and put pressure on her fingers, his eyes looking at her, signaling to go along.

Again gasps, but this time from the mamas. The men were smiling, believing the duke may have been away but he was steady and sure about what he wanted.

So he and Uncle James were playing games at my expense, were they? Well, we'll see.

"I suppose, *Your Grace,* if you insist, I could possibly write your name on my calendar. Of course, however, you must not change your mind as once you're committed. I'm stubborn, you see, and I mean to have my way."

Derrick's eyes twinkled. "That is good to know. Do you ride, Miss Marvalea Durand?"

Everyone stood near listening, some bristling over the fact that the Duke of Grenfell was tolerating this untitled woman.

"I do, probably not well, but I manage."

"Wonderful." He let go of her hand and was about to turn to go, then said, "If the earl will permit my calling, we can decide on a day."

"I suppose, but do not wait too long or I may decide to cancel." Gasps!

Laughing, Derrick said, "As you wish, Miss Marvalea Durand." He moved to one side to talk with several gentlemen.

Marcella worked her way over to her daughter and James stood beside her. Smiling, but speaking just to the two of them, Val said, "Just wait!" And she moved off to mix with the guests. Now that the duke had showed her special attention, others wanted to get to know her.

Derrick mixed with the *ton*, making no conversation about his disappearance or of his reappearance, always covertly keeping an eye on his angel.

Marvalea pretending to be charmed at the attention suddenly thrust upon her, finally taking the opportunity to slip out of the ballroom and into the hall. Where to go to collect her thoughts… she knew of the linen room off the far hall knowing it would be open in case of the need of replacing cloths. Hurrying, not looking, and finally alone in the hall, she slipped into the linen closet and leaned against a fresh stack of tablecloths. *So pirate, you're a duke,* she giggled; *well, it makes no difference to me. I still want to marry you and I will, but not before I give you a bit of nuisance… just to get even.* She took a deep breath, ready to return when the door swung open and then shut quickly.

"Hello, Angel."

Her heart pounding and her legs barely able to keep her standing, she said, "Pirate!"

Derrick laughed. And without another word reached for her and she fell into his arms. "I've missed you." And his kiss was gentle, slow yet persuasive and she met him with desire of her own. Brushing his lips against hers, he spoke, "Will you marry me, Angel?"

There was nothing in this world that she wanted to hear, but he had his payback coming and so did Uncle James. She moved out of his arms, using the back of her hand to press her forehead, the light being dim in the room, so he couldn't see her eyes, she said, "Thank you, Your Grace, but I don't think so. A duke? No, you see, I'm in love with *my* pirate. A duke will never do."

Derrick wanted to laugh, but he didn't have time to play games, he'd be missed and so would she. "Oh no you don't, Spitfire… I've got to go. We can't be caught here alone." He put two fingers to his lips and then pressed them to hers and just as quickly as he had entered, he was gone.

Marvalea smiled as she touched her lips with her fingers and still feeling his kiss, she knew to wait a few more minutes before returning to the ball. *Oh pirate, you are in for one big surprise.*

Chapter Fifty

At four o'clock in the morning, Marvalea sneaked out of the earl's home, dressed in britches she had brought with her from the island and having taken one of her uncle's hats, she filled it with her curls pulling it easily down on her forehead. Wearing her leather riding gloves and boots, she prepared to dupe her pirate.

Changing her voice as low as possible, she hired a hackney to take her to a certain corner. The driver didn't give the lad a second look, only wondered where he got the blunt to pay.

Walking to the Duke of Grenfell's stable, she banged on the door; a young lad, rubbing his eyes stared at her. "Whatcha' want?"

"I'm supposed to take the duke's horse for a run this morning. Have you got him saddled?"

"No one told me and the stablemaster isn't here till six."

"Do you think I'd get up this early for nothing? I got my orders from the duke himself. Now saddle up Valiant, and let me do my job. I need the blunt." The lad didn't argue further and got busy.

Marvalea climbed on Valiant. The stallion wasn't happy, but held steady as she patted his neck whispering to him.

"You got some nerve to take on his horse. I'd never do it."

"The duke knows I can handle him." Valiant was anxious to get going, feeling the reins loosely held, evidently not caring that it wasn't his master taking him for a gallop.

Marvalea, trotting out and heading for the road to Richmond that everyone talked about when wanting to take a fast gallop, beamed a smile. *I did it.* Dawn beginning, she had to hurry to get out of town.

Following the road north and seeing a few other riders ahead, she knew she was going in the right direction.

Valiant was trying to sidestep, anxious to go, she leaned forward. "Easy, I'm going to let you have your way as soon as we're out of town." Her heart pounding, not with fear but excitement to be riding again, feeling freedom.

Leaving the mansions and then more moderate houses and finally coming to open land with the open road and riders in front, she leaned into Valiant's ear, "Okay, let's show them what you've got." She took off, sitting straight and comfortable, having only to nudge Valiant slightly and giving him free rein; the black horse took off leaving dust and stunned riders behind. Whether they paid her any attention she knew not or cared; with the cool morning dampness blowing against her face, she felt alive. And Valiant, doing what he liked most of all, raced on.

The sun began to awaken the sky when Marvalea spied a stream and slowed Valiant, guiding him to the water. "We'll rest and decide what to do," she told the horse.

She sat on a boulder with her chin resting on her hand when two riders steered their horses to drink. Knowing dressed as a boy she'd not draw attention, she didn't move.

"That's a fine horse you have there," one man said.

She turned and just nodded, not daring to speak as her voice would give her away.

These men weren't that sleepy lad at the duke's stable. "Let's go, Dunnston, I've got a meeting this morning."

"Right. We've exercised our horses. I'm ready."

They got on their horses and said not another word and left.

Marvalea smiled. She got away with that too. She was having a good morning with her deception. *See how you like it, Mr. Pirate.*

From the boulder, she mounted and Valiant was ready. "We'll go nice and easy for a while. We have all day."

Meanwhile, back at the duke's stable, Derrick went out just after six o'clock to take Valiant for some exercise and also to enjoy a gallop.

Her hat fell off and her blond curls were all over her face. Laughing, she proceeded to push them back under her hat when she heard the pounding hoofs and looking, recognized the Duke of Grenfell. Without thought, grinning, she loosened Valiant's reins and said, "Come on, let's see what you can do." Dust flying, her laughter floating out into the air, Marvalea was in heaven, she was ahead of her pirate and she had the better horse.

Derrick was enraged, but he admired the young lad's grip on the reins, just as he would let him do, Valiant thrived using his speed at will. But he couldn't figure out why his prized horse was stolen and where was it being taken. He'd find out. Knowing the horse he was riding wasn't going to catch Valiant, he did what he knew would slow Valiant and get him to stop. He whistled. And like magic, the beautiful black stallion began to slow and in no time, Derrick raced up and grabbed his reins bringing Valiant to a halt.

He grabbed the thief's arm and felt its thinness, but that was no excuse. But before he voiced his anger, he heard, "Really, Pirate, don't pretend you aren't happy to see your horse and me." She was cocky. "Don't we make a charming couple?"

"You?" He couldn't believe and then just as quickly, he did. But he wouldn't give her the satisfaction of admiration for her ruse.

Relieved to find both his angel and horse unhurt, he wouldn't give Spitfire the satisfaction of knowing it.

"I should have you arrested for stealing or better yet, I should spank your bottom. Which do you prefer?"

"Guess?" Her voice filled with underlying sensuality and she gave him a conspiratorial wink.

Derrick's eyes never left hers for an instant. He couldn't stay angry. He burst out grinning. "Spitfire, I've got to hand it to you, you have my stable in an uproar and I didn't make it easy for them, though once I learned Valiant left peacefully, I wondered *who* would have the nerve to blatantly come and order my horse be saddled. I could think of only one person, but I had to be sure before I put out an alarm. My worry is which way you went. And luckily, I came upon Dunnston and he told me about a young lad on a black stallion. In fact, he was in awe that such a small lad you could handle the beast."

Releasing Valiant's reins, Derrick said, "Let's go over to that chinaberry and talk."

"Just talk?"

"Angel, you are out here unescorted… we're alone. That's not the way things are done. You're not in Port Charles. I do not want to give you a reputation." He got off his horse and went to lift Marvalea down, but she was too quick—she slid down off Valiant and dropped lightly on her feet.

Derrick tied the horses to a tree branch. Sitting down, he patted the ground. "Come here."

Not bothering to look around, not caring if anyone was about, she leapt on Derrick knocking him over. Laughing, she began kissing his face. And between her kisses, she said, "Tell me you love me." She kissed his mouth and he pushed her up and away.

"Listen, Spitfire, we can't carry on in public. Especially you being a lad and me… a man." When he saw her disappointment, he went on, "But yes, I do believe I love you in spite of all the grief you cause me." He jumped up and took her into the growth of the hanging branches. "Kiss you? Oh yes…"

"Then kiss me, Pirate, like you mean it."

He had every intention, but now he was the one in control and he'd have his way. "First, say you'll marry me, Angel. No kisses until you say yes and no more games, you must really mean it."

"Of course, I'll marry you, haven't I always said we'd be married."

"Yes, but now I'm proposing."

"It's important to you?"

"It is."

Marvalea's warm smile brightened the shadows under the trees' laden branches of leaves. "Yes, I will marry you, Pirate… or if you prefer… Your Grace."

Derrick's eyes traveled over her face, scrutinizing her dewy green eyes and saw the truth in them, with tears sitting on her lids. "Pirate will do just fine," he whispered as he kissed away her tears and then his kiss started slow before shattering the calm with his hunger for her. She met his every move and felt goose bumps spiral all over her body.

Derrick's fingers raked through her curls as he pulled her to him. Out of the morning sun, in the shade of the chinaberry, the air cooled, yet passion raced rampant as she snuggled against him. On her toes she kept kissing his neck, chin, and nipping at his lips. He stopped to catch his breath and did what he had to—gently separating them from each other. "My angel," his voice simmering with checked passion.

"I want to stay like this forever."

"I wish, but not until we marry. It has to be, Angel, the only way." He bent and picked up James' hat and put it on her head, doing his best to stuff in her curls.

"I'll do it and you tell me if I missed any."

With one last light kiss, they were ready to mount. Derrick grinned. "I don't suppose you'd be willing to trade horses?"

"No, *Your Grace.*"

"Sassy, aren't you? Well, because you're going to be my duchess, I'll permit you to have your way."

"Permit?"

"Let's just say it's a bad choice of words." He looked up and said for her benefit, "Lord have mercy on this man in love."

Marvalea was all smiles.

"Let's go, my sweetling, and when I stop over to see you this evening, be ready to set our wedding date."

"You can count on it!"

Epilogue

Eight months later

The celebrated Wedding-Ball of the Duke and Duchess of Grenfell at Penumbra was equivalent to an unexpected thunderclap, it shook the ton. The ton overtly voiced their opinions at having a wedding and ball as one. It just was not the thing and then that the duchess wore the famous Grenfell jewels with her wedding gown—it was outrageously taboo though many wished they could be so blessed.

Gossip floated along when seeing the duke's twin and his lady having arrived from the Continent. Lady Eudora appeared detached until she spied the Grenfell jewels on the beautiful bride. Unable to take her eyes off the necklace she began to walk toward the bride—where? Where were they hidden? Where? His Grace stepped beside Eudora while Delbert on her other side raised his wife's hand and laid it on his arm keeping it in place. The guests noted their thinness and pallor believing they were unwell. It appeared the brothers were in conversation as the duke seeming to nod led them off where unknowingly they were escorted to a carriage.

The one incident that kept on-dits going was when the future Duke of Tayford joined the set of odd persons on the far side of the open terrace. Rutley, known to be the duke's mentor on horses, a young boy that constantly tugged at his collar and a petite black woman sitting with her hands in her lap. Then a tall black man offered Bender the biggest smile and not bowing but shaking his hand. A broad red headed man stood aside with laughter and didn't seem to be embarrassed. The duke and duchess joined them with friendly warmth. So very odd to the ton yet none would have the audacity to inquire. Remembering the young lord's temperate manner; now as duke he exuded an unexpected indisputable skill with a demanding stance yet his demeanor remained genial.

Still, the most unforgettable on-dit of the Duke and Duchess of Grenfell's Wedding-Ball was when the duchess was overheard whispering to the duke, "Pirate, when can we get out of here?" His Grace's smile broadened at his new duchess.

The mystery remains; why was the duke missing and why the duchess called his Grace Pirate.

Made in United States
North Haven, CT
09 January 2024

47253126R00157